Christopher Fowler is the award-winning author of more than forty novels – including thirteen featuring the detectives Bryant and May and the Peculiar Crimes Unit – and short story collections. The recipient of the coveted CWA 'Dagger in the Library' Award for 2015, Chris's most recent books are the Ballard-esque thriller *The Sand Men* and *Bryant & May – Strange Tide*. His other work includes screenplays, video games, graphic novels, audio plays and two critically acclaimed memoirs, *Paperboy* and *Film Freak*. His weekly column 'Invisible Ink' was a highlight of the *Independent on Sunday*. He lives in King's Cross, London, and Barcelona.

To find out more, visit www.christopherfowler.co.uk

D0417795

Praise for Christopher Fowler's Bryant & May mysteries

'Quirky and original . . . the relationship between
Bryant and May is done brilliantly'
Mark Billingham

'Imagine the *X-Files* with Holmes and Watson in the place of
Mulder and Scully, and the books written by P.G. Wodehouse,
and you have some idea of the idiosyncratic and distinctly
British flavour of the Bryant & May novels'
Black Static

'What Christopher Fowler does so well is to
merge the old values with the new . . . he's giving
us two for the price of one'
Lee Child

'Fowler, like his crime-solvers, is deadpan, sly,
and always unexpectedly inventive'
Entertainment Weekly

'I love the wit and playfulness of the Bryant & May books'
Ann Cleeves

'Invests the traditions of the Golden Age of detective fiction
with a tongue-in-cheek post-modernism'
Evening Standard

'One of the quirkiest and most ingenious pleasures
to be found in the genre: atmospheric, sardonically
funny and craftily suspenseful'
Barry Forshaw

'Witty, sinuous and darkly comedic storytelling
from a Machiavellian jokester'
Guardian

'Atmospheric, hugely beguiling and as filled with tricks and sleights of hand as a magician's sleeve'
Joanne Harris

'Mr Fowler has no trouble convincing readers that London is a place where the occult lives on, the dead might rise, and a detective might absently pluck a kitten out of his pocket. Their very credibility puts quaint old Bryant and May in a class of their own'
The New York Times

'Quirky, touching, profound and utterly original'
Peter James

'Slow burning, adroitly plotted, with a distinct atmosphere . . . goes against the grain of most detective fiction and is the better for it'
Daily Telegraph

'Devilishly clever . . . mordantly funny . . . sometimes heartbreakingly moving'
Val McDermid

'Exciting and thoughtful . . . one of our most unorthodox and entertaining writers'
Sunday Telegraph

'Bryant and May are hilarious. *Grumpy Old Men* does *CSI* with a twist of Dickens!'
Karen Marie Moning

'Witty, charming, intelligent, wonderfully atmospheric and enthusiastically plotted'
The Times

'A proper old-fashioned puzzle. You feel pleased when you spot stuff. This is Golden Age detective story-writing'
Kate Mosse

BRYANT & MAY
London's Glory

CHRISTOPHER FOWLER

BANTAM BOOKS

LONDON · TORONTO · SYDNEY · AUCKLAND · JOHANNESBURG

TRANSWORLD PUBLISHERS
61–63 Uxbridge Road, London W5 5SA
www.penguin.co.uk

Transworld is part of the Penguin Random House group of
companies whose addresses can be found at global.penguinrandomhouse.com

Penguin
Random House
UK

First published in Great Britain in 2015 by Doubleday
an imprint of Transworld Publishers
Bantam edition published 2016

Copyright © Christopher Fowler 2015

Illustration of the Peculiar Crimes Unit on page 25 copyright © Keith Page

Christopher Fowler has asserted his right under the Copyright,
Designs and Patents Act 1988 to be identified as the author of this work.

This book is a work of fiction and, except in the case of historical fact, any resemblance to
actual persons, living or dead, is purely coincidental.

Every effort has been made to obtain the necessary permissions with reference to copyright
material, both illustrative and quoted. We apologize for any omissions in this respect and will
be pleased to make the appropriate acknowledgements in any future edition.

A CIP catalogue record for this book
is available from the British Library.

ISBN 9780857503121

Typeset in 11/13 pt Sabon by Kestrel Data, Exeter, Devon.
Printed and bound by Clays Ltd, Bungay, Suffolk.

Penguin Random House is committed to a sustainable future for our business, our readers and
our planet. This book is made from Forest Stewardship Council® certified paper.

MIX
Paper from
responsible sources
FSC® C018179

1 3 5 7 9 10 8 6 4 2

For Clare, with love and pride

CONTENTS

Introduction

STILL GETTING AWAY WITH MURDER

Why have crime novels stuck around for so long? In theory they should have died out decades ago. After all, there's nothing remotely realistic about them. In real life the murder rate is falling and there are very few clever killers, so why do we want to believe in fictional crime tales?

Let me try to answer this with an illustration of the problem.

Some years ago, I found myself locked inside a Soho taxi late at night while my driver was viciously attacked by a pair of City bankers. The driver had shouted at the men, who were drunk and had hammered on the bonnet of his cab, and the drunks had dragged him through the window of his vehicle and beaten him senseless. I agreed to act as the driver's witness, but outside the courtroom the police persuaded the plaintiff to drop his case in exchange for enough cash to repair his vehicle and compensate for his injuries. The officers said court proceedings would only cause everyone more hurt and trouble. It was a reasonable solution, if an unexciting one. The police shifted a case off their books and the victim seemed happy, but I couldn't shake the feeling that he had lost out.

In Britain, we have 'equality of arms', which allows the same resources to be made available to both defence and prosecution, and broadly speaking this idea of balance filters down through the system. There's a reason why the Old Bailey's statue of Justice holds scales. It means we don't get such outrageous courtroom dramas as O. J. Simpson fiddling with a glove, but the end result is often fairer.

If you've ever been the victim of a crime, you'll know that it's a very different experience from its fictional equivalent. Police stations are like hospitals: utilitarian, brightly lit, overflowing with paperwork, staffed by over-worked people who barely notice you, and most of what goes on takes place behind the scenes. The rest is just waiting around and trying to reconcile your anger and frustration with the orderly procedures you have to face. If crime fiction accurately reflected this reality it would be dead, so we augment it.

Yet we writers are still keen to convince you that our latest murder mysteries are grittily realistic. They aren't. They never were and never will be. How many killers are captured while they're in the middle of their slaughter sprees? How many have ever planned a series of murders according to coded biblical signs? How many leave abstract clues for a single detective and get caught just as they're about to strike again? Only some of the psychological-suspense writers are exempt from these lunacies.

Crime fiction is a construct, a device for torquing tension, withholding information and springing surprises. Yet every month dozens of crime novels appear that promise us new levels of realism, when they patently supply the reverse. We'll happily believe that the murder rate in Morse's Oxford equals that of Mexico City if the story is told with conviction, or that the villages of the *Midsomer Murders* are thatched-roof hellholes more like the Bronx in the 1970s.

The latest census data about Britain reveals that the country is changing fast, and economic mobility is a major catalyst. However, there is a part of England that forever has an alcoholic middle-aged copper with a beloved dead wife, investigating a murdered girl who turns out to be an Eastern European sex worker. This idea might have surprised us a couple of decades ago, but it's still being sold to us with monotonous regularity. It's not gritty, it's a comforting cliché.

While judging the CWA Gold Dagger Award I had to read a great many books which were interchangeable. It was shocking to think that they made it through the process of agent, reader, editor, commissions panel and proofer without anyone pointing out that opening a novel with a detective being called to a patch of waste ground to look at a slaughtered girl was not original. Originality has a tendency to decrease one's popularity.

Crime fiction accounts for more than a third of all fiction published in the UK, but there are relatively few contemporary London stories being told with audacity and flair. This is odd, because crime with an element of black comedy is something we do incredibly well, from films like *The Ladykillers* and *Kill List* to authors like Kyril Bonfiglioli, Joyce Porter and the wonderful, underrated Pamela Branch. Few crime writers stray from the narrow path set by publishers in the wake of Nordic Noir. Stieg Larsson's books were proof that you could get away with anything if you said it with a straight face. They're very enjoyable reads, but patently absurd. Shows like *The Killing* and *The Bridge* made for excellent television, but their success has only exacerbated the problem for authors. As Tony Hancock once said, 'People respect you more when you don't get laughs.'

We are told that readers want veracity, but readers will accept that a murderer is stalking London according to the rules of a Victorian tontine, even though they'll ask why your detective doesn't age in real time. I've coped with the fact that Bryant and May are ancient and getting older by providing a suitably outrageous explanation in one of the later books.

Britain's Golden Age mysteries frequently featured surreal crimes investigated by wonderfully eccentric sleuths. From Gladys Mitchell and Margery Allingham in the thirties to Peter Van Greenaway and Peter Dickinson in the sixties, the form was treated as something joyous and playful. *The Notting Hill Mystery*, which many regard as the first detective novel, was republished by the British Library and consists of letters, reports, floor plans and notes. Dennis Wheatley created a similar set of whodunnit-dossiers containing photographs, blood-stained material, a burned match, a lock of hair and other pieces of evidence in little bags. Even though his mysteries weren't very good they were at least great fun.

They have been followed by too many doorstops of unrelenting grimness. Meanwhile, a handful of characters have become TV brands: Poirot, Holmes, Morse, Marple. Every year delivers another crate of old wine in new bottles. Kim Newman, whose own excellent Holmes books have a wonderful Gothic quality, has pointed out that TV doesn't need to purchase new ideas so long as it can get away with stealing old ones.

I would argue that what we once loved, and what we're not getting very much of these days, is murder mysteries which are as enjoyable from one page to the next as they are puzzling in their denouements. The beauty of crime tales from writers like Charlotte Armstrong, Edmund Crispin and Robert Van Gulik is that they were first and foremost fine reads, sometimes to the point where the solution to the crime was almost incidental.

Crime as a Confection

There's a quote from Barnes Wallis, the inventor of the bouncing bomb that destroyed the Ruhr dams in the Second World War, who said, 'There is nothing more satisfying than showing that something is impossible, then proving how it can be done.' That was what interested me about mystery writing from an early age. Well, that and my mother saying, 'If you write a book it will remain in the library long after you're dead.' If any of you have read my memoir *Paperboy* you'll know it's typical of her to say 'after you're dead' to a nine-year-old.

I write a weekly column for the *Independent on Sunday* called 'Invisible Ink', about once massively popular authors who have now become a minority taste or who have disappeared altogether, and it's surprising how many wrote over a hundred books before vanishing into collective forgetfulness. They fade from popularity because tastes change, or their readers change, or the authors themselves change.

While I was researching the now virtually unread but once incredibly popular crime writer Margery Allingham, I discovered that she regarded a crime novel as a box with four sides: 'a killing, a mystery, an enquiry and a conclusion with an element of satisfaction in it'. Her plan – which I think is a good template for all popular novels – was to reduce books like stock, to boil them to a kind of thick broth of a language that tasted rich enough to satisfy and left you wanting to copy down the recipe. Allingham believed in the 'plum pudding principle': you provide your readers with a plum every few bites, to keep them interested in the whole pudding. Dickens famously did this, of course, and so in his own way does Mr Dan Brown. Allingham has an extraordinary richness to her writing – it's allusive, witty, bravura stuff – but it's a window to an English mindset that is now completely lost.

I fell for Sir Arthur Conan Doyle because he conveyed the creeping pallor of Victorian street life, the fume-filled taverns where a man might find himself propositioned by a burglarizing gargoyle, the Thames-side staircases where gimlet-eyed doxies awaited the easily duped. Even his cheerful scenes felt vaguely gruesome: shopkeepers would drape a Christmas goose around a character's neck like a feather boa; and the welcoming yellow light of a first-floor window could somehow suggest that its tenant was lying dead on the floor. Fog muffled murderers' footsteps and London sunlight was always watery. The Holmes adventures were virtually horror stories. Men went raving mad in locked rooms, or died of fright for no discernible reason. Women were simply unknowable.

And even when you found out how it was done or who did it, what kind of lunatic would choose to kill someone by sending a rare Indian snake down a bell-pull? Who in their right mind would come up with the idea of hiring a ginger-haired man to copy out books in order to provide cover for a robbery?

Graduating to the Agatha Christie books, the initial thrill of discovering such plot ingenuity also created a curious sense of dissatisfaction. How were you supposed to identify with any of the characters? On my street there weren't any colonels, housemaids, vicars, flighty debutantes, dowager duchesses or cigar-chomping tycoons. Certainly, none of our neighbours had ever attended a country house party, let alone found a body in the library. Nobody owned a library, and country houses were places you were dragged around on Sunday afternoons. I never went shooting on the estate – although sometimes there *was* a shooting on an estate.

At least Conan Doyle's solutions possessed a kind of strange plausibility, whereas Christie's murder victims apparently received dozens of visitors in the moments before they died, queuing up outside their bedrooms like cheap flights waiting to unload, and the victims were killed by doctored pots of jam, guns attached to bits of string, poisoned trifles and knives on springs.

'It is a childishly simple affair, *mon ami*. Brigadier Hawthorne removed the letter-opener from the marmalade pot *before* Hortense the maid found the burned suicide note in the grate, *after* Doctor Caruthers hid the viper, easily mistaken for a stethoscope, under the aspidistra, *at exactly the same time as* Lady Pettigrew was emptying arsenic over the jugged hare.' The only thing I ever learned from an Agatha Christie novel was the lengths to which county people would go to show how much they hated each other.

Traditionally, authors who write more books featuring

their detectives survive over ones who write fewer, but there are exceptions. Sir Arthur Conan Doyle and R. Austin Freeman post similar numbers: Sherlock Holmes starred in 56 stories and 4 novels, while Freeman's terrific Dr Thorndyke appeared in 40 short stories and 22 novels. Agatha Christie used Hercule Poirot in 33 books, while her contemporary Gladys Mitchell used her detective Mrs Bradley in 66 volumes. Dorothy L. Sayers only wrote 11 Lord Peter Wimsey novels, while Robert Van Gulik wrote 25 Judge Dee novels, although as each of these contain several cases in the Chinese style do we count them as more?

When it comes to totals, Christie also wrote an additional fifty short stories featuring Hercule Poirot, so she wins on volume. This is important as readers develop a loyalty, but it also creates its own problems. How do you keep a series fresh?

It's not all about numbers, of course. Colin Dexter wrote surprisingly few Inspector Morse novels, but an exemplary TV series kept his character alive with stories often created by respected playwrights, and despite the death of the superlative actor John Thaw, they continued into both the future and the past with spin-off series. The *Bryant & May* books are slightly unusual in that they're simultaneously fictional pastiches full of real London history, but also contain quite a large cast of characters – what I term 'the Springfield effect' – all of whom I have to keep track of. Then there are the plots . . .

The Impossible Sleuths

I rarely watched TV as a child, but I did love *The Avengers*, joining at the start of the Emma Peel series, where strange plots were the norm – the field in which rain drowns people, the village where nobody dies but the cemetery fills up, killer nannies, clocks with missing hours, houses that send you mad – and I failed to realize that these were Golden Age plots transposed to the medium of television.

Many years later I came back to the classic mysteries I'd found in the library, with their academic eccentricities and timeless view of an England that never really existed. If you're going to describe the investigation of a crime, you might as well have fun with it.

I did some homework. I read Sexton Blake and Raffles, who were so chinless you had to wonder how they managed to put a pillowcase on by themselves, but the early French masters were fun because they were sometimes dashing, like Arsène Lupin, or stubbornly peculiar, like Vidocq and Fantômas. There were the afore-mentioned R. Austin Freeman's charming Edwardian mysteries featuring Dr Thorndyke, showcasing the opposite of the whodunnit, the 'inverted mystery', the how-will-he-be-caught? puzzle. And there was Edmund Crispin, the spirited, funny man who composed six scores for the *Carry On* films and wrote the majority of his joyous Gervase Fen books between 1945 and 1952. Fen is the crime-solving Professor of English Language and Literature, and assumes that the reader can keep up with him as he spouts literary allusions while cracking crimes over a pint. There were also those mordant mysteries by Gladys Mitchell, starring pterodactyl-like Mrs Bradley. Mitchell was once judged the equal of Dorothy L. Sayers and Agatha Christie.

I wanted to create my own detectives like theirs, so Bryant and May were born. I made my sleuths elderly because I was fed up with the ageism that suggests only the young can carry out their jobs well, and wanted to show that older characters could bring knowledge and experience to crimefighting.

The plan – as much as there was one – was to explore my detectives' careers from beginning to end, so *Full Dark House* was an origin story, kicking off with their very first meeting during wartime. I used the setting of old London theatres because they have hardly changed in decades. London is full of unusual characters, so I use people I've met, including a British Museum academic who finds his enthusiasm getting him into trouble with the law, artists, lecturers, a white witch, a disgraced scientist, members of a Gilbert and Sullivan society – all real. Unlike my stand-alone novels, such as *Plastic* and *Nyctophobia*, the *Bryant & May*s feel as if they write themselves. I'd be lying if I denied they're hard work to put together – they are – but I have more confidence now.

To invent your own detective you have to ask yourself about the sleuths of the past. When Sir Arthur Conan Doyle conceived Sherlock Holmes, why didn't he give the famous consulting detective a few more quirks: a wooden leg, say, and an Oedipus complex? Well, Holmes didn't need many physical tics or personality disorders; the very concept of a consulting detective was still fresh and original in 1887.

But most detectives of the past have very few defining characteristics. By the time you get to Hercule Poirot all you have is some Euro-pomposity, an egg-shaped head, 'ze little grey cells' and a moustache. It's interesting that we could talk about our friends using the shorthand templates of Dickens's characters, saying 'He's a regular Harold Skimpole' or 'She's a real Mrs Jellyby', those being just minor roles in *Bleak House*, but you can't do that even with a main character in many crime novels. Past mystery writers tended to be driven by the mystery, not the investigator.

How does a writer create a detective? I started with a matchbox label that read 'Bryant & May – England's Glory'. That gave me their names, their nationality, and something vague and appealing, the sense of an institution with roots in London's sooty past. London would be the third character; not the tourist city of guidebooks but the city of invisible societies, hidden parks and drunken theatricals, the increasingly endangered species I eagerly show to friends when they visit.

Every night, my detectives walk across Waterloo Bridge and share ideas, because a city's skyline is best sensed along the edges of its river, and London's has changed dramatically in less than a decade, with the broken spire of the Shard and the great Ferris wheel of the London Eye lending it a raffish fairground feel.

By making Bryant and May old I could have them simultaneously behave like experienced adults and immature children. Bryant, I knew, came from Whitechapel and was academic, esoteric, eccentric, bad-tempered and myopic. He would wear a hearing aid and false teeth, and use a walking stick. A proud Luddite, he was antisocial, rude, erudite, bookish, while John May was born in Vauxhall, taller, fitter, more charming, friendlier, a little more modern, techno-literate and a bit of a ladies' man. Their inevitable clash of working methods often causes cases to take wrong turns.

'A Lovely Bit of Dialogue'

The hardest part was accepting the fact that after writing a great many books I was once again starting on the first rung of a new learning ladder. Smart plotting wasn't enough; situations needed to be generated by character. Recurring staff members appeared pretty much fully formed. The rest of the team had to have small but memorable characteristics: a constable with a coordination problem; a sergeant who behaved too literally; a socially inept CSM; you can't give them big issues if they're going to be in several books, because you don't want their problems to steal the spotlight from your heroes.

One of my favourite ancillary movie characters wasn't from a crime film at all. Police Constable Ruby Gates was played by Joyce Grenfell in the early St Trinian's films. It was a very funny idea to have a lovestruck PC missing police broadcasts because she had retuned her radio to a romantic music station. Her response to her sergeant was: 'Oh Sammy, you used to call me your little blue-lamp baby.' This is only amusing if you can picture her. There was also the hilariously stern Sergeant Lucilla Wilkins played by Eleanor Summerfield in the film *On The Beat*. Forced to operate undercover in a hairdressing salon, she had to keep getting her hair permed to garner information, and became increasingly gorgon-like through the film. There are also bits of Diana Dors, Liz Fraser, Sabrina and other pin-up models from the 1950s, but to create Sergeant Janice Longbright I added the toughness of a real constable I knew and characteristics of Googie Withers in *It Always Rains on Sunday*. The film is explicitly mentioned in one of the PCU bulletins that always start off the novels.

Arthur Bryant's landlady started out as an Antiguan version of Irene Handl in *The Rebel* (with whom I once spent an enjoyable afternoon). The name of Dame Maude Hackshaw, one of Maggie Armitage's coven, is an homage to a short-lived headmistress in a St Trinian's film, which also inspired the idea of the two workmen who never leave the PCU office. There are many other hidden influences in the books, some drawn from friends, some from childhood books and movies.

I stuck by my character outlines, even though a couple of interviewers told me I should have made them younger, which would allow for more sex and violence – the very thing I didn't want to do. It wasn't a matter of prudery; rather the fact that a sexual bout or a fist fight is a lazy exit from an awkward scene. I wanted the tone to be light and funny, all the better to slip in serious moments.

I linked the Bryant & May novels with compounding clues and recurring characters as reward-points for loyal readers. Following the Barnes Wallis rule, I started the first Bryant & May novel with an explosion that destroys the detectives' unit and kills Arthur Bryant. I created a police division, the Peculiar Crimes Unit, loosely based on a real experimental unit founded by the government during the Second World War, and added younger staff members who would be knowledgeable about the 'new' London. I listened to oral histories of Londoners stored in museums, and ploughed through the diaries, note-books and memorabilia hoarded by their families. This wasn't strictly necessary; I just enjoyed doing it.

For my second Golden-Age-detectives-in-the-modern-world mystery, *The Water Room*, the research was literally on my doorstep; my house was built on top of one of London's forgotten rivers, the Fleet, so the tale concerned a woman found drowned in a completely dry room. I usually explain that the strangest facts in my books are the real ones.

As a location, London offers more anachronistic juxtapositions than most European cities – you're likely to find a church on the site of a brothel – and it was important to find a way of reflecting this. Each story tries out a different kind of Golden Age mystery fiction: *Full Dark House* is a whodunnit; *The Water Room* is a John Dickson Carr-style locked-room mystery; *Seventy-Seven Clocks* is an adventure in the manner of Bulldog Drummond; and so on.

The unlikeliest elements of these tales turned out to be mined from London's forgotten lore: tales of lost paintings, demonized celebrities, buried sacrifices, mysterious guilds and social panics had casts of whores, mountebanks, lunatics and impresarios who have been washed aside by the tide of history – but their descendants are still all around us, living in the capital city.

In the sixth book, *The Victoria Vanishes*, I dived into the hidden secrets of London pubs. When you've got established characters your readers root for, you can start playing games. So far I've had Bryant and May release illegal immigrants into the social system, disrupt government offices and even commit acts of terrorism in order to see that justice is done. *Bryant & May On the Loose* dug into the murky world of land ownership in London, and *Bryant & May Off the Rails* did something similar for the Underground system. *The Memory of Blood* looked at how the English subverted the legend of Punch and Judy to their own ends.

One of the joys was always tackling the duo's dialogue. They had known each other for so long that they could almost see each other's thoughts. A writer friend said, 'I'm not much of a drinker but I do like a visit to the pub to find a lovely bit of dialogue.'

One criticism levelled at me by a reader was that my books were 'too quirky to be realistic'. I took him to my local pub, the King Charles I in King's Cross. It sometimes hosted the Nude Alpine Climbing Challenge, which involved traversing the saloon dressed only in a coil of rope and crampons, never touching the floor. The pub was always either packed or closed, according to some mysterious timetable that the owner kept in his head. On that particular night everyone in the place had a ukulele. It was heaving, and what appeared to be a stuffed moose head or possibly the top half of a deformed donkey was lying on the bar billiards table. The owner was attempting to attach it on the wall in place of a barometer, 'from where,' he said, 'it can gaze across to the gazelle opposite with a loving look in its eyes'.

While we were supping our beers, a man reached past my companion for a giant, well-thumbed volume. 'Let me pass you the telephone directory,' my friend offered. 'No, mate,' the drinker replied, 'this is the pub dictionary. It gets a lot more use in here than a phone book.' The crowd started playing the theme from *Star Wars* on their ukuleles, led by Uke Skywalker. And then Iain Banks wandered in. After that my friend concluded that perhaps I had not exaggerated the books' quirkiness.

Londoners remember Soho's Coach & Horses pub for its rude landlord Norman Balon, but few realize that it was the drinking hole of the Prince Edward Theatre's scenery-shifters. One evening I overheard a huge tattooed shifter at the bar telling his mate, 'I says to 'im, call yourself a bleeding Polonius? I could shit better speeches to Laertes than that.'

Well, write such dialogue down and you follow authors like Margery Allingham, Gerald Kersh, Alexander Baron and Joe Orton, who were clearly fascinated by London's magpie language and behaviour.

In the process of finding subjects for investigation, I've covered the Blitz, theatres, underground rivers, pre-Raphaelite artists, tontines, highwaymen, new British artists, the cult of celebrity, London pubs and clubs, land ownership, immigration, churches, the tube system, the Knights Templar, King Mob, codebreaking and Guy Fawkes, and still feel as if I'm only scratching at the surface of London history.

All writers are influenced by the things they've experienced, read and watched, by people they've met or heard about. The resulting books should not, I feel, reveal the whole of that iceberg. There must always be something more for the reader to discover.

Which brings me to this volume. Short fiction is rather out of favour these days, but I couldn't resist the opportunity of fleshing out some of the missing cases from the files of the Peculiar Crimes Unit. Think of this as a Christmas annual, a throwback to the days when such collections came with a few tricks and surprises. Ideally I would have included a selection of working models you could cut out. Maybe next time . . .

The Peculiar Crimes Unit as drawn by Keith Page, Age 14, Upper 4B

BRYANT & MAY: *DRAMATIS PERSONAE*

Raymond Land, Acting Temporary Unit Chief

The Temporary Unit Chief dreams of escaping the PCU, but never manages to get away. An obsessive, meticulous member of the General and Administrative Division, he graduated in Criminal Biology, but often misses the point of his investigations. It's said of him that 'He could identify a tree from its bark samples without comprehending the layout of the forest.' He can't control his detectives. Or his wife.

Arthur Bryant, Senior Detective

Elderly, bald, always cold, scarf-wrapped, a wearer of shapeless brown cardigans and overlarge Harris tweed coats, Bryant is an enigma: well-read, rude, bad-tempered, conveniently deaf and a smoker of disgusting pipe tobacco (and cannabis for his arthritis, so he says). He's a truly terrifying driver. He wears a hearing aid, has false teeth, uses a walking stick, and has to take a lot of pills. Once married (his wife fell from a bridge), he worked at various police stations and units around London, including Bow Street, Savile Row and North London Serious Crimes Division. He shares a flat with long-suffering Alma Sorrowbridge, his Antiguan landlady.

John May, Senior Detective

Born in Vauxhall, John is taller, fitter, more charming and personable than his partner. He's technology-friendly, three years younger than Bryant, and drives a silver BMW. A sometimes melancholy craver of company, he leaves the TV on all the time when alone. He walks to Waterloo Bridge most nights with Bryant for 'thinking time'. Vain and a bit of a ladies' man, he lives in a modernist, barely decorated flat in Shad Thames. He's divorced; his son and granddaughter now live in Canada.

Janice Longbright, Detective Sergeant

Janice is a career copper; her mother Gladys worked for Bryant. She models herself on 1950s and 1960s film stars, and prides herself on looking glamorous. She's smart but tough, and hates to show her true feelings. Dedicated to Arthur and John, she always puts work before her personal life. She lives a solitary existence in her flat in Highgate, and keeps a house brick in her handbag for dealing with unwanted attention.

Dan Banbury, Crime Scene Manager/InfoTech

The unit's crime scene manager and IT expert is almost normal compared to his colleagues. He's a sturdy, decent sort, married with a son, although he gets a little over-enthusiastic when it comes to discussing crime scenes and can bore for England on the subject of inefficient internet service providers.

Jack Renfield, Desk Sergeant

This sturdy former Albany Street desk sergeant is a brisket-faced by-the-book sort of chap who used to be unpleasant and dismissive of the PCU. Blunt but honest, he tends to think with his fists, and had an ill-fated relationship with Janice Longbright. He plays footie for the Met.

Meera Mangeshkar, Detective Constable

The stroppy, difficult, Kawasaki-driving DC comes from a poor South London Indian family, but beneath the (very) hard shell she has a good heart. However, she's determined to resist the advances of Colin Bimsley, her co-worker.

Colin Bimsley, Detective Constable

The fit, fair-haired, clumsy cop is hopelessly in love with Meera, and suffers from Diminished Spatial Awareness, which can make him a liability. His father was also a former PCU member. Colin trained at Repton Amateur Boxing Club for three years, and will only give up trying to date his co-worker if there's a restraining order placed on him.

Giles Kershaw, Forensic Pathology

The Forensics/Social Sciences Liaison Officer is naturally curious, winning, posh and plum-voiced. Promoted to the position of Chief Coroner at the St Pancras Mortuary, he has relatives in high places who can occasionally help the unit out of tight spots.

Liberty and Fraternity DuCaine

These virtually identical West Indian brothers are auxiliary officers who help the detectives in key cases. After Liberty was brutally murdered, his brother Fraternity stepped in to help out at the unit.

April May

May's granddaughter was severely agoraphobic until re-solving issues about her mother, killed by a man the press dubbed the Leicester Square Vampire. Thin and ethere-ally pale, she joined the unit and was good at making connections, but left after the stress became too much for her. She now lives in Canada near John May's estranged son.

Crippen, staff cat

Everyone thought he was a boy-cat until he had kittens. Named after the first murderer to be caught by telegraph.

Maggie Armitage

The good-natured Maggie runs the Coven of St James the Elder, in Kentish Town. A Grand Order Grade IV White Witch, she is permanently broke but lives to help others in need of her dubious services. She's part of a network of oddballs, academics and alternative therapists who help the unit from time to time.

Leslie Faraday

The government's most pedantic civil servant, an outspoken, thick-skinned Home Office Liaison Officer who is thoughtlessly rude and never forgets a grudge. The Peculiar Crimes Unit makes his life miserable, so he tries to return the favour.

Surrounding these main characters are what could loosely be described as Arthur Bryant's 'alternatives', consisting mainly of fringe activists, shamans, shams and spiritualists, astronomers and astrologers, witches both black and white, artists of every hue from watercolour to con, banned scientists, barred medics, socially inept academics, Bedlamites, barkers, dowsers, duckers, divers and drunks, many of them happy to help the unit for the price of a beer or a bed for the night.

When I was a child the highlight of the year was to visit Santa Claus at Gamages department store in Holborn. There was always a magical journey to reach him (knocked together with rotating bits of scenery and hand-rocked modes of transport) and when you arrived His Ho-Ho-Holiness would sit you on his knee and ask you if you'd been good all year. Gamages began with a tiny shop front in 1878, but by 1911 its catalogue ran to nine hundred pages. In the early 1970s it was replaced by offices and 'exciting retail spaces'. It went the way of other great London department stores – Swan & Edgar, Marshall & Snelgrove, Bourne & Hollingsworth, Derry & Toms and Dickins & Jones. The idea for this story came from something that actually happened to me.

BRYANT & MAY
AND THE SECRET SANTA

'I blame Charles Dickens,' said Arthur Bryant as he and his partner John May battled their way up the brass steps of the London Underground staircase and out into Oxford Street. 'If you say you don't like Christmas everyone calls you Scrooge.' He fanned his walking stick from side to side in order to clear a path. It was snowing hard, but Oxford Circus was not picturesque. The great peristaltic circle had already turned to black slush beneath the tyres of buses and the boots of pedestrians. Regent Street was a different matter. Virtually nothing could kill its class. The Christmas lights shone through falling snowflakes along the length of John Nash's curving terrace, but even this sight failed to impress Bryant.

'You're doing your duck face,' said May. 'What are you disapproving of now?'

'Those Christmas lights.' Bryant waggled his walking stick at them and nearly took someone's eye out. 'When I was a child Regent Street was filled with great chandeliers at this time of the year. These ones aren't even proper lights, they're bits of plastic advertising a Disney film.'

May had to admit that his partner was right. Above them, Ben Stiller's Photoshopped face peered down like an eerie, ageless Hollywood elf.

'We never came to Oxford Street as kids,' Bryant continued. 'My brother and I used to head to Holborn with our mother to visit the Father Christmas at Gamages department store. I loved that place. You would get into a rocket ship or a paddle steamer and step off in Santa's grotto. That building was a palace of childhood magic. I still can't believe they pulled it down.'

'Well, you're going to see Santa now, aren't you?' May reminded him.

'Yes, but it's not the same when you feel like you're a hundred years old. Plus, there's a death involved this time, which sort of takes the sparkle off one's Yuletide glow.'

'Fair point,' May conceded as Bryant tamped Old Holborn into his Lorenzo Spitfire and lit it.

They passed a Salvation Army band playing carols. '"Silent Night",' Bryant noted. 'I wish it bloody was.

Look at these crowds. It'll take us an age to reach
Selfridges. We should have got off at Bond Street.'

'Can you stop moaning?' asked May. 'I thought that as
we were coming here we could pop into John Lewis and
get my sister a kettle.'

'Dear God, is that what she wants for Christmas?'
Bryant peeped over his tattered green scarf, shocked.
'There's not much seasonal spirit in that.'

'It's better than before. She used to email me Argos
catalogue numbers,' said May. 'When I first opened her
note I thought she'd written it in code.'

A passing bus delivered them to the immense department store founded by Harry Selfridge, the shopkeeper
who coined the phrase 'The customer is always right'.
The snow was falling in plump white flakes, only to be
transmuted into liquid coal underfoot. Bryant stamped
and shook in the doorway like a wet dog. With his
umbrella and stick he looked like a cross between an
alpine climber and a troll.

By the escalators, a store guide stood with a faraway
look in his eye, as if he was imagining himself to be anywhere but where he was. 'I say, you there.' Bryant tapped
an epaulette with his stick. 'Where's Father Christmas?'

'Under-twelves only,' said the guide.

'We're here about Sebastian Carroll-Williams,' said
May, holding up his PCU card.

The guide apologized and sent them down to the
basement, where 'O Come, All Ye Faithful' was playing
on a loop along with 'I Saw Three Ships' and 'Ding
Dong Merrily on High'. The Christmas department
was a riot of fake trees, plastic snow, glitter, sledges,
wassail cups, cards, robotic Santas, dancing reindeer,
singing penguins, North Poles, Christmas logs, candles,

cake-holders, cushions, jumpers and chinaware printed with pictures of puddings, holly, mistletoe and fairies. 'It's been this jolly since October,' said the gloomy sales girl, directing them. In her right hand she held some china goblins on a toboggan. 'It makes you dead morbid after a while.'

Beyond this accretion of Yuletidiana, a large area had been turned into something called 'The Santa's Wonderland Sleigh-ride Experience'. 'Why do they have to call everything an "experience"?' asked Bryant irritably. 'It's tautological and clumsy. It's like *Strictly Come Dancing*. The BBC obviously couldn't decide whether to name it after the old show *Come Dancing* or the film *Strictly Ballroom* so they ended up with gibberish. Two verbs and an adverb? How is that supposed to work? Does nobody study grammar any more?'

'It's hard to learn that stuff,' said May. 'English is the only language I can think of where two negatives can mean a positive, and yet conversely there are no two positives that can mean a negative.'

'Yeah, right.' Bryant turned around. 'Look out, floor manager.'

Mr Carraway was a man so neatly arranged as to appear polished and stencilled, from the moisturized glow of his forehead and his carefully threaded eyebrows to his shining thumbnails and toecaps. 'Thank you so much for coming,' he said, pumping each of their hands in turn. 'We didn't know if this was a matter for the proper police or for someone like you, and then one of our ladies said you dealt with the sort of things they couldn't be bothered with.'

'Oh yes, we were just sitting around knitting and doing jigsaws, waiting for your call,' said Bryant. 'You'd better tell us what happened before I'm tempted to bite you.'

The floor manager eyed him uncertainly. 'Er, yes, well, perhaps we should go into Santa's Wonderland,' he said, leading the way.

'I thought it was Alice who had a Wonderland,' said Bryant as they walked.

'No, this is Santa's Wonderland,' said Mr Carraway.

'Yes, but, you know – Alice in *Wonderland*.'

'We narrowed it down to Wonderland or Christmas-ville. It could have gone either way.'

A tunnel of black light illuminated Bryant's dentures, turning him into a Mexican Day of the Dead doll. They emerged from the other end to find an immense cyclorama of the North Pole as imagined by a very gay man who had seen too many Disney films, complete with geographically misplaced polar bears and a variety of non-reality-based fauna including elves, goblins and little people in pointed hats and dirndls, some of whom were real and presumably taking time out from their busy performance schedules as gold-mining dwarves or Oompa-Loompas.

'Mickey,' called Mr Carraway, 'where's Father Christmas?'

'He's gone to the toilet,' said Mickey, one of the dwarves. He looked up at the two detectives, studying each of them in turn. 'Are you here about the lad who died?'

'Yes,' said May. 'Were you here when it happened?'

'Yeah, we're here for the full season,' said Mickey. 'We were supposed to be in panto at the Fairfields Hall, Croydon, but we got laid off after Snow White put in a sexual harassment claim against us. She said we touched her bum but we were just trying to get her into the glass coffin. She's a hefty lass.'

Just then Father Christmas came back on to the Arctic set doing up his flies. 'Ah, the rozzers,' he said, rolling his Rs in a plummily theatrical brogue. 'I suppose you want to know how the magic happens. Of course, I'm just filling in doing this. Normally I'm treading the boards. I had to come out of a *major* role, but who can resist helping out at Christmas?'

'What were you doing?' asked May.

'The Duke of Ephesus, *Comedy of Errors*, "Five summers have I spent in farthest Greece, Roaming clean through the bounds of Asia . . ."'

'Whereabouts?'

'Crawley Rep. It's a nice short play and I was in a toga so I could be in the pub by ten.'

'Can you talk us through what happened?' asked May.

Father Christmas pulled down his white beard and scratched his chin with the end of a biro. 'Sorry, these things get damnably hot. It was the day before yesterday, just before six o'clock, wasn't it, Mickey?'

The dwarf nodded.

'This lad, Sebastian Carroll-Williams, about eleven, small for his age. I saw him come in with his mum. She was fussing around him something chronic. Normally that's my cue to take over and have a chat with them about what they want for Christmas. I always tell the same joke.'

'What sort of a joke?' asked Bryant.

'*What did the elf get while he was working in Santa's toyshop? Tinsellitis.* We don't sit them on our knees any more, not since Jimmy Savile. We're all very carefully vetted. And we're on camera.'

'Last year we had a Father Christmas with creeping hands,' said Mr Carraway. 'Dreadful.'

'Then we get them ready for their selfies,' said Santa.

'What selfies?' Bryant asked.

'They get a choice of outfit: polar bear, Santa's helper or toy soldier,' said Mickey. 'Princess gown for a girl. The girls only get one choice. Me and the other dwarves put the costumes over their heads. It just takes a few moments. Velcro. We're on turnover.'

'Then what?'

'The photographer takes his shot,' said Santa, 'I give them their gift and they're slung back on the sleigh. It's like processing hamburgers.'

'What did the boy pick for his outfit?' asked May.

'He didn't have a preference. He didn't want to be here at all. I think his mother pushed him into it, so he finally went for a polar bear. A real sense of entitlement about him. Dead stroppy. Mickey had to help him get into his outfit because he was angry and got all tangled up in it.'

'They're hyperactive at that age,' said Mickey. 'And they fart a lot. Nerves.'

'What did he ask Father Christmas to bring him?'

'A machine gun.' Santa rolled his eyes. 'Kids. So he got a gift from the sack and was sent on his way. He took the sleigh-ride back to the tunnel exit.'

'What was the gift?' asked May.

'I've no idea,' Santa admitted. 'We just work from the colour-coded boxes. The girls get tiaras and cuddly toys and games, the boys get more gadgety stuff. It all comes from China. Mind you, some of the gifts are pretty good. I never got things like that when I was a kid. We encourage them to open their presents after they've left

Wonderland, just so they don't get bits of cardboard all over the place.'

'Do you know anything about what happened after the boy left?' Bryant asked.

Santa shrugged. 'You'll have to ask Mr Carraway about that.'

'I saw him just as he came out of the tunnel, back into the main store,' said the floor manager. 'He was holding the torn-open box in his hand and appeared to be in a state of distress. His mother was nowhere in sight. You get an instinct about trouble.' He touched a plucked eyebrow as if securing it in place. 'I started walking towards him and suddenly he threw the box across the china hall. Luckily, nothing broke. I went after him but by this time he had reached the escalator. I got there as quickly as I could, but it was hard to see him, being so small. He ran between the make-up counters and out into the road.'

'Where he was hit by a number 53 bus,' said May, checking his notes.

'He went straight under the wheels,' said Mr Carraway. 'He never regained consciousness. The doctor reckoned he didn't feel anything.'

'We interviewed Carroll-Williams's mother,' said May. 'She went running after him but the store was very crowded and she lost sight of him.'

'So the boy was fine when he left you and got back into the sleigh,' said Bryant.

'Yeah, it only goes halfway round a bit of track. He could barely wait for it to stop.'

'But when he emerged from the tunnel he was distraught. Was there anyone else in the tunnel with him?' May asked.

'No, we were finishing for the evening. There were just the six of us: Mickey, me, the photographer, the kid, the kid's mother and the other Father Christmas. We were all still here in Wonderland when the boy left.'

'Wait, I'm confused,' said Bryant. '*You're* Father Christmas.'

'No, I'm *a* Father Christmas,' said Father Christmas. 'There's two of us, working in rotation. It would be too knackering otherwise.'

'Wait, so you saw everything from where you were backstage but it was the *other* Santa who asked Sebastian what he wanted for Christmas?'

'You've grasped it,' said Santa. 'I'm Edwin, he's – What was his name, Mickey?'

'God knows,' said Mickey. 'We get through them at a rate of knots.'

'I'm embarrassed to say I'm not sure either,' said Mr Carraway. 'He was only here a few days. The incident probably upset him. It must have done because he didn't come in yesterday.'

'But you have a contact number for him?' May asked with a sinking feeling.

'Certainly,' said Mr Carraway. 'Our Santas are vetted very carefully.'

'You need to find it for us as soon as you can,' said May.

Bryant was thinking. The loss of one Father Christmas didn't seem to bother him. 'So the boy must have opened his gift as he walked out through the tunnel.'

'It looks that way.'

'What on earth did he find inside the box to upset him so much that he would run out into the street without watching for traffic?'

'That's the oddest part about it,' said Mr Carraway.

'He threw it away just after opening it. It was completely empty.'

'He wasn't carrying the gift? It wasn't on his person?'

'No, there was nothing inside the box or on him at the accident site,' said Santa.

'If it was empty, it must have felt lighter than the usual gift packages,' said Bryant.

'No, because some of them just have vouchers inside that you can take to the electronics department.'

'You didn't notice anything out of the ordinary about this particular box?'

'It was just like all the others. You can see the CCTV footage if you want,' said Mr Carraway. 'There's nothing on it that's remotely unusual or different from any other Santa experience.'

'Do you still have the box?' asked Bryant.

'Yes, I had one of my girls put it in a plastic bag for you,' said Mr Carraway. 'It's in my office.'

The detectives examined the box and found nothing unusual about it. Then they watched the CCTV footage of the other Father Christmas with Sebastian Carroll-Williams. In terms of identification, it didn't help that Santa wore a wig, a hat and a beard. The footage had no sound, but the actions of both made everything pretty clear. Santa told his joke, helped the boy into his polar-bear outfit, posed with him for the selfie, gave him a gift and sent him on his way. At no point was there any physical contact between them.

'It's obvious that whatever happened to the child occurred in the tunnel,' said Bryant. 'But I'll need you to find the contact for your other Santa, just to corroborate the sequence of events.'

'Has it occurred to you that the kid might just have

had anger-management issues?' May asked as they trudged back through the sludge to the tube station. 'He could have been upset about the box being empty or just annoyed with his mother. He might have discovered that he was claustrophobic and freaked out in the tunnel or the crowds. Any number of things could have happened.'

'No,' said Bryant. 'He'd walked in through the crowded store and was fine. You heard what his mother said. It was only after he saw Father Christmas that he panicked. We have to track down the missing Santa. And get Dan Banbury to go over every inch of the tunnel. If that's where he opened the box, he might have discarded evidence.'

That night, as the detectives sat working late in their offices and the crusted snow on their window ledges started to roast black from car exhaust fumes, Dan Banbury turned up, ridiculously underdressed. 'I'm glad you're still here,' he told them, pulling off his scarf to reveal a short-sleeved Hawaiian shirt. 'I was supposed to be at a party tonight. The trains are up the spout. Why does London have to grind to a stop when it snows? They manage all right everywhere else. Look at Russia. They can't even produce an edible salad but their trains run on time. We've just finished at Selfridges. I think we've got something.'

'I hope you have,' retorted Bryant. 'We've got nothing. It's starting to look like our Santa's done a bunk.'

'Well, don't get too excited. There was nothing on or in the box, but we lifted this from the tunnel.' Banbury unclipped his forensics box and took out a small clear bag, emptying its contents on to the desk.

Bryant donned his trifocals and squinted at the object.

It appeared to be a tiny, ragged scrap of dark-blue cloth. 'What's that?' he asked. 'It looks like there's something written on it.'

'It's hard to read but definitely a signature. "Branways",' said Banbury. 'Picked out in gold and silver thread. I thought you might have an idea what it means.'

'Not a clue. Did you run a search?'

'I just got back,' said Banbury. 'I thought you'd like to do that.'

'Found it,' said May, checking online. 'It's an old-fashioned school-uniform shop, supplies exclusively to St Crispin's School for Boys. It says here the school was founded in 1623 by the Right Honourable Sir Thomas Lindsay. "For almost four hundred years the institution has prospered, with many of its Old Boys going on to great achievements in the world of politics, sport and the liberal arts." Did Sebastian go there? The mother said something . . .'

'I made a note somewhere,' said Bryant, scrubbing about among the rubbishy scraps of paper on his desk. 'Ah, it would seem he did. We've missed the shop tonight. You might as well go to your party, Dan.'

'I'm supposed to take a pineapple,' said Banbury.

'The Asian place over the road will be open,' said May. 'Take a tin.'

The next morning, the detectives headed for the Covent Garden shop. It had snowed again overnight and then frozen hard, which made the pavements as treacherous as mountain paths. 'I'm not breaking a hip over this,' Bryant complained, picking his way through stalagmites of ice and frozen bags of restaurant garbage.

'Don't worry, I'll catch you if you go over,' said May.

The idea of requiring a helping hand did not, of course, appeal to Bryant, who would rather have plunged to his death than shown the need to accept assistance. The young man who had once cycled to work every morning and knew every pothole in the Strand had given way to the old man who sometimes struggled to get off the sofa, but his mind was as sharp as ever.

The outfitters' shop proved to be one of those odd anomalies London has a habit of producing from no-where. Its windows were decorated with gilt shields and its interior was dark wood, but it was wedged between a mobile-phone store and a Pret A Manger. Its manager, Miss Prentice, was a formidable presence, as stately as a galleon in full sail. Bryant imagined that she might have once been a headmistress, reluctantly released by the board of governors for being too free with the cane.

'Branways has been supplying school uniforms to St Crispin's for nearly four hundred years,' she said with fierce pride. 'My staff can get the measure of a child in a single glance. Of course, they're getting chubbier these days, but boarding school soon knocks that out of them.'

'I bet they hide the doughnuts and save the dosh,' said Bryant. 'Schools like St Crispin's are a closed book to me. What's to stop the parents from shopping elsewhere?'

'We hold the licence for the uniforms,' Miss Prentice explained. 'No other stylings are allowed. Lapels, ties and belts must all be a certain width, collars must be a specific distance from the hair, sleeves and cuffs have rigidly dictated lengths and cuts. And of course no one else has the right to hand-sew pocket badges, heraldic devices or crests. They're unique and impossible to duplicate. St Crispin's sportswear is renowned for its quality. Our pants have a double-lined gusset for those chilly mornings on the rugger pitch.'

'So it's fair to say you have the school uniform racket stitched up,' said Bryant, laughing at his own joke. Miss Prentice shot him a look that could have dented a frying pan.

He placed the plastic bag on her counter and shook the scrap of material out of it. 'I presume you've seen one of these before?'

Miss Prentice pushed back her iron-grey hair and peered closely. 'That's one of ours. It's the manufacturer's tag from the school tie. It's been cut off. They can't be torn. And it's not more than eighteen months old.'

'How can you tell?' Bryant asked.

'We briefly flirted with nylon thread but switched back to our own blend after complaints. This is from the new stock.'

'Can you provide us with a list of all the customers who have bought a tie like this?' asked May.

Miss Prentice pursed her lips alarmingly. 'I'd rather not divulge our client details.'

'Good Lord, you're not a doctor, you're flogging togs to nippers,' said Bryant, exasperated. 'Everybody's a big shot. I want a list of all the parents who bought this tie, right now, please.'

'There are one hundred and sixty boys in Covent Garden day school and four hundred and twenty in the main boarding school in Sussex.' Miss Prentice was suddenly agreeable. She had been stood up to, and respected that.

'Is there any way of narrowing that number down?' asked May.

'Let me see. Actually, yes. There are three ties, first

year, junior and sixth form. They're all slightly different in length and colour. This label is from the first-year size.'

'We only need you to check the boarding school,' said Bryant.

May was puzzled. 'Why?'

'This boy's family lives in Lewes. He and his mother had come up to town for the Christmas lights. He was in the first year so the tag is likely to be from someone of the same age.' He turned to Miss Prentice. 'St Crispin's. I'm sure it provides a wonderful education but I vaguely remember it being in the news.'

'I – heard something . . .' Miss Prentice began tentatively. 'There was a culture of bullying among the new boys. Of course, you tend to get these things in boarding schools but this one was particularly unfortunate.'

'Unfortunate in what way?'

'I think a boy died.'

'How long ago?'

'About a year, right around this time.'

May had already found a report of the case on his phone. 'Andrew Gormley, aged eleven,' he said. 'Hanged himself in the school dorm. An independent investigation carried out by the board of governors found a culture of persistent bullying existed among the first-year students.'

'I remember Andrew.' Miss Prentice suddenly softened, and Bryant saw kindness in her grey eyes. 'He was a sweet little boy. I remember fearing for him.'

'What do you mean?' Bryant asked.

'He didn't want to board,' she said. 'He was a very gentle, rather fragile-looking child. You worry about the ones who can't stand up for themselves.' Her steeliness returned. 'But it's important that they learn to do so. It's a training course for later life. The world is a cruel place, Mr Bryant, as I'm sure you know all too well.'

Mr Gormley lived in Redington Road, one of those twisting Hampstead backstreets that had once been filled with gruff artists and lady novelists but was now entirely the province of international bankers. Bryant preferred to catch those he interviewed by surprise, but as Gormley was liable to be out he phoned first to arrange a meeting. That evening the detectives walked down the road from the tube, and found themselves inside a Christmas card. The thick snow had rendered the winding hillside road more picturesque than ever. The laden trees and holly bushes, the terracotta chimneypots beneath lowering yellow skies, the odd red robin on a gatepost . . . there were only a few tyre tracks to mar the perfect scene.

'I'm sorry, gentlemen, I've only just got back. I may have to take some calls,' said Edward Gormley, shaking their hands. 'We've got a wildly fluctuating exchange rate on our hands tonight. It's all about finding the most favourable rate for our clients. Can I get you anything?'

'We just have a few simple questions, then we'll get out of your hair,' said May. Gormley was completely and prematurely grey. He looked as if he hadn't taken a day off work since his son died. The detectives were shown into a sterile, elegant front room with charcoal walls, filled with scenic sketches and watercolours. There were odd spaces, Bryant noted, as if someone had removed a number of items. He could smell an acrimonious divorce a mile away.

'It's about your son,' said May. 'We understand there was an investigation into his school's culture of bullying.'

'Yes, but as it was conducted by the school's own board

of governors nothing happened as a result of it,' said the financier. 'They were scared of putting parents off. Why, has there been a development?'

'It's an ongoing investigation,' May explained. 'I know it's a matter of record now, but we'd like to hear what happened to your son, if you wouldn't mind.'

'Andrew hated it at St Crispin's and wanted to come home,' Gormley explained. 'I was persuaded that this was the initial reaction of many children away from home for the first time, and told him he had to stay. I later found out that he tried to run away on several occasions.'

'Did you ever find out who was bullying him, or why?'

'Not really. There had been some cruel things posted online, but Andrew never named anyone in particular.'

'So the name Sebastian Carroll-Williams doesn't ring any bells?'

'I think he might have been in Andrew's class. Why?'

'He's dead,' said Bryant.

'How? What happened?'

'He ran out into the road after being frightened by someone.'

The financier remained motionless, simply staring back at them. All that could be heard was the mantelpiece clock ticking loudly. The phone rang suddenly. 'Excuse me,' he apologized, 'I have to take this.' He left the room.

'What just happened?' asked May.

'Something interesting.' Bryant rose and walked to the window overlooking the back garden. At the other end of the lawn was a bird table. A single set of tracks led out to it and back, through the otherwise pristine snow. Bryant frowned.

May knew that look all too well. 'What are you thinking?' he asked.

'Hang on a minute.' Bryant left the room, heading towards the rear of the house. He was gone for less than a minute, scooting back just in time to reseat himself before the financier returned.

'I'm sorry,' said Gormley. 'Where were we?'

'Winter's tough on the birds, isn't it?' said Bryant. 'It's nice to see you've been feeding them.'

'Oh.' Gormley turned around to look out of the window. 'It's very calming, having them around.'

'The wellingtons,' said Bryant.

'I'm sorry?'

'By the back door, still wet. I thought you'd only just made it back. It's not normally the first thing you'd do when you come in, is it? Feed the birds?'

Gormley checked his watch. 'Well, I may have been in a little longer.'

'An unusual colour for wellington boots,' said Bryant. His partner shot him a where-are-you-going-with-this look. 'Red, I mean. What did you do with the rest of the outfit?'

Gormley held his eyes again with the same unnerving stare. 'I don't know what you mean.'

'I think you do, Father Christmas.'

This time the stare could not hold. The boots were hard evidence. 'They don't supply the outfits,' he said, his voice thinning in pain. 'You have to buy your own.'

'Didn't they think it was strange, someone like you applying for a temporary job as a department store Santa?'

'You'd be surprised who takes a job as a Santa. People you'd never expect.'

'And you didn't know that the boy went under a bus.' Bryant took out the tie tag and placed it on the coffee table between them. 'I made a mistake,' he admitted, 'thinking this tie label belonged to your son. It didn't, did it?'

'No,' said Gormley softly.

'Tell me how it worked,' said Bryant.

'I never had the chance to go to a good school,' Gormley said. 'Our divorce was tough on Andrew. He was a bit of a cry-baby about the whole thing. I could afford to give him a decent education. I thought it would toughen him up. Instead he got picked on. They called him "Gormless" – not much of an imaginative leap there. It only takes one boy to poison the rest.'

'And that boy was Sebastian Carroll-Williams.'

'I complained about him, but my complaints were ignored. "It's what happens," they told me. "It'll pass. Strong metal must be forged in flames." But it didn't pass. The bullying got worse. I take it you know about the ties.'

'Why don't you tell us?' said May.

'The only time they ever come off is when you go to bed. They're a mark of respect and honour. Schools like St Crispin's have strange old customs. If someone cuts the tag off your tie, your life at the school is over. You lose any respect you might have won. You become an object of ridicule. Sebastian cut off Andrew's tag while he was in the showers, so after that it wasn't a case of my son being picked on by one kid; they all did it. They sent him to Coventry, took away his pocket money, ate his lunches, tore up his schoolwork, defaced his books. And there was nothing I could do to stop it.'

A look of devastation crossed Gormley's face. 'I was busy trying to sort out the end of my marriage and keep the business afloat. I should have done something about it earlier. After Andrew died, I kept an eye on that little thug. I talked to some of the other parents and found out that his mother was bringing him up to London to do some Christmas shopping. One parent told me that Mrs Carroll-Williams had a tradition of forcing her child to visit Santa, to have his picture taken. It was the perfect opportunity. I paid one of the Santas to get lost for the afternoon and took his place. You can't tell who's who behind those beards. As Sebastian was struggling to get into his polar-bear outfit I moved his tie over his shoulder so that he could get the suit on. I cut off the tag and slipped it into a gift box. I wanted him to suffer the same punishment my son suffered. I guess when he realized what had happened he fled.' He looked even more haunted now. 'I didn't kill him, I just made him feel the same way Andrew felt. There's nothing you can arrest me for, except perhaps impersonating Father Christmas.'

'If you hadn't panicked the child he'd be alive today,' said May. 'The prosecution will play on that.'

'I lost my wife and son, and I'm losing my business,' said Gormley. 'For God's sake, isn't that enough?'

'You created another grieving parent,' said May angrily. 'No one should lose their child, at Christmas or at any other time.'

It was a conclusion that satisfied no one. As they trudged back up the hill in the snow, Bryant was silent and thoughtful. Finally, just before the pair reached Hampstead Heath, he spoke. 'You think about them a lot, don't you?'

May looked up. 'Who, my son and granddaughter? Of course I do. He won't speak to me, and she's so terrified of turning into her mother that she had to leave the country to feel at peace. Of course I think of them, especially around this time of the year.'

'Christmas is hard on people like us,' said Bryant, poking at a frozen pigeon with his walking stick.

'One tends to think of what might have been,' said May sadly.

'Well, you've always got me,' said Bryant. 'Come on, I'll buy you a pint in the Flask.'

They made their way past an amateur theatrical group in Victorian dress loudly performing *A Christmas Carol* outside a supermarket. It was a very Hampstead scene.

'I suppose Christmas serves its purpose, if only in reviving memories of happy times,' Bryant conceded as he eyed the declaiming theatricals. 'But if that Tiny Tim comes anywhere near me with his collection bucket I'll break his other leg.'

It's hard to explain the genesis of some of these stories without giving away too much. This one had its roots in a trip I took and a story I read in my local newspaper, one of those lazily written rags filled with baking contests and arguments about parking. Often stories arrive from two conflicting pieces of information. Also, I'm a huge lover of locked-room mysteries, and have learned that they don't simply have to take place in a room. John Dickson Carr was the master of this form and wrote variations that increased in ornate complexity. He wasn't remotely interested in offering his readers realism or relevance, and instead provided instances involving witchcraft, automata, snowstorms, impossible footprints, corpses that walked through walls, and in one case a victim who dived into a swimming pool and vanished. I'll never beat him but I can try . . .

BRYANT & MAY IN THE FIELD

'Remember that parachutist who was alive when he jumped out of his plane but was found to have been strangled when he landed in a field? Well, you're going to love this one, trust me.' John May took the car keys away from his partner and threw him an overcoat. 'Come on, I'll drive. You'll need that, and your filthy old scarf. It's cold where we're going.'

'I'm not stepping outside of Zone One,' Arthur Bryant warned tetchily. 'I remember the last time we left London. There were trees everywhere. It was awful.'

'It'll do you good to get some fresh air. You shouldn't spend all your time cooped up in here.'

The offices of the Peculiar Crimes Unit occupied a particularly unappealing corner of North London's Caledonian Road. Most of the building's doors stuck and hardly any of its windows opened. Renovations had been halted pending a budget review, which had left several of the unheated rooms with asbestos tiles, fizzing electrics, missing floorboards and what could only be described as 'a funny smell'. Bryant felt thoroughly at home in this musty deathtrap, and had to be prised out with offers of murder investigations. It was particularly hard to prise him out today as his cardigan had got stuck to the wet varnish on his office door lintel. 'All right,' he said grudgingly, 'if I have to go. But this had better be good.'

As the elderly detectives made their way down to the car park, May handed his partner a photograph. 'She looks as though butter wouldn't melt in her mouth, but don't be deceived. The Met has had its collective eye on her for a couple of years now. Marsha Kastopolis. Her husband owns a lot of the flats and shops along the Caledonian Road. He's been putting her name on property documents as some kind of tax dodge. The council reckons it's been trying to pin health-and-safety violations on them, but no action has ever succeeded against her or her husband. I think it's likely they bought someone on the committee.'

'Yes, yes. I take it she's dead,' said Bryant impatiently.

'Very.'

'That doesn't explain why we have to drive somewhere godforsaken.'

'It's not godforsaken, just a bit windswept. The body's been left *in situ*.'

'Why?'

'There's something very unusual about the circumstances. Yes, look at the smile on your podgy little face now; you're suddenly interested, aren't you?'

'We'll see, won't we?' Bryant knotted his scarf more tightly than ever and climbed into the passenger seat of Victor, his rusting yellow Mini.

'Have you got around to insuring this thing yet?' asked May, crunching the gears.

'It's on my bucket list, along with climbing Machu Picchu, visiting the Hungarian Museum of Telephones and learning the ocarina. Where *are* we going?'

'We need to climb Primrose Hill.'

Bryant perked up. 'Greenberry Hill.'

'Greenberry?'

'That's what it was once called. After the executions of Messrs Green, Berry and Hill, who were wanted for the murder of one Edmund Godfrey in 1679. Although nobody really knows for sure if the legend is true.'

'Incredible,' May muttered, swinging out into Euston Road. 'All this from a man who can't remember how to open his email.'

The night before it had snowed heavily again. Now the afternoon air was crisp and frosty, and the rimes of snow that formed tidemarks around King's Cross Station had turned black with traffic pollution. The Mini slushed its way past the grim bookies and pound stores of lower Camden Town, up and over the bridge still garlanded with Christmas lights, and into the wealthier environs of those who paid highly for living a few more feet above sea level. It finally came to a stop at the foot of the fenced-off park, a great white mound surrounded by the expansive, expensive Edwardian town houses of Primrose Hill.

'Local officers have sealed the area,' said May, 'but the council wants the body removed before nightfall. The hill is a focal point for well-heeled families, and as the shops in Queen's Crescent are all staying open late over Christmas they're worried about the negative impact on local spending.'

Bryant wiped his glasses with the end of his scarf and peered across the bleached expanse, its edges blurred by a lowering silver sky. Halfway up, a green nylon box had been erected. 'You can tell them they'll get it cleared when we're good and ready to do so,' he said, setting off towards the body.

'Wait, you can't do that, Mr Bryant.' Dan Banbury, the PCU's crime scene manager, was sliding through the pavement slush towards them.

'Can't do what?'

'Just go off like that. I've established an approach path.' He pointed to a corridor of orange plastic sticks leading up the hill. 'You have to head in that way.'

'I'm a copper, not a plane,' said Bryant, waving him aside.

'There are already enough tracks out there. I don't want to have to eliminate any more.'

Making a sound like a displeased tapir, Bryant diverted to the narrow trodden channel, and the detectives made their way up the snow-covered slope to the tent, with Banbury anxiously darting ahead. 'She was found just after six twenty a.m. by a man out walking his dog,' he told them.

'Why did it take so long to get to us?' asked May. 'It's after two.'

'There was a bit of a dispute about jurisdiction. They were going to handle it locally but all fatal incidents in Central North get flagged, and we put in a claim that was challenged.'

'Meanwhile the victim's been lying there like an ice lolly,' said Bryant. 'So much for the dignity of death. Show me what you've got.'

They reached the tent and Banbury went in ahead of them. The woman lay on her back on the frozen ground, her beige overcoat dusted with snow. From the alabaster sheen of her skin she might have been a marble church effigy reclining on a bier. A single battery lamp illuminated the wound on her upper throat. Blood had coagulated around the parted flesh and had formed a hard black puddle beneath her left shoulder. Her eyes were still open but had lost their lustre as they froze.

'You've moved her,' said Bryant, noting the snow on the front of her clothes.

'That was the dog-walker,' said Banbury. 'All he could see as he got closer was a woman's body lying in the middle of the common. There was a bit of a mist earlier. He thought maybe she had collapsed until he turned her over and saw she'd been stabbed.'

'Looks like a very sharp kitchen knife or a cut-throat razor,' said May. 'The wound's very clean, straight across the carotid artery. A real vicious sweep.' He checked her palms and fingers and found them crimson. 'No defence marks. Maybe she raised her hands to the wound and tried to stem the bleeding. Any other cuts to the body?'

'Not that I can see, but bodies aren't my field of expertise,' Banbury admitted. 'I'm more interested in where she fell.'

'Why?' May asked.

'She's in the exact centre of the common, for one thing, about a hundred and fifty metres in every direction. The dog-walker was met by a DS from Hampstead who called in his team. We took a full statement from him. I picked up the initial report and established the corridor to the site.'

'Why did you do that before anything else?'

'Because there are no footprints,' Bryant cut in, waving his gloved hand across the virgin expanse of the hill.

'That's right, Mr Bryant. We've got hers, out to the middle but not back, the dog and his owner's, also there and back, and the DS's. Nothing else at all. Six is a bit early for the Primrose Hill crowd. Victim was last seen around eleven p.m. last night by one of her tenants. She was coming out of a restaurant. No more snow fell after about five a.m. According to the dog-walker, there were just her footprints leading out to the middle of the hill-slope and nothing else. Not a mark in any direction that he could see.'

'He must have been mistaken.'

Banbury blew on his hands. 'Nope – he's adamant, reckons he's got twenty-twenty vision and there were no other prints at all.'

'Then it's simple – she must have taken her own life.'

'What with? There's no weapon.'

'You haven't had her clothes off yet; you can't be sure of that,' Bryant said. 'Can we take the body or do we have to use the local resource?'

'They're happy for her to go to St Pancras if you sign it off.'

Bryant didn't answer. He was peering at the victim, trying to conjure her last moments.

'Could someone have swept away their footprints?' asked May.

Bryant pulled a sour face. 'Look at this snow – it's crusted solid. Besides, why would anybody try to do such a thing? This is an urban neighbourhood, not Miss Marple country. There has to be a more obvious explanation. Got her mobile, have you?'

'She received a call from a nearby phone box just after six this morning.'

'A *phone box*,' said May.

'Yes, you might want to check last night's – No!' Banbury snatched the plastic bag back from Bryant, who had begun to open it. 'Can you not take it out until I've finished with it?'

'Just send us the call list, then.' May was always keen to keep the peace. His partner was like a baby, reaching out to grab the things he wanted without thinking. Except that he was always thinking. 'Come on, Arthur,' he said, 'we've enough to be getting on with.'

'Where did she live?' Bryant asked as he was being led away. Below him the skyline of London formed an elaborate ice sculpture that shone pink and silver in the gelid afternoon air.

'Canonbury, I believe,' Banbury said.

'What was she doing over here so early on a Tuesday morning? Get those lads on it.' He indicated the members of the Hampstead constabulary who were standing around in the car park. 'She might have stayed somewhere nearby; maybe she has family here. Have them check taxis running from Canonbury to Chalk Farm early this morning.'

'Why Chalk Farm?' asked May.

'To get here from there you either have to drop off your fare by the footbridge near Chalk Farm station or go all the way around,' Bryant explained. 'This place is a peninsula that's a pain in the arse to reach because of the railway lines. That's why the rich love it. They don't have to rub shoulders with us plebs. Get someone to walk all the way around the perimeter, check for any kind of break in the snow. There must be *something*.'

After a brief stop at the PCU, the pair headed across to the gaudy offices of North One Developments Ltd, the property company Marsha Kastopolis had owned with her husband. Bypassing the confused staffers at their computer terminals, they found Phantasos Kastopolis in the building's basement, sweating on an exercycle. The beetroot-faced property tycoon was leaking from the top of his dyed combover to the bulging waistband of his electric-blue nylon tracksuit. He grabbed a towel and mopped at his chain-festooned chest, annoyed at having his journey towards a coronary thrombosis interrupted.

'If this is about burst pipes, there's nothing I can do,' he said. 'It's bloody freezing, innit, and them students haven't paid their rent this month so they got no bloody complaining to do.'

'It's about your wife,' said May, and he proceeded to explain the circumstances of Mrs Kastopolis's death while Bryant wandered around examining the Californian gym equipment with ill-disguised distaste.

'What was she doing out at that time?' Kastopolis asked after he had demonstrably absorbed the news, a process that involved a fair amount of ranting but not much grief. 'She never goes for a bloody walk.'

'We were hoping you could tell us. Does she know anyone in Primrose Hill?'

'I don't know where her bloody friends live.'

'Do you know if she had any enemies?'

'She had enemies because I have enemies!' Kastopolis exploded, throwing his towel on the floor. 'They all got it in for us, 'cause they don't like Cypriots owning their streets.'

'I thought your wife was English.'

'Yeah but she was married to me. I came here with nothing but the clothes I stood up in and bought the shops one by one. My father was a farmer, his fingers in the dirt, and look at me now. Thirty years of bloody hard work.' He raised his spatulate fingers before them in an attempt to prove the point. 'Of course I have enemies. They're jealous of me. They try to ruin me. But I tell you what, my friend, I do a lot of good in this community.'

'You infringe a lot of building regulations, too,' said Bryant, unimpressed. He pulled a plastic folder from his overcoat. 'Fire hazards, illegally blocked-off hallways, substandard materials, contractor lawsuits, environmental-health injunctions, it's all here.'

'Listen, if I waited for council approval before starting to build, I'd never get anything done.'

'Let's get back to your wife,' said May. 'You think someone was trying to get at you through her?' He thought: *If that was the plan, they didn't succeed. He's not upset or even surprised.*

'Why else would anyone bother with her?' Kastopolis pushed past them and began slicking down his hair before an elaborate gilt mirror. 'She didn't know nobody important.'

'But she worked for you.'

'Secretary stuff – posting the mail, making coffee, that sort of thing. I made her come to work just to keep her out of the shops, spending my bloody money. And to stop her eating. She was getting as fat as a pig.'

'When was the last time you saw her?'

'When she left the office yesterday evening. She was going out with her mates to some cocktail bar maybe. I don't know what she does no more.'

'She didn't come home?'

'We got a lot of places, and she's got keys to them all. She stays in different ones when she's had a few drinks.'

'Alone?'

'Of course alone! She belongs to me! What are you bloody saying?'

'And you, do you stay in these flats without her?'

'That's got nothing to bloody do with it.'

'It has if you can't vouch for your whereabouts between last night and today.'

Kastopolis nearly ruptured a vein. 'Ask my boys upstairs where I was. They was with me all evening. We left here at eight and went to the Rajasthan Palace until midnight. They was all with me again from six o'clock this morning. We work long hours here. Why you think we make so much money? Are you sure she's dead?'

'Very sure. She was stabbed.'

'Primrose Hill, eh? No blacks around there – don't know how she got stabbed. I can't bloody believe this! I gave her everything. She didn't have nothing when she met me, came down from Liverpool without a penny to her name. She owed me big time, and this is how I get paid for my kindness.'

'What do you mean?'

'Stands to reason, innit? She was seeing someone behind my back.' Kastopolis checked his hair in the mirror and turned to them. 'Where do I pick up her body?'

*

'What a revolting man,' said Bryant as they headed back along the Caledonian Road. 'All that grey chest hair poking out between his chains, it made me feel quite ill. Surely no one would speak about his wife like that if he'd killed her.'

'Obviously it's a long time since he cared anything for her,' said May. 'It sounds to me as if the arrangement of staying in empty apartments was more for his benefit than hers.'

'I think we should talk to someone she counted as a friend,' Bryant replied, 'rather than a husband.'

They found Kaylie Neville seated alone in the Lion & Unicorn. The dishevelled forty-year-old was nursing an extremely large gin and tonic. Judging by her swollen red eyes and the number of lemon wedges in her drink, she had already been informed of her friend's death. The pub was so still and quiet that the detectives stirred the dust motes in the late-afternoon sunlight as they sat down beside her at the copper-topped table.

'Phantasos called me and just started having a go, yelling and carrying on like I'm to blame,' she said, anxiously searching their faces. 'You mustn't believe anything he says about her. Nothing true or kind has ever come out of his mouth. He cheats, he steals, he has affairs. There's not a decent bone in him. The things he gets up to in those flats, you don't want to know.'

'Forgive me,' said Bryant, 'but if Mr Kastopolis is such a terrible man, why did Marsha marry him?'

'She'd had a rough time of it. She came to London to escape a bloke in Liverpool who said he would kill her.'

'Why did he say that?'

Kaylie tapped nervously at her glass with bitten purple nails. 'He was staunch Irish Catholic, and she had an abortion. He threatened to come down and cut her up. She was a lousy judge of men. But a kind heart, a good heart. I did what I could for her. You do what you can, don't you? She met Phantasos and he offered to look after her. Then she found out what that involved.'

'What did it involve?'

'Keeping the clients sweet. Doing anything they wanted. I mean, *anything*.'

'You're saying he prostituted her out to them?' said Bryant, always one to title a gardening implement accurately.

'She said no, of course. But he found plenty of other ways to compromise her.' Kaylie took a sudden alarming gulp from her gin, nearly finishing it. 'She told me he started using her identity to hide cash in different accounts, all kinds of dodgy goings-on. I keep away from him. If he knew half the things I know, I wouldn't fancy my chances.'

'Do you think he had something to do with his wife's death?' asked May.

'He must have done,' Kaylie replied, prodding the table-top. 'See, she was smart. She kept everything written down in a little notebook, just in case there was ever any trouble.'

'What sort of things did she write down?'

'Account numbers, deposit dates, details of all the rental contracts he faked, the councillors he bribed, everything.'

'I don't suppose you know where she kept this book?'

'She never told me. Not at home. Maybe in one of the rented properties, but there's forty or fifty of those. He's got people everywhere. They're always on the lookout for trouble, that lot.'

'And you think that's why she died? Because she was keeping track of him?'

'You have to understand, he goes on about arriving in London without a penny, how he built up an empire, how no one can stop him. Then she started standing up to him. She told me she'd had enough. She was going to take the notebook to the police.'

'When was this?'

'She said it again last night. She'd said it loads of times before, but this time I think she was really going to do it.'

'We're going to find out who killed her,' said May.

'If we can find out how he did it,' said Bryant.

The temperature was dropping again, and the froth of brown pavement ice had become treacherous once more. May kept a tight hold of his partner's arm as the pair made their way around the corner to their unit. Central London in the snow was never picturesque for more than the first hour.

'It doesn't make any sense,' said Bryant. 'You can see the kind of a man Kastopolis is, a feral throwback, something out of the 1970s, crafty but not too bright. His wife was lured out into the middle of that park and killed – that's why somebody called her from a phone box just before her death, to make sure that she was keeping her appointment. You heard what Miss Neville said: Kastopolis has men everywhere. Central North is his turf. Everybody knows the local villain, and that's the way he likes it. He needed this to happen off his patch. What I don't understand is how he did it, and he knows that we don't know.'

'Maybe he's smarter than you think he is,' said May. 'Perhaps he wants to divert our attention into trying to work out how it happened.'

'Let's talk to Giles,' Bryant decided. 'He might have had a chance to examine her properly by now. Perhaps he's turned up something.'

They found Giles Kershaw in the darkened forensic pathology office at Camley Street, where he had recently taken up the position of coroner for St Pancras. 'You've caught us at a bad time,' warned Giles, ushering them in. 'The power's out. Ice pulled down the lines. The fridges are on a separate grid but we're working by torchlight until tomorrow morning. I don't know how Canada manages. A few millimetres of snow here and the whole of London grinds to a halt.'

'What did you get from Mrs Kastopolis?' asked Bryant. 'Is there any tea going? I'm perished.'

'I didn't get much from her, and it's probably not what you're after,' said Giles, leading the way. 'I don't think she stayed overnight in Primrose Hill. Went there first thing this morning, I imagine, but you'll know that once you've checked her Oyster card.'

'How do you know?'

'What, that she went by tube or that she'd been in Islington?'

'Both.'

'She had no purse and no cash unless it was taken, just the travel card. No make-up, and she'd dressed in a hurry. She was wearing boots that had some fragments of French gravel in the grooves. They hadn't been there long because there was ice underneath them. Islington uses different tarmac surfacing to Camden, so it looks to me as if she crossed boroughs this morning. I've got a home address for her in Canonbury, Islington.'

'Her husband says she didn't come home last night, but she had several empty flats she could have gone to in the Canonbury area. Anything else?'

'We have a time of death because of the phone call. She fell face down and died quickly. There was no weapon of any kind on her, or anything that could conceivably be used as one. It looks like there were two wounds, one opening the carotid artery and the other grazing the trachea.'

'Grazing – you mean cutting it?'

'Yes, just lightly.'

'So the air escaped from her lungs and she couldn't breathe in,' said May.

'Exactly. Slashes rather than stabs – they're not very deep. She's five six, which would make her killer six feet at least, because the cuts are downward.'

'Except that he couldn't have been standing in front of her because he left no footprints,' added Bryant. 'How do you account for that?'

Kershaw flicked back his blond fringe. 'Well, I can't. Most seemingly impossible situations are the fault of poor information-gathering. Are you sure Dan's got his facts straight? The obvious answer is that the dog-walker killed her and threw the weapon away.'

'That won't fly,' said May. 'He walks his dog at the same time every day, along the same route. He was searched at the site and came up clean, and he has no connection with the deceased. The officer said he was badly shaken. There's no reason to suspect him.'

'Oh come on,' said Giles, 'you're a policeman, you suspect everyone. What about her enemies?'

'An ex-boyfriend in Liverpool. Turns out he died of

a barbiturate overdose nearly a year ago. We've good reason to suspect the husband, but he has alibis in the form of half a dozen employees, so he must have got someone else to do it. Dan's searching every inch of the field but so far he hasn't found any marks in the snow other than the ones we've accounted for.'

'A throwing dagger,' said Bryant suddenly.

'They'd have found it,' said May, shaking his head.

'Not if it cleared the field.'

'Thrown three hundred metres?'

'With rockets attached. Or a boomerang. Circus performers. A crossbow with razorblades on the front.'

'I'm going to take him back to the unit now,' May told Kershaw, patting his partner's arm. 'It's time for his medication.'

'Not yet,' Bryant insisted. 'Let's check Kastopolis's alibi. His employees are going to say anything he tells them, aren't they? The Rajasthan Palace, Cally Road, didn't he say he spent most of last night there?'

'Marsha Kastopolis died this morning.'

'But if he hired someone else to kill his wife it was because of what she'd told Kaylie Neville, and maybe he planned it in the restaurant. Besides, it's been ages since I had a decent Ruby Murray.'

'Don't you ever stop thinking of your stomach?' asked May.

'I need to keep the boiler functioning in this weather,' said Bryant. 'If my pilot light goes out, I might never get it started again.'

From the outside it was not the most appealing of restaurants. The splits in the yellow plastic fascia had been repaired with brown parcel tape, and computer printouts of takeaway menus were plastered over the windows, but the staff were smartly uniformed and the interior was clean enough. May selected a salad while Bryant followed the time-honoured British tradition of ordering twice as much Indian food as he could possibly eat, topped off with a Peshwari naan and a pint of Kingfisher. As the waiters got busy he attempted to question them, but they proved reluctant to be drawn on the subject of their customers and anxiously fetched the manager, Mr Bhatnagar, who tentatively tiptoed out towards them.

'Mr Eddie is our very great friend,' the manager explained, beaming eagerly. 'Everyone calls him Mr Eddie. He is coming here regularly for dinner and staying a very long time.'

'When was the last time you saw him?' asked May.

'Last night, same as always. He arrived soon after eight and stayed until we closed.'

'What time was that?'

Mr Bhatnagar silently calculated the validity of his drinks licence. 'Midnight,' he assured them.

'You remember who he was with?'

'His colleagues from the office, all very nice but very fond of a tipple, I think. Very – energetic.'

Bryant assumed he meant loud and ill-mannered. 'Does he bring anyone else here apart from his colleagues?'

'Sometimes he comes here with his lovely wife.'

'Does she eat here with her own friends?'

'No, just with Mr Eddie.'

'And who else does Mr Eddie bring to dinner?'

'Many people. Mr Eddie has many, many friends. He is very well known in this neighbourhood.'

'And your staff' – Bryant waved his hands at the young

waiters illuminated by the pale light of their mobiles behind the counter – 'they were all working here last night?'

'All except these two, Raj and Said.'

'You manage several restaurants along this road, I suppose.'

'Yes, half a dozen or so.'

'And Mr Eddie owns them. Do your staff take shifts in the others?'

'What do you mean?'

'Do the waiters move around?'

'Indeed so.'

'I don't suppose you overheard any conversation last night?' asked Bryant, already sure of the answer.

'Oh no, sir,' came the hasty reply. 'We would never eavesdrop on our esteemed customers, certainly not.' Mr Bhatnagar gave them both a friendly, reassuring smile.

'What was all that about?' asked May as they stepped back into the street.

'I like to get a thorough picture,' replied Bryant evasively. He was carrying a foil package shaped like a swan containing two-thirds of the meal he'd ordered.

'Yes, and I also know when there's something funny going on in your head. One more stop and we'll go back to the PCU. The Islington Better Business Bureau. It's the council's outsource in charge of the licences for properties along Upper Street and the Caledonian Road. Let's see what they make of Mr Kastopolis.'

'Do we have any friends there?' asked Bryant.

'We're not their favourite people. You gave them grief over a corpse found in one of their properties, remember? A headless body stuffed into a chip-shop freezer? Ring any bells?'

'Oh, *that*. Not someone called Anderson, by any chance?'

'The very one. He's Kastopolis's liaison officer. I'm sure he remembers you. You made him go to the old Bayham Street mortuary to identify the victim.'

'Why did I do that?'

'You didn't like him.'

'Ah. I wonder if he remembers.'

'I imagine it might have stayed in his memory, yes,' said May. 'Better let me do the talking.'

May held a twanging glass door open for his partner. They entered a lobby that resembled a spaceship's flight deck from a low budget film in the late 1980s. David Anderson came down to meet them, waving them anxiously towards a minuscule pink and blue glass meeting room beside the reception area, a holding pen for those not worthy of being granted full access to the executive suites upstairs. He was slightly plump, slightly balding, slightly ginger, slightly invisible, the kind of man who makes you feel old when you realize with a shock that he's probably only in his early thirties.

'Our relationship with Mr Kastopolis has been some-what fractious in the past,' he explained, placing himself between the detectives and the waiting area outside, for he was none too pleased about having the law visit council offices. 'He's quite a larger-than-life character, as I'm sure you've discovered.'

'We're more concerned that he may—' *be a murderer*, Bryant was about to say, but May kicked him under the table. As this was also made of glass, everyone saw him do it.

'—have done more than just bent a few bylaws this

time,' concluded May diplomatically. 'Perhaps it would be better to discuss this somewhere less open.'

Anderson was clearly upset by the idea, but was hardly in a position to argue. The trio headed up to his third-floor office and settled themselves in plusher, more traditional surroundings. Bryant had to be surreptitiously cautioned against rummaging about on Anderson's desk. The meeting did not go well. The planning officer was prepared to admit that the bureau suspected Kastopolis of flouting property regulations, but was unwilling to divulge any personal doubts.

'What about outside of work?' Bryant asked. 'Do you see each other socially?'

'Good Lord, no.' Anderson seemed genuinely horrified by the idea. 'We're expressly forbidden from seeing clients outside of the building. There's a sensitivity about undue influence, you understand. And after the MPs' expenses scandal, it's more than our lives are worth. Can you give me more of an idea why he's of particular interest to you at the moment?'

'No,' said Bryant offhandedly, trying to read the liaison officer's paperwork upside down.

'The seriousness of the matter at hand means we must limit information until there's a case to be made,' said May, 'if indeed there is one to be made. But we appreciate the help you've been able to give us.'

'Was there any need to be quite so diplomatic?' asked Bryant as they left the building. '"We must limit information until there's a case to be made." You don't get anything out of people if you don't frighten the life out of them. A typical council man, wet as a whale's willy, reeking with the stench of appeasement, utterly incapable of confrontation. Kastopolis runs roughshod over the lot of them and they do nothing.'

'You don't know that,' said May. 'Kastopolis has spent the last thirty years finding ways to balance along the edges of the law. Men like that eventually make mistakes.'

'I can't wait for him to make a mistake. I'm too old.'

'What do you want to do, then?'

'Head back to the PCU,' Bryant said with a sigh. 'There's something I need to check.' May was glad they had brought the car. The iced-over pavements had become bobsleigh runs, and his partner was unstable at the best of times.

As the hours passed, May worked on with the rest of the PCU team while Bryant remained holed up in his office with the door firmly closed to visitors. Finally, when he could no longer bear the suspense of not knowing what his partner was doing, May went to check on him.

'You should put the overhead lights on,' he said. 'You'll strain your eyes.'

'She's here,' Bryant said, looking up sadly. He had printed out everything he could find on Marsha Kastopolis, and had stacked it all in the centre of his desk. His hands were placed over the file, as if trying to conjure her presence. 'I can sense her.'

'What do you mean?' asked May.

'She was a bright girl. Then she was abused by her new stepfather. Her mother did nothing. The social services failed to protect her. She became withdrawn and lost. Her school grades dropped away. She was made pregnant by a junkie, came to London and started again. By this time she had grown a tough hide, and was determined to make something of herself. She must have been able to see through her husband, so why did she put up with him? What did she get from the relationship? Stability? Money? No, something else. That's the key to this.'

'Funny,' said May.

'What?'

'Nothing. I thought you'd be in here trying to work out how he did it. You know, the mechanics. The nuts and bolts. More up your street than people.'

'Don't be so rude. I hate to see promising lives ruined. As it happens, I know how it was done.'

'You do?'

'Most certainly. And I think I want to handle the last part by myself.'

'I don't understand you, Arthur.'

'I want to do the right thing for her. You can see that, can't you? I don't anticipate a problem, but it might be better if you stayed within reach of your mobile. I'm not going very far.' With that he rose stiffly, jammed on his squashed trilby and burrowed into his old tweed overcoat. May watched him go, flummoxed.

'What's up with the old man?' asked Banbury as he passed.

'You know how possessive some people are with their books?' said May. 'Arthur's like that with crimes. Sometimes I think I hardly know him at all.'

Bryant pushed open the wire-glass door of the Rajasthan Palace and seated himself by the window. An impossibly thin, hollow-eyed waiter who looked as though he'd not slept well since Gandhi's death approached and placed a red plastic menu before him.

'I'll just have a hot, very sweet *chai*,' said Bryant. 'But you can send Mr Bhatnagar out to me. I know he's there, I just saw him peep through the curtain.'

Moments later the portly little manager appeared from behind the counter and made his way over to the table, bouncing on the balls of his feet. 'Mr Bryant,' he said, 'what a pleasure to see you again, so very soon.'

'You may not think so in a minute.' Bryant gestured at the seat opposite. Mr Bhatnagar's smile showed sudden strain, and he remained standing. 'Mrs Kastopolis,' said Bryant. 'She ate at the Bhaji Fort last night. Your boy Raj saw her, didn't he? More to the point, he overheard her. Who did he tell you she was with?'

'Raj is a good boy,' said Mr Bhatnagar anxiously. 'Mrs Kastopolis was with another lady, a friend, that's all, not somebody my boy knew.'

'Then why did he bother to call you?' asked Bryant. 'I'll tell you why.' And he proceeded to do so. By the time he had finished, Mr Bhatnagar had visibly diminished. His mouth opened and closed, but no sound came out. Finally, he sat and dropped his head in his hands, not caring about his staff, who were nervously peering out at him from their counter. Mr Bhatnagar realized that his eagerness to please had finally been the undoing of him, and wept.

'I thought you didn't like the fresh air,' said May, slapping his leather-clad hands together in an effort to keep warm. His breath condensed in dragon-clouds as he looked down from the pinnacle of Primrose Hill over the frost-sheened rooftops of London.

'I don't,' said Bryant, dislodging the snow from his trilby by violently beating it. 'But it's windy today, and I wanted you to see this. How it was done.' He pointed to the far edge of the hill, where several young Indian men were standing. May followed his partner's extended index finger up to the burnished winter sky. 'Can you see them now?' he asked.

Overhead, half a dozen diamonds of indigo and maroon silk soared and swooped around each other like exotic fish fighting for food. 'Kite-flying is a very popular pastime in Rajasthan. But it's far from a gentle sport. It's a matter of kill or be killed, and sometimes huge bets ride on the outcome. The idea is to destroy your enemies by bringing them down. The only way to do that is by severing their strings. So the kite-warriors coat their cords with a paste of boiled rice mixed with glass dust. It makes them as sharp as any cut-throat razor. And they can control the lines to go exactly where they want. Our assassin only had to bring his kite down from the sky and touch it across her throat.'

May was incredulous. 'You're saying Mrs Kastopolis was killed by a *kite*?'

'By the cord of a kite flown by an expert, yes,' said Bryant. 'Mr Bhatnagar looked out for his friend and protector, the landlord of all his properties. He made sure his waiters kept their eyes and ears open. When one of them overheard Marsha Kastopolis telling her friend that she was going to talk to the police about her husband, he stepped in to help. He called the man who had repeatedly asked him to stay vigilant.

'Obviously, if anything bad happened to Marsha on her husband's home turf suspicions would have been aroused. So one of the waiters was paid to draw her away. Mr Bhatnagar called her pretending to be an ally, and said he had important information for her. He lured her to the meeting on Primrose Hill. He thought he could get rid of her in a quiet place, and made his waiter, Raj, do the dirty work, using the one special skill he possessed.

I don't suppose the lack of footprints in the snow even crossed anyone's mind. Unfortunately for him, it made the case unique enough to attract our attention.'

'Why would this waiter Raj agree to do such a thing?'

'He had no choice. He was in debt to Mr Bhatnagar.'

'Have you sent someone around to arrest Kastopolis?'

'No, you've misunderstood,' said Bryant. 'Kastopolis didn't ask Mr Bhatnagar to keep an eye out for problems. It was the liaison officer, Anderson. Your first instinct was right: Kastopolis had bought someone on the committee. That was how he got away with breaking the law for so many years. Anderson got kickbacks and watched out for his client in return. Ultimately it was Anderson who forced the waiter, Raj, to commit murder.'

May was mystified. 'But how did you know it was him?'

'Anderson vehemently denied ever consorting with his client, remember? But when I rummaged about on his desk I saw a receipt for the Rajasthan Palace. He'd eaten there the night before. He couldn't resist slipping the dinner through on his expenses.'

'All these people, working to protect one corrupt man,' said May, 'and they're the ones who'll go down for him while Kastopolis walks away again. It's not fair.'

'You're forgetting one thing,' said Bryant. 'The notebook is still out there somewhere. We just have to find it before he does.'

The elderly detective turned back to watch a shimmering turquoise kite as it looped down and slashed the string of its nearest rival. The other kite, a fluttering box of emerald satin, was caught in a tight spiral and plunged into a dive, collapsing on the frozen earth.

'Alluring and dangerous,' said Bryant. 'The winners are

raised up on the sacrifices of the fallen. That's how it has always been in this city.' He smiled ruefully at his partner and turned to watch the turquoise diamond weaving back and forth across the silvered clouds, savouring its brief moment of glory.

Here's a short, simple tale hinging on something I found in an old book. There's rarely enough time to pull off a whodunnit in a very short story, so you tend to concentrate on another mysterious aspect of a case. Those who know me well will recognize the influence of Norman Wisdom in the title.

BRYANT & MAY ON THE BEAT

'I'm completely out of ideas.'

John May, senior detective at the Peculiar Crimes Unit, studied the living room of the chaotic tenth-floor apartment. Its contents were sealed beneath a cowl of clear plastic, designed to prevent contamination of evidence. 'His body was found over there by his landlady and was taken straight to University College Hospital. The last time anyone saw him was Christmas Eve, four days ago. The doctors want to know if he was a farmer or had visited a farm in the past two weeks.'

'Seems a bit unlikely,' said Arthur Bryant, his partner, laboriously unwrapping a rhubarb and custard boiled sweet. 'Living in the Barbican, hardly the most rural spot in London, although I suppose it does have a lake. Why farming?'

'They think he died of anthrax. He had mouth ulcers,

had complained of stomach cramps and feeling sick. Anthrax is a virus that's more likely to be used for bioterrorist attacks.'

'I remember. In 2001 it was sent through the American Postal Service and infected more than twenty people. Turned out to have been mailed by a US government scientist with a grudge, didn't it? Maybe the same thing happened here.' The boiled sweet rattled against Bryant's ill-fitting false teeth as he turned the problem over. 'What do we know about him?'

'William Warren, forty-seven, part-time musician, played with a jazz band in pubs, ran a stall in Camden Market, no known affiliations with any political organization, moved here after he broke up with his wife last year. It seems an amicable enough split. He was still seeing his kids at the weekends. Nothing much else to go on.'

Bryant lifted a corner of the plastic seal, raised a piano lid and gave an impromptu, unrecognizable rendition of 'Chopsticks'.

'Don't do that – the room hasn't been dusted for dabs yet.'

'Not my fault you have a tin ear. "Music hath charms to soothe a savage breast."'

'It's too early in the morning to start quoting Shakespeare.'

'It's not Shakespeare, it's William Congreve, the first line of his play *The Mourning Bride*. It's there.' He pointed to the wall, where the phrase had been neatly painted in gold script. 'He must have loved his music.' Bryant put the piano lid back down. 'I suppose you checked his mailbox.'

'The landlady says there was nothing out of the ordinary. She always opened his stuff for him.'

'Why?'

'He had a habit of avoiding his bills. Didn't like paying "the man". Bit of an old hippie, didn't approve of financing fat cats.'

'Bet he didn't mind supporting the black economy, though.' Bryant picked up a macramé mandala and grimaced. 'Pub jazz sessions and market stalls: I don't suppose he got around to paying tax on his earnings. Do we know his movements over Christmas?'

'Same as always, apparently. He saw his kids, played his gigs, ran his stall, went drinking with his mates.'

'*Cherchez la femme?*'

'Well, I think there's something going on with the landlady. She's a bit of an ex-rock chick.'

'He doesn't sound like the sort of person who gets targeted by an international terrorist gang. Selling anything dodgy on the side?' Bryant loosened his moulting pea-green scarf and sniffed the air. 'Doesn't smell very fresh in here.'

'Not that I know of. All we have to go on is what's in this apartment.' May carefully stepped over a pile of dirty laundry and surveyed the cluttered room. Some partially repaired musical instruments were arranged in one corner. The sofa and two armchairs were piled with sheet music, volumes of poetry, bits of home-made pottery, hand-woven woolly hats, a flute, bongo drums and various hand-painted ethnic bits of wood.

'You can tell a lot about someone by looking at his home,' said Bryant, raising an empty plastic pudding pot and peering into it. 'It's all a bit knit-your-own-muesli. I bet he was a vegetarian. Probably poisoned by a rogue sprout. The thing is' – Bryant gingerly replaced the tub on the windowsill – 'people like Mr Warren are colourful and vaguely tiresome but they don't usually have any enemies. Why do you think he was murdered?'

'Anthrax is hard to catch,' said May. 'You can get it from tainted meat, except, as you rightly surmise, he was a vegetarian. It's one of the diseases that comes flagged with a red alert on the system because of its terrorist connotations, so we were asked to check it out.'

Bryant wasn't listening. He had twisted himself under the window and was squinting up at the sills.

'What are you doing?'

'These locks have been painted over at least half a dozen times. People can't be bothered to take the old paint off any more. What's wrong with a blowlamp?' He pottered over to the door and flicked experimentally at the hasp. 'Was he a skinny man? Not much meat on his bones?'

'Yes, I believe so. Why do you ask?'

'Jumpers everywhere, rubber seals on the door, draught excluder. The flats in the Barbican are notoriously overheated, and yet he obviously felt cold. It's suggestive.'

'Of what?' May wondered.

Bryant ignored the question. He withdrew a pair of old brown leather gloves and tightened his scarf, then produced an enormous pair of kitchen scissors from within his rumpled overcoat. Stabbing the plastic evidence seal, he knelt and rooted about in the cardboard boxes that stood behind the sofa.

'You really shouldn't . . .' May began, then gave up.

'He made those ghastly Tibetan hats and drums for his stall and sold them, along with ethnic musical bits and bobs, is that right?' asked Bryant.

'I believe so.'

'And he was an enthusiastic musician?'

'The neighbours say he drove them mad.'

'Well, there you go. This place should be sealed off.'

'It was until you arrived. Where did you get those scissors from, anyway?'

'I keep them on me just in case.' Bryant smoothed the plastic back in place like a naughty child hoping no one would spot something he'd broken. 'The neighbours. Did they say what he played?'

'I didn't ask them.'

'You see, that would have been my first question.' Bryant's knees creaked like coffin lids as he rose and dusted himself down. 'Mr Warren wasn't involved in a terrorist attack. And it wasn't murder or suicide, either. Accidental death. Let's pack up here and go to the pub.'

'That's it?' said May, amazed. 'Is that all you have to say? That's the sum total of your investigative technique? "Pack up here and go to the pub"?'

'It's either that or return home to Alma's gruesome leftover Christmas creations. It was thinking about her overcooked turkey drumsticks that did it. You see? Drumsticks?'

'No,' said May, 'I really don't.'

'Oh for goodness' sake, do you need it spelled out?' Bryant's aqueous blue eyes widened in innocence. 'The windows were *sealed shut*. The door was closed tight, too. There was no fresh air. He made his own music! Look!'

He pointed through the plastic at the stack of home-made bongo drums arranged on the sofa.

'He covered the drums with uncured animal skins,' said Bryant. 'They're cheaper, and they're also illegal. And when he thrashed them with his drumsticks he released their toxic bacteria spores, and accidentally ingested them.'

Bryant picked up his battered trilby and found that the trim had been sewn with festive tinsel. 'How long have I been wearing this?'

'Since the Christmas party. The girls put it there. They thought it would brighten you up.'

Bryant almost smiled. 'Only death brightens me up.' He glanced back at the room. 'Poor bugger,' he said, pulling the door closed with funereal respect. 'He should have realized that music can also kill you.'

*I make no apologies for chucking my detectives into the past;
I've established on numerous occasions that Arthur Bryant's
memoirs are unreliable in the extreme, especially when it
comes to dates. This particular moment in London's history
has often intrigued me – it happened before I was born but
something about it haunts, especially in atmospheric photographs of the period. I found a monochrome study of a sturdy
policeman leading a car through an empty street, the kind of
eerily deserted photograph you can never take any more in the
metropolis . . .*

BRYANT & MAY IN THE SOUP

It was the thickest fog London had ever seen.

Acrid and jaundiced, it rolled across London on
5 December 1952, and lasted for four days. It was impossible to keep at bay; yellow tendrils unfurled through
windows, crept under doors and down chimneys until
it was difficult to tell if you were inside or out. The fog
stopped traffic and asphyxiated the cattle at Smithfield's
Market. At Sadler's Wells, performances were halted
because it invaded the auditorium, choking the dancers
and the audience. Down near the Thames, visibility
dropped to nil. Cars crashed into pillar boxes, cats fell

out of trees and residents became lost in their own front gardens. On the lowly, lowland Isle of Dogs, it was said that people could not even see their own feet. Only the highest point of Hampstead Heath rose above the dense yellow smoke. From there, all you could see were the hills of Kent and Surrey on the far side of the sulphurous cauldron.

This bizarre phenomenon had been caused by an unfortunate confluence of factors. The month had started with bitterly low temperatures and heavy snowfalls, so the residents of London piled cheap coal into their grates. The smoke from their chimneys mixed with pollutants from the capital's factories, and became trapped beneath an inverse anticylone. The resulting miasma caused over twelve thousand fatalities and stained London's buildings black for fifty years. The young and the elderly died from respiratory problems. Their lungs filled with pus and they choked to death.

The thought of suffering in so horrible a fashion clouded Harry Whitworth's thoughts. In the last few minutes he had found it difficult to catch his breath. Cramps were knotting his stomach, and he had to keep stopping beside the gutter to spit. When he reached his place of employment, the coachworks in Brewer Street, he was surprised to find the place almost deserted.

'Where is everybody?' he asked Stan, the slack-boned young apprentice who helped the mechanics tune the engines.

'Ain't you heard, Harry? The place has been closed until the fog lifts. We can't take anything out in this, not without someone walking in front of the vehicle, and we ain't got the staff. Charlie was supposed to phone you and tell you not to come in.'

'We're not on the phone,' Harry explained. 'Why are the engines running?'

'Maintenance. A couple of them are dicky. I thought if we couldn't take the coaches out, I'd at least be able to get some soot off the pistons.'

'I think my ticker could do with a decoke,' said Harry, patting his chest. 'I feel proper queer. I was sick a few minutes ago, and I've got a chronic pain in my guts. I've been coughing like a good 'un. Can't catch me breath. Let me get the weight off me feet, at least.'

'You know you're not supposed—'

Too late. Harry had climbed up into the driver's seat of the nearest coach, sat down and placed his hands on the wheel. With a weary sigh, he closed his eyes.

Two minutes later, he was dead.

Arthur Bryant realized how bad the fog had become when he tried to post a letter in a Chelsea Pensioner. Earlier that day he had asked a lamp-post for a light.

He was on his way to meet John May, his fellow detective at Bow Street Police Station, but had somehow lost his way in the few short streets from Aldwych. Luckily, knowing that his partner was capable of getting lost inside a corset, May had come looking for him. Bryant had a distinctive silhouette, like a disinterred mole in a raincoat, and was easy to spot. When a hand fell upon his shoulder, he jumped.

'Ah, there you are,' said Bryant, as if it were he who had found the other. 'You left a message at my club?'

'You don't have a club, Arthur. It's a pub, and not a very nice one either.' May linked his arm in Bryant's and steered him out of the road.

'Perhaps not, but at least they've managed to keep

out this blasted muck.' Bryant was lately in the habit of frequenting a basement dive bar underneath Piccadilly Circus that served high-quality oysters to low-quality clientele. 'Your note said something about a coach garage.'

'That's right. It's nearby.' May wiped his forehead and found it wet with sooty black droplets. 'I'd keep your scarf fastened tightly over your mouth; there's a lot of dirt in the air. You know you've always had trouble with your lungs.'

It took them ages to feel their way to Brewer Street. 'I got a call from my sister,' May explained. 'Her neighbour's boy, Stan, told her he had a dead body on his hands and didn't know what to do.'

The main gate to the coachworks was shut, but there was an unlocked side door. The interior of the building was wreathed in mist, but at least it was thinner than the air outside. A gawky lad with a face of crowded freckles lolloped towards them. He waved behind him, distraught. 'He's over here, sir. Come with me.'

They found Harry Whitworth behind the wheel of the green and cream coach. His skin was blanched to a peculiar shade of khaki. 'Did you find him like this?' asked May.

'No, sir. He came in for work late this morning, about nine o'clock. He normally starts at eight but I think he had trouble finding his way because of this fog.'

'Did he complain of any health problems?'

'Yes, sir, he told me he was having trouble breathing. He'd been sick, and had a sore tummy. And he was coughing a lot.'

Bryant climbed into the seat next to Harry Whitworth,

reached over and opened his mouth. 'He's got a tongue like a razor strop.'

'Red, you mean?' asked May.

'No, dry. Anybody else here?'

'No, sir,' said Stan, 'they've all been given the day off.'

'So none of the coaches were running their engines?'

'Two of them were running. I was making some repairs, so the day wasn't wasted.'

'Any fog get in here?'

'Some, sir. It's difficult to keep out.' Stan looked distraught.

Bryant looked around. 'But the doors and windows were all shut?'

'Yes. On the radio this morning they were telling people to stay indoors and keep everything sealed.'

'But you're in an enclosed space, lad. Did you not think about the exhaust fumes?'

'No, sir. Couldn't be any worse than the fog.'

'Actually it could.' Bryant eased himself out of the coach cabin. 'I think this chap died of carbon monoxide poisoning.'

Stan's thin hands flew to his mouth. 'You're not saying I killed him?'

'Not exactly,' said May, anxious to placate the boy. 'It would have been an accident.'

'Surely you knew the danger of running the engines in here?' asked Bryant sternly. 'You could have asphyxiated yourself. The engines are off now, though.'

'Yes, sir, I turned them off to attend to Harry.'

'How old are you?'

'Seventeen, sir.'

'In good health?'

'As far as I know. I've always been good at P.E.'

'And Mr Whitworth?'

'He had a bout of pneumonia last year.'

'He's a driver, yes?'

'No, sir, not any more, not since his illness. He does the drivers' rosters.'

'So Harry Whitworth had a chest weakness, which is why the lad survived and he didn't,' May told Bryant. 'Open-and-shut case.'

'Do you know how we can contact Mr Whitworth's family?' Bryant asked.

'That's easy enough,' the boy told them. 'His son Clive works over at the ABC café on Wardour Street.'

'I'll call ahead and make sure someone informs him before we get there.' May tugged at his partner's sleeve. 'Come on. Let's get the rest over with.'

'I won't go to prison, will I?' Stan was wringing his handkerchief in his hands.

'No. But you're not to go anywhere until our men get here, do you understand? You're on your honour. They'll only be a few minutes.'

Bryant was still hanging around the coach as May made to leave. 'What's the matter?' May asked.

'Nothing.' Bryant didn't sound certain.

'What?'

'It's funny, that's all.'

'What's funny?'

'If Harry Whitworth had a desk job, why did he get behind the wheel?'

The two detectives left the coachworks and made slow progress through the thickening fog. Their hearing became almost as muffled as their sight. May was forced to yank his partner out of the path of a recklessly driven taxi. 'Do you mind?' Bryant complained indignantly. 'This is my best coat.'

'You were nearly buried in it,' May snapped back. 'There's the café. On your left. No, your other left.'

Ahead was a soft glowing rectangle of glass. Bryant felt around, located the door handle and pushed. The pair tumbled into the café, which smelled of boiled cabbage and roly-poly pudding. The radio was playing, its thin treble making Winifred Atwell's honky-tonk piano sound even tinnier than usual. Fewer than half a dozen customers sat at the tables; the fog was keeping everyone out of the West End. A pretty waitress with pencilled eyebrows stood listlessly examining her nails. Bryant went to the kitchen counter and rapped on it with his knuckles. 'Anyone at home back there?'

A red-eyed young man in a chef's hat appeared. One glance at the alarming profile of his nose told the detectives that they had found Harry Whitworth's son.

'Are you Clive Whitworth?' May asked. When the young man warily nodded, he continued: 'I take it you've heard the bad news about your father.'

They seated him in the kitchen and gave him a tot of brandy from Bryant's hip-flask. 'When did you last see him?' May probed gently.

'This morning.' Clive looked down at his hands. 'He often comes in for breakfast. Mum died a couple of years ago. He doesn't cook for himself. Always makes a mess when he tries.'

'You live in the same house?'

'I'd like to get my own place, of course. We usually come in together from East Finchley. Not today, though. I had to start early.'

'How did he seem to you?'

'He was coughing a lot. I think the fog was getting to him. He said his stomach hurt. I told him he shouldn't have come in.'

'How did he get here from the station?'

'He'd have walked, I'm sure. In spite of the fog. He was stubborn like that.'

'Well,' said May, waiting for a suitable break in the conversation, 'we should be getting along. We'll make all the necessary arrangements for your father; you needn't worry yourself about that side of things.' He gave Clive Whitworth a comforting pat on the back and led the way from the kitchen.

Bryant was unusually quiet as they returned to Bow Street through the sickly yellow fumes. May knew better than to assume it was simply because he was heavily muffled.

'All right,' he said as they unwrapped themselves back at the police station, 'what's the matter?'

Bryant regarded him with innocent blue eyes. 'What do you mean?'

'I always know when there's something on your mind. You're not happy. Out with it.'

'Well, it's really unimportant.' Bryant dropped behind his desk and began to doodle aimlessly on a blotter.

'Really, getting information out of you is like pulling teeth some days. Are you going to tell me or not?'

'I've been thinking. Harry Whitworth had weak lungs, and had been out in the fog. The bloodless dry tongue is a classic sign of oxygen starvation, and it's also consistent with carbon monoxide poisoning. In both cases it's a form of hypoxia leading to death, but which of the two causes of death was it?'

'Does it really matter?' asked May. 'Most likely it was a little of both.'

'He told the boy he had an upset stomach when he arrived. Perhaps we should wait until Oswald Finch has had a chance to conduct a post-mortem.' Finch was the coroner used by the Bow Street police.

'Well, it's terribly sad, but I'm sure there'll be similar cases before the fog lifts.' May opened his report folder, happy to fill it in and move on.

They worked quietly until lunchtime. At ten to one, Bryant rose and knotted his scarf around his face once more, leaving only his eyes and the tops of his ears exposed. 'I thought I'd pop out and get something to eat,' he mumbled. 'I'll bring you something back.' And he was gone. This in itself was extraordinary, as May knew his partner always brought sandwiches in gruesome combinations that involved cheese, jam and sardines. Sure enough, today's greaseproof-paper packet was still in the top drawer of his desk. *What's he up to?* he thought.

Half an hour later, he received a phone call. Bryant was ringing from the blue police box on Shaftesbury Avenue. 'I wonder if you'd be so kind as to meet me back at the coachworks?' he asked.

Harry Whitworth's body had been removed, but Stan the apprentice was still seated glumly in the manager's office, waiting to be released. He rose in anxiety as the detectives arrived. 'Will it be all right for me to go home soon, sir?' he asked. 'It's been a terrible morning.'

'Of course, Stanley, I just want you to repeat what you told me a few minutes ago.'

'About Harry and his son?'

'That's right.'

Stan turned to John May. 'I was telling Mr Bryant that they didn't get on. Ever since Harry's wife died he hardly allowed Clive out of his sight.'

'Not that part, the part about why Harry seated himself behind the wheel of the coach.'

Stan looked sheepish. 'He missed it, see. He'd been banned from driving.'

'And why was he banned? Tell Mr May here.'

'After Mrs Whitworth died, Harry started drinking. He had a bit of an accident. He's been here all his working life, though, so Charlie put him in charge of the rosters. You don't need to drive for that position. He missed taking the coaches out.'

'And that little tidbit of information was of interest to me because?' asked May as he was virtually dragged back into the shrouded street by Bryant.

'Next stop, the ABC café,' said Bryant, ignoring him.

When they reached the café, Bryant prevented his partner from going in. To May's astonishment, Bryant knocked on the window and the pretty little waitress slipped out. She sucked her crimson bottom lip and widened her eyes at May in a way that reminded him of Betty Boop.

'Our prearranged signal,' Bryant explained. 'Dolly, tell Mr May what you told me.'

Dolly was clearly excited to be part of an investigation. 'Just that Clive and the old man had a terrible bust-up the other day, right in the middle of the restaurant.' May couldn't help noticing that she had upgraded the ABC from a mere caff. 'Clive and me went out to the dance hall last Saturday and got back late, and the old man was furious, told him he couldn't go out no more, and

Clive said, "I'm twenty-one, I've got the key of the door and can do what I like," and the old man said, "Over my dead body," and Clive said he wished the old man would hurry up and die.'

Released, Dolly reluctantly returned to her station in the café.

'What is the point of all this?' asked May tetchily.

'Harry Whitworth was already sick when he got to the coachworks.'

'Yes, so you said.'

'He hopped on a bus from the tube. Dolly was arriving for work, and saw him getting off at the bottom of Wardour Street. So he wasn't out in the fog for very long at all.'

'What about at the other end, from his house?'

'He lives right next door to the station, and leaves a minute before the train arrives. She's a mine of information, Clive's little lady.'

'So you're telling me he didn't die of either cause?'

'No,' said Bryant, 'but I think somebody would like us to think he did.'

'Not Stan.'

'Stan was at the coachworks an hour before Harry, and even though he had been running the engines all that time there couldn't have been enough carbon monoxide in the air to hurt either of them. There's a ventilation shaft at the back of the shed.'

'Then what made him sick?'

'Harry came to work separately from his son this morning. I think they had another argument last night. The only thing he did before reaching his place of employment was have a bite to eat.'

'You think Clive poisoned him?'

'I'm just saying that I think we should search the kitchen.'

Harold Whitworth had eaten some scrambled eggs and had drunk a bowl of Brown Windsor soup, his favourite. His son watched on blankly, seeming barely present as the two detectives went about checking every canister of ingredients. Rationing meant that powdered eggs were still in use, but May tasted them and found nothing wrong. Bryant tried everything from the lard to a piece of mutton shin that had been used for the soup. It was hard to tell if he was testing them or grabbing a quick snack.

'This is ridiculous,' May complained. 'Dolly, how many eggs and Brown Windsors have you got through serving today?'

Dolly check the larder and returned. 'About two dozen eggs and six soups,' she told them.

'And did Harry Whitworth's come from the same place as all the others?'

'Oh yes, sir.'

'There you have it.' May threw up his hands in despair, but he knew that once Bryant was convinced of something, nothing would disabuse him of the notion until every last particle of doubt had been combusted. He turned to the son. 'Clive, did you have words with your father this morning?'

'No, he had one of his sulks on. Barely said a thing, just ordered from the menu, ate and left without even paying.'

Bryant turned to Dolly, the waitress. 'Where did Harry sit?'

'Over there,' she said, pointing to a small Formica-topped table in the corner, beneath a doubtful painting of the Bay of Naples.

'Does he always sit in the same place?'

'No, of course not. We do have other customers, you know. We're very popular.'

'I can't imagine why.' Bryant wandered over to the table, tasted the salt, pepper and tomato sauce, and returned more dissatisfied than ever.

'Well, I'm sorry to have taken up so much of your time,' he told Clive finally. 'I'll let you attend to your customers.'

The moment they stepped outside the café, Bryant slapped his partner in the chest and brought him to a standstill. 'I need you to stay in the doorway opposite, by the Craven "A" sign, and not let that young man out of your sight until I get back,' he said.

'In this fog? You must be joking.'

'Then take my scarf.' Bryant unwrapped it from his own neck and began to mummify May before he could protest.

Helpless, May was forced to install himself in the shadowed doorway of a tobacconist's shop, but found he could barely see across the narrow road. The city had entered a state of limbo. Trucks and taxis hove into his blurred line of vision like prehistoric beasts, only to vanish just as mysteriously. He could see black particles floating in the air. He wondered how much poison the people of London were being forced to consume, and how it would affect them.

The bell on the door of the café tinkled with each arrival and departure. The customers appeared as little more than phantoms, and it was hard to keep track of them all. May stamped his feet and wiped the beads of black water from his brow. He readjusted the scarf, and was alarmed to note that the patch covering his mouth was thick with grime. He wanted to go home and scrub himself in a hot bath.

Two hours and ten minutes after he had left, Bryant returned. His stumpy figure was as unmistakable as ever in the gloom. He was panting. 'Sorry to leave you so long,' he apologized, 'but I had to get a preliminary result from a friend of mine who runs a chemist's shop in Oxford Street. Has he come out?'

'Who, Clive Whitworth? A result on what?' asked May.

'I tipped some of the salt and pepper into my handkerchief before I left the café. Dolly told me the old man didn't like ketchup, so I thought it had to be in the condiments.'

'You mean poison?'

'What else would I mean? The pepper was fine. The salt has been cut with an industrial chemical that causes hypoxia. But it's a very low dosage, too low to do any damage, no more than one grain to every thirty of salt. Hang on, someone's coming out.'

They both peered across the road. 'I can't see a blinking thing,' Bryant complained.

'It's Clive,' said May.

'Damn, he's leaving early. I've arranged to have him placed under arrest, but the others aren't here yet. This blasted fog. We'll have to follow him.'

Tracking their quarry through the chaotic backstreets of Soho would have been tricky enough without the obscuring murk. But at least if they could not see him, Clive Whitworth could not spot that he was being followed. At one point, when he disappeared behind a stack of fish-crates, the detectives feared they had lost him, but he emerged the other side, crossing into Greek

Street and then Soho Square. The watery sun threw shafts of strange green light through the branches of the plane trees, as if London was in the throes of an apocalypse.

'He's heading for St Peter's,' Bryant pointed out. The red-brick tower of the Roman Catholic church rose in the east quadrant of the square. The detectives followed their suspect inside.

Even here, blossoms of yellow mist were unfolding beneath the doors of the church. Fog hung in the air like the manifestation of holy spirits. Clive seated himself at a pew and dropped forward on to his knees in fervid prayer. The detectives crept into the row behind him and quietly listened.

After a few minutes, Bryant stood. 'A confession of guilt, I think,' he told his partner. Clive turned to look at them and started.

'I am arresting you for the murder of Harold Whitworth,' Bryant began, placing a hand on his shoulder. He liked to do things the traditional way. 'Anything you say . . .'

Clive tried to rise, but was restrained by May's rugby-strengthened arms.

'Come on,' said Bryant, 'hold him tight and let's get out of this fog. I've had enough poison for one day.'

Back at Bow Street, Clive Whitworth did not attempt to rescind his confession. He looked utterly defeated. The detectives retreated to their cluttered first-floor office. It was so gloomy that they had to turn on the lights. May placed a kettle on the gas ring, and Bryant filled his pipe.

'You're not going to smoke your navy shag in here,

are you?' May complained. 'The air's thick enough as it is.'

'I'm replacing the coal smoke with the healthy aroma of high-grade naval tobacco.' Bryant tipped back in his chair and began to puff. 'Come on, then, I know you're dying to ask me how he did it.'

'All right then. I can't for the life of me see how.'

'Clive and Harry Whitworth had a fight last night. Harry told his son he would never have the house. Clive took a powerful poison from his garden shed and carried it to work. He added a tiny amount to the salt. Harry always came in for something to eat before the start of his shift, even when they had argued.'

'But surely he couldn't know where the old man would end up sitting.'

'Precisely. So he measured out the poison and added it to each of the salt cellars in the room. It didn't matter where Harry sat.'

'Then why didn't any of the other customers become ill?'

'Harry used more salt than anyone else. Clive knew he would.'

'I really don't see how he could know that.'

'After the argument, Harry went down the pub and got drunk. You heard what Stan said; since the death of his wife he had become an alcoholic and lost his licence. Excessive drinking removes the salt from your system. Alcoholics always oversalt their food, especially when they're hungover. Harry had no choice but to do so – it was a biological necessity. And for every thirty grains of salt, he consumed a grain of poison.'

'Well I'm damned,' said May. 'I wonder what gave him that idea?'

'Look out of the window,' Bryant replied. 'The city poisons us all. It's just a matter of degree.'

He blew a satisfying cloud of smoke into the air, and watched in amusement as John May had a violent coughing fit.

*One of my favourite Golden Age authors is Margery Allingham.
The first time I read* The Tiger in the Smoke, *the book widely
regarded as her masterpiece, I kept losing my place. The chase
to track Jack Havoc, jail-breaker and knife artist, in the London
fog is as densely confusing as the choking gloom through which
he carves his way. There's a central image of a hopping, running
band of ragtag musicians silhouetted in the murk that stays
beyond the conclusion. It's a dark, strange read that leaves its
mark.*

*Anyway, every year there's a Margery Allingham award for
the best short mystery story. I'd done fog – see the last story
– so I wrote this. It didn't win but it did make the shortlist, and
I'm proud of that.*

BRYANT & MAY
AND THE NAMELESS WOMAN

'There's someone to see you,' said Janice Longbright,
dropping Monday morning's mail on John May's desk in
a way that didn't destroy her freshly painted nails. Arthur
Bryant had been confined to his apartment, having recently
suffered a debilitating bout of memory loss, and May did
not enjoy working alone. He was worried about his old
friend. Bryant was supposedly due back at the Peculiar

Crimes Unit today but there had been no sign of him yet.

'Who is it?' he asked.

'Oh, *someone*.' Longbright raised a stencilled eyebrow, indicating that the someone was a woman, and an attractive one. 'You might want to comb your hair. She specifically asked for you.'

'You'd better show her up, then.'

'I'm not your secretary and you're not Sam Spade,' said Longbright. 'Get her yourself.'

'What is wrong with everyone today?' May asked the empty room, knowing all too well what was wrong: his partner was away and although nothing ran smoothly when he was here, without him the place was worse.

He found her on the landing, waiting to be collected. 'Please, come in and take a seat,' he said. 'I don't think we've met.'

The woman had cropped blonde hair and was elegantly dressed in grey silk. Tall and slender, she had a pleasant smile and an aura of calm control. She was wearing white cotton gloves, May noted, an odd affectation in this day and age. She avoided giving him her name, and somehow made the omission seem like the most natural thing in the world. She looked like someone they'd once interviewed as an accessory to murder – what had her name been?

May behaved differently around such women. He felt somehow vulnerable and awkward, as if he was a teenager again. The change was obvious enough to wring sarcastic responses from those who knew him well, but there was absolutely nothing he could do about it.

Opening her handbag, she took out a monochrome photograph and pushed it across the desk. 'I thought I should let you know what I'm going to do,' she said. 'I want there to be no mistakes or misunderstandings.'

'I'm sorry, I'm not quite with you,' said May uneasily, sensing something bad approaching.

'In one week's time I'm going to kill this man. There's nothing you can say or do that will make me change my mind.'

For a moment May wondered if he had indeed wandered into a 1940s noir movie. 'We're not a private detection agency,' he said, 'we're a unit seconded to the City of London Police. You can't just come in here and tell me you're going to kill someone.'

The woman raised an eyebrow. 'Then who *should* I tell?'

'No one. Well, I mean, you're not actually allowed to kill anyone. Who is he? Your husband, your boyfriend? What has he done that makes you think he deserves to die?' The photograph showed a handsome, tanned businessman in early middle age, sleek and well groomed.

'If I told you, you wouldn't . . .' She searched carefully for the right words. '. . . appreciate the problem.'

'If anything happens to this man, you'll be arrested. Am I allowed to know who he is?'

'His name is Madden. He's rich and successful.' Slipping crimson nails under the photograph, she dropped it back in her bag.

'And he's hurt you?'

'No.'

'Then why come here and tell me this?'

'Because in a week's time he'll be dead, and you'll come looking for me.'

'I don't know who you are,' said May, exasperated.

'No, but you will,' she said, rising and leaving.

*

Against his better judgement May had a look for Madden, but with only a surname and his memory to guide him he drew a blank. One week later, the PCU received a call about a man who had drowned in the rooftop swimming pool of an exclusive City club near the Guildhall. He had indeed been identified as Joel Madden. A young woman had been picked up on the building's CCTV, and was now being sent to them for questioning. And so it was that John May found himself in the unit's interview room sitting opposite the very same woman, once again clad in dark couture.

'You refused to give your name to the officers, is that correct?' he asked, determined not to let her undermine him a second time, which was fine until she said:

'I told them I would only talk to you.'

'Why me?'

'Because we've already met.' Her relaxed attitude astounded him.

'You were seen leaving the swimming pool,' said May, emptying out the evidence bag that had been placed before him. Inside were several photographs of the deceased that Giles Kershaw had sent over. Madden did not look like a drowning victim, more like someone who had just drifted off to sleep. He read Giles's report. Chlorinated water in the lungs; no external markings beyond a faint red line on the left wrist. He turned his attention back to the suspect.

'Do you want to tell me in your own words exactly what happened?'

The woman sat motionless, her bag on her knees, but she allowed herself the smallest of smiles . . .

*

Joel Madden swam with the same languor, the same sense of luxury he possessed out of the water, his tanned arms lifting and falling through the cool blue shadows.

He was happiest at night on his own in swimming pools, during business trips to faraway hotels, or even here at the club near his office. He liked to watch the pool glazing on his exit, the last one to leave. Rolling on to his back, he studied the rivulets of rain sliding down the glass canopy as he lazily drifted beneath it. He had already swum his thirty lengths; now he could relax in these final few minutes of freedom before heading home for the weekend. The Beijing contract had been renegotiated this week, and he had led the team to a hard-won victory. It was a pity he couldn't stay on in town and have fun, but duty called.

The tight-fitting plastic goggles locked him into a cool green world. Chlorine affected his vision adversely. More than ever he found himself wearing shaded lenses of some kind; his eyes were becoming sensitive to the bright strip-lighting at work. He had considered buying photochromic glasses, but wondered how they would affect his appearance.

He was forty-one and in good shape, vain about his ability to maintain a flat stomach. He felt he still had his pick of the females, and his current girlfriend, an astonishingly athletic nineteen-year-old from Poland, watched him with a possessiveness that made every one of his male colleagues feel bitter about themselves. His wife pretended everything was fine, and spent her days with the children or at her laptop, taking courses in Spanish and figure-drawing or wandering around malls looking at hideous hand-woven rugs, for which she had developed a penchant. She seemed to be happier when not having to think about him, which suited both of them. She looked after their house near the coast and he lived in an overpriced City apartment from Monday to Friday, reasonably arguing that it lessened his commute and increased his productivity. The last time he failed to turn up for her birthday party he bought her a horse by way of compensation, so everyone was happy.

At this time of night there was usually no one else left in the swimming pool. The rest of the lane-ploughing high-flyers had showered and dressed, to disperse in every direction from the City, having burned off the aggression they would otherwise have taken out on their families. One other swimmer remained, a slender young woman with cropped blonde hair, seated motionless at the left-hand corner of the deep end. She was wearing a white bikini that was cut outrageously low. To be honest, he was surprised the club had allowed her in dressed like that. The bikini bottom slimmed to a single silver string at the sides and left very little to the imagination.

The young woman rested her palms on the edge of the pool and leaned back, staring up into the fluttering mesh of reflected light that danced arabesques on the glass canopy.

'I went for a swim,' she told John May. 'The club was getting ready to close. Mr Madden was the only other person in the pool. I swam for a short while and left.'

'You didn't speak to him, have anything to do with him?'

'No.'

'You didn't touch him?'

'No.'

'What was Mr Madden doing when you left?'

She held his gaze just long enough to make him feel foolish. 'Swimming.'

May checked the evidence bag again. There was no CCTV coverage in or around the pool for the sake of propriety. A private club, old school. They operated under their own rules. Madden had been found at the bottom of the deep end. There was nothing else out of the ordinary anywhere. The changing rooms had already been searched, and nothing had been found out of place except a small pair of nail scissors left in the ladies' dressing area.

'The City Sports Guild,' he said. 'You're a member of this place?'

'No.'

'Then how did you get in?'

'I walked in.'

'And nobody stopped you?'

'No.'

He didn't doubt her word. She had a look that could open doors, and some of the City clubs were so discreet that they always appeared to be deserted. But there was supposed to be somebody on the reception desk.

'Can you give me exact timings for when you arrived and when you left?'

'Of course.'

May was starting to understand the situation he was in. If he failed to establish any link between her and the dead man, he would have to let her go. In a heavily chlorinated pool there was unlikely to be salvageable DNA evidence. There was even a possibility that she had picked the Peculiar Crimes Unit because it was not a police station; visitors weren't filmed. There were supposed to be cameras in the ground-floor corridor, but the two Daves, the Turkish workmen who never seemed to leave the building, had yet to put them in place. Someone had done their homework very carefully.

'Is there anything else you can tell me about what happened?' May asked, puzzled.

Madden lowered his feet, reaching down to touch the sloping floor of the pool. He stood still and allowed the water to settle. Through his green lenses the woman looked confident and attractive. It could do no harm to swim up beside her. He took his time, windmilling slowly, kicking once in a while, then gliding to the tiled edge.

He decided not to remove his goggles because his hair dripped chlorine into his eyes, and besides, they left oval rings on his face. Resting the soles of his feet against the wall of the deep end, he gripped the edge and flexed his muscular arms, looking up at her.

When she turned her face down, it was to look past him. Fascinated by the slivers of light that pierced the pool and descended into pale helices, she seemed determined not to look his way.

'Come on in,' he said. 'The water's perfect.'

The young woman allowed a moment to pass before she turned to him. 'I'm not a good swimmer. It's a little too deep for me.'

'It's the best time to swim,' he said, 'when it's quiet like this.'

She glanced around. 'Isn't there supposed to be a lifeguard on duty?'

'It's a private club, not a municipal pool. Tucker likes a drink. He usually goes off once the bar's open upstairs.'

'Ah. I've never been here before. I'm using a friend's membership.'

'I'm not sure that's in the rules,' he said. 'Perhaps you should come in and get wet, just for appearances.'

'I'm fine here. The water relaxes me. I just have to look at it. I like the reflections.' She pointed over to the diving board, where buttresses of light danced around the ladder and dropped into the refracting depths.

His smile broadened to reveal perfect bleached teeth. He thought it made him look boyish, but against the wavering blue it gave him the appearance of a marine predator.

'What's your name?' he asked.

'You already know it.' Her voice was as cool as the water. 'We've met before.'

'No, I don't think so.'

'We most definitely have.'

'Trust me, I never forget a . . .' The sentence hung unfinished. He studied her through the green lenses until she began to look uncomfortable. He raised his goggles in order to see her a little more closely. Now he could see that she had remarkably blue irises.

'You could be right,' he told her. 'Did we go for dinner somewhere?'

'You *do* remember.'

'It's distracting, seeing people without their clothes on. One doesn't tend to look at the eyes. Yes, we did, didn't we? We went for something to eat. It was one night in the week. Did we have a date?'

'Not really. But I felt like I got to know you.'

'How was I?'

'You were very funny.'

'Was I? I wonder what put me in such high spirits.' It

was like fishing. He liked the pull on the line, the turn of the reel, the way the fish tacked back and forth behind the boat, gradually growing tired, being brought ever closer. 'When was this?' he asked.

'Mmm.' She thought for a moment. 'About four years ago.'

'That long?' She didn't look more than twenty-five. 'Where did we go?'

'A restaurant in Soho with a French name. L'Escargot, I think. The food was very nice. Expensive. You ordered a dozen green-lipped oysters.'

'Really?' That wasn't much of a clue. He always ordered a dozen oysters when he'd just met an attractive girl. Oysters had the taste of victory. He maintained the smile, intrigued.

'Yes,' said the young woman, remembering. 'You insisted on paying for absolutely everything.'

'Now that doesn't sound like me at all.' He laughed. 'What did we do after?'

'We went to a club just across the road from the restaurant and drank cava at champagne prices.'

'And I paid again?'

She nodded slowly. 'You must have done. I think I was out of work at the time. I remember your name. It's Joel. And you can't remember mine.'

'I'm not good with names. Faces and bodies, though, I'm usually good with those.' The amusement faded slowly to a warmth between them, but the water started to feel cold on his back and thighs. He moved a little closer to her.

'So tell me,' he coaxed, 'where exactly did we meet?'

'I'm sure you'll remember if you put your mind to it,' she teased. 'You paid for all the drinks in the club as well. Do you always pay for everything?'

'I consider it the gentlemanly thing to do. I like your bikini.'

'Do you?' She fingered the side-string. 'You paid for this too. In a roundabout way.'

'Now that's impossible. I only buy presents for—'

'For your wife.'

He was growing a little uncomfortable. He liked to be in control. There was something about her that bothered him.

'I told you I was married?'

'You even showed me her photograph. It was in your wallet.'

'You know what? I think you're bluffing.' He wagged his finger at her. *Naughty girl.* She pretended not to feel patronized. 'You're making all this up. Lots of men like oysters; lots of men keep photos of their wives in their wallets.'

'To be fair, you were a little bit drunk when we met. You'd been celebrating a deal. Some kind of merger.'

He shrugged, shook his head. He was growing tired of this game. But then she shifted her position at the pool edge, opening her thighs slightly. Her bikini bottom was no bigger than a cocktail napkin folded in half. He felt himself heating up.

'You still don't know who I am.'

'I give up,' he said impatiently, 'just tell me.'

'OK. Come here and I'll let you in on a little secret.'

She said this very slowly. If he hadn't known better, he would have sworn she was trying to beat him at his own game. Without moving another inch she somehow managed to beckon him closer, and knew he would follow because she was young and attractive and he was intrigued.

A sixth sense told him that something was not right.

It was the kind of sense that made one halt at a kerb, take a foot off an accelerator or step back from an excited animal, but he was not a man to be intimidated by common-sense rules. Pulling his broad arms up on the pool edge, he drew himself closer still. As much as he wanted to fathom her motives, his eyes could not resist following the outline of her body. His arm was almost touching her thigh.

Suddenly he realized what was bothering him. Why on earth would he have shown her a picture of his *wife*?

Just as he paused to consider this, she brought her right hand around in a swift, practised movement and closed a white plastic tie over his wrist. He looked down in astonishment and found the tie zipped into place. It was the unbreakable kind they put on packing crates, with a small square lock that could be moved forward but not back, the kind his own factory workers had frequent cause to use.

She looped the tie through something imbedded in the walkway. He recognized it as the grille of an oblong steel drain; they sat in recessed trays around the pool's tiled edge.

Knowing better than to pull on the tie, he yanked himself close and tried to grab at her leg, but she moved too quickly for him.

'I remember you,' was all he could manage. 'You wouldn't come home with me. Take this damned thing off.'

May felt inside the evidence envelope on his desk to see if there was anything else at all. Giles had included a photograph of the only mark on the body, a very faint red line on Madden's left wrist, underneath the slender silver band he wore. That bothered him. How had the band left the mark? It didn't appear to be very tightly fixed to his arm.

One other detail. The thumbnail on Madden's right hand was split. He was the kind of man who had regular manicures and never undertook any manual work. So why was the nail torn almost to its base?

He looked back at the young woman opposite, who was calmly waiting for him to finish. 'Do you have any-thing at all to add to your statement?' he asked.

'No,' she replied. 'Do you have any further questions?'

'She was a piece of work,' he later told Bryant. 'I've never dealt with anyone so calm.' But right then he won-dered what she was really thinking.

She smiled at Madden reassuringly. 'The tag is just there to make sure that I have your full attention. I'll take it off once we've talked. You still don't remember my name, do you?'

'No,' Madden admitted. 'I don't remember your name. Sophie, Emma, Kate. Names are all the same. But I re-member who you are. I met you a second time. You're the shopping woman.'

'That's right. I told you I was looking for a job, and you said your wife needed a personal shopper for when she came to town. You wrote down her number for me. But then I wouldn't come back to your flat. You got pretty steamed up about that.'

'And you still had the nerve to call my wife about the job?'

'She didn't really need someone to shop for her, she just needed someone to talk to. She was lonely and desperate to tell someone about her life.'

He remembered their second meeting now – he had

been buying a gift for his girlfriend at Harrods, and had bumped into his wife and the personal shopper. To cover his guilt he'd offered to pick up his wife's bill. Without batting an eye she'd added a pair of amethyst earrings to it, putting a price on her pain.

'I've heard all about you,' said the young woman.

'What, from my wife?' he said scornfully. 'Have you also heard about all the holidays and trinkets and parties I pay for?'

'She pays for them.'

'How do you work that out?'

'By putting up with the insults. The cruelties. The infidelities. The little hurt looks you give her when you're after sympathy. She knows all about your girlfriends. And other things.'

'Then why doesn't she leave?'

'Because of the children. And because she's too scared of you to do anything about her situation.'

'She confides in you about all this, does she?' he asked heatedly. 'The personal shopper? You shouldn't listen to anything she tells you. She's got her art classes and her cookery clubs and her clothing allowance, what more does she want? And anyway, what the hell has it got to do with you?' He plucked at the plastic strap, leaving a red mark on his wrist. A second attempt to break it split his thumbnail.

'You're right, it has nothing to do with me,' said the young woman. 'Do you know what my job is actually about? It's not helping my clients to choose cushions or curtain materials. It's listening.'

'Rather you than me,' said Madden. 'I don't need to do that. You all sound the same. A distant background noise, chirruping away about your feelings.'

'Well, it seems to me that you're listening now.'

'What do you want? Is this about money?' He pulled at the strap but knew that he would never break it.

'I'm a very good personal shopper,' said the young woman. 'We've become quite close, your wife and I.'

'Well, that's fine when it comes to cushions,' said Madden, his voice honeyed with sarcasm. 'I'm her husband. She listens to me.'

'That's true,' she said. 'Women do all the listening. I told your wife I could get her anything. That it was just about cutting the best deal. Do you know what she asked me for, what she wants most in the world?'

Madden stopped tearing at the cable tie long enough to look at her. 'What?'

'Freedom. She wants you to die.'

'You mean she wants a divorce. Well, she's welcome to it. I'll sign the bloody papers tomorrow.'

She bit her lower lip. 'No, she actually wants you to die. A divorce settlement wouldn't be freedom, it would be a negotiation, and that's what you do for a living, isn't it? Always looking to increase your advantage?'

'I honestly don't understand what she expects,' he said, hurt. 'We'll sit down with lawyers. I promise I'll give her a reasonable deal.'

'That isn't what she'd get, though. Your lawyers would tear her to shreds.'

'Well, that's business.'

'Your wife trusts me.' She leaned forward, resting a cool hand on his shoulder. 'In my own small way I'm a negotiator too. We're both looking for the seller's break point.'

He glowered at her. 'If you don't let me go in the next ten seconds you'll be in so much trouble—'

'Ah, threats and consequences,' she said, as if remembering a section from a negotiation handbook. 'I can tell I'm dealing with a professional. Let's not waste any more time. I'll make you an offer. If you can remember my name, I'll advise your wife to meet with your lawyers. If you don't . . .' She reached forward and pulled the plastic cable tie one notch tighter on his wrist.

For the first time he felt a twitch of panic. What the hell *was* her name? Lisa? Hannah? Sarah? Usually when he asked a woman her name he didn't bother listening to the answer, and called them *darling* or *sweetie*. His mind rushed back to the restaurant . . . Nothing, a total blank. What about when they came face-to-face in the department store? He tried to recall the exact conversation between them.

He suddenly remembered the earrings his wife had casually added to the bill. He remembered the look on her face, the glance she gave the woman in front of him. She hadn't been buying them for herself.

'Amethysts,' he said aloud, triumphant. 'I knew I'd get it. You're Amy.'

She turned her back to him, and for one joyous moment he thought she was crumpling in defeat. But she was trying to lift the grating from its place in the trough. That was the thing about an old-fashioned club like this. Their builders had no love of lightweight modern materials. They had opted to use solid steel grids around their pool. She turned to him with the grating hoisted in her hands, forcing him to move his wrist with it.

'Amy,' she said.

He nodded frantically.

'You're quite sure of that.'

'Absolutely.'

'What colour are amethysts?' She sounded almost regretful as she asked.

John May leaned forward, looking into his suspect's eyes. 'Who are you?' he asked. She was wearing a strong perfume but he had never been any good at identifying scent.

'I'm someone you'll never have to see again,' said the young woman. She checked her watch. It was the first time she had betrayed any anxiety, and was a mistake.

'I think we need to go over this from the top in much more detail,' said May with a friendly smile that said, *I have all the time in the world.*

'What colour are amethysts?' she asked again.

When no answer was forthcoming she released the heavy steel block, which toppled into the pool with a bass splash, setting the surface in motion once more as it swiftly dragged Joel Madden down to the bottom of the pool.

His ears popped as he sank. The breath burned in his lungs. He fought against the weight of the water but in his panic he accidentally sucked the stinging chlorine into his throat. He coughed, choked and breathed in again, and now his fate was sealed. Something burst behind his eyes. Crimson floated through aquamarine to become—

Violet, he thought. *Oh God, Violet.*

'Goodbye, Joel Madden,' said Violet.

May listened, of course, but he watched her more carefully than ever. In all the time she had been in the unit's interview room she had barely moved a muscle.

Her self-control was superb. He found himself grudgingly admiring her.

The file on Joel Madden didn't make for very pleasant reading; he negotiated deals for a living and specialized in mercilessly crushing his competitors. He treated his wife and girlfriends the same way. Three A4 pages held the bare facts; it wasn't much of a total for a man's life.

But if this young lady had killed him, she deserved to be punished. He thought about the mark on the dead man's wrist. The longer he studied the photograph, the more convinced he became that the bracelet hadn't caused it. But what else could it have been? There was nothing else in the evidence envelope, only a brochure from the sports club which was proud to point out the attractive specifications of its amenities. In particular it mentioned the swimming pool, and the fact that its deep end was a full ten feet. Joel Madden was five feet ten inches tall. It was almost as if she had managed to drag him down to the pool's floor and hold him there until he drowned, but she didn't appear capable of such a feat . . .

Violet stood by the edge of the pool's light-cracked surface, staring into the glaucous corner where Madden's body slowly thrashed, his brown limbs waving hopelessly beyond reach. He released a blast of bubbles that rose to the top like silvered jellyfish, but it took another minute for him to stop plucking at the grate and grow still, and for the pool to glaze over once more.

Violet climbed the ladder and executed a perfect dive into the water, swimming down to him and snipping the plastic tie free with a pair of nail scissors. It was hard work dragging the drainage block back to the shallow end, then hoisting it out and replacing it in the floor, but she had trained for it, so it didn't take very long.

As she changed from her bikini into a little black dress and heels, she started to think about treating herself to a dozen oysters.

John May looked up at the interview room's clock, sensing that it would make no difference how long he kept her here; she would never crack. A woman who could walk into a police unit and calmly announce she was going to kill a man in a week's time would have thought of every last detail.

If he could just find out how she did it, how she *might* have done it, he would have a reason to keep her here until the wife could be brought in and further connections surfaced.

The pair of them sat facing each other, a staring contest in which nobody cracked, as the time ticked slowly past.

Suddenly the door banged open and Arthur Bryant wandered in carrying a large cardboard box. 'Sorry I'm late,' he said, unfurling his scarf. 'I just ran over the neighbour's cat. He made an incredible fuss about it. I offered to buy him a new one as the old one looked worn out anyway but he threatened to punch me in the face.' He turned to face the young woman in the chair. 'Sorry, miss, I hope I'm not interrupting anything.' He waved his snub nose above her hair. 'What a lovely smell. Violets, isn't it?'

May saw a faint shift in her features.

Bryant turned his attention back to his partner. 'Anyway, here's the rest of your mail. Janice just threw a strop about having to lug it upstairs.' He dropped the box on the desk.

May looked at the box. It was held together with two white plastic ties.

'And good luck getting that open,' Bryant said as he left. 'Janice just split her thumbnail on it. You'll need a pair of nail scissors.'

May looked back at the nameless woman and smiled. 'Violet,' he said.

The circuses and freak shows of the past always had a sinister side to them. A few years ago I went to a display of period sideshows, and they confirmed my worst fears – that the old displays of headless women, two-headed creatures and lizard babies were far creepier than anything you could see today. I have a painting that shows a carnival barker calling to the crowds while, partially hidden by his sideshow curtain, an unconscious man is being dragged offstage, and I always remember Tobe Hooper's underrated monster movie The Funhouse, *so pitting Bryant and May against a criminal in one of these travelling shows was a no-brainer.*

BRYANT & MAY AND THE SEVEN POINTS

'I've reached the age,' said Arthur Bryant with the weariness of a man who has just realized that his library card's expiry date is later than his own, 'when my back has started to go out more often than I do.'

'That's because you have no social life,' his Antiguan landlady Alma Sorrowbridge pointed out as she passed him a fresh slice of buttered lavender cake sprinkled with hemp seeds. 'You spend all your time in that filthy old office of yours. And you do go out. You went to see your old friend Sidney Biddle the other day.'

'Alma, I went to his funeral,' said Bryant testily. 'I don't call that much of a day out. He was as adamantine in death as he was when he was alive.'

'I don't know what that word means.'

'Unyielding, like your sausage rolls. Mind you, the ones at the wake were better than yours. I swiped some and ran chemical tests on them. Caramelized onions, apparently. You may wish to take note.'

'Those who are taken from us don't always leave the earthly realm,' said Alma, who had been following a more spiritual line of thought.

'You may be right,' Bryant admitted. 'I imagine most of them end up working for the post office. Has this cake got nuts in it?'

'Of course not,' said Alma. 'I know how they get under your dental plate.'

Bryant examined his slice with suspicion. 'Everything comes with a warning about containing nuts these days. Except the general population. Do you know there's no common consensus on what constitutes insanity in society?'

'Really,' said Alma flatly. Bryant had been poring over a tattered volume entitled *An Analysis of Uncommon Psychoses* all morning. She didn't hold with too much reading.

'Benjamin Franklin said that insanity was doing the same thing over and over again and expecting different results. But psychosis suggests a spectrum of behavioural patterns defined by abnormal thought processes and violations of societal norms, a flagrant disregard for accepted moral codes.'

'I'll remember that when I'm doing your ironing. Do you always have to harp on about murderers? You know what I think about all that sort of thing – it's unwhole-some.' Alma rose and tidied away the tea things. 'Why don't you get your mind off all this morbidity? Come to church with me this evening.'

'You never give up, do you? I'm not that desperate for something to do,' Bryant replied, dusting crumbs from his stained waistcoat. 'Besides, I remember what happened the last time I went. The vicar told me off for praying too loudly.'

'You made God jump,' said Alma. 'And your singing nearly deafened us. It would have helped if you'd known the tune. Or the words.'

'I couldn't read the hymn sheet because I'd forgotten my spectacles, so I had to make up the lyrics. I think I did a better job than all that rubbish about winged chariots and spears of fire.' Bryant sighed and looked about himself impatiently. 'I suppose I could make myself useful, plant the window boxes, scrape the oven out, clear the guttering, put some dubbin on my boots. It's just that I've got no cases on at the moment.'

'Then Mr May is probably at a loose end, too. Why don't you give him a call?'

As Alma rose and prepared to wrap herself up against the grim deluges of a blustery February morning, Bryant rang his partner, John May.

Don't think too harshly of Mr Bryant; since Christmas, London had been alternately drenched and frozen by squalls heading down from Iceland, until its massed buildings looked like something one would find at the bottom of a stagnant pond. Everyone who ventured out soon became cold, wet and bad-tempered, and Arthur, who took the chill in his aged bones for a sign as ominous as the appearance of Elsinore's ghost, suffered more than most. It is a testimony to John May's persuasive skills that the most senior detective in London's Peculiar Crimes Unit was soon following his partner across the rainswept upper reaches of Charlton Park, looking for a closed funfair.

'He's been missing for three weeks,' said May as they made their way through the wet grass. 'Left work at seven p.m. on the last Friday in January, detoured here for reasons we don't know, and never reached home.'

'And it took him all this time to be flagged as missing?' asked Bryant, incredulous. 'Slow down a bit. My walking stick's sinking into the mud.'

'It's a little more complicated than that. As far as we know, Michael Portheim is an MI5 officer and mathematician specializing in codes. He was seconded to MI5 from Porton Down for reasons no one will tell us, although an inside contact of mine suggested he was involved in certain aspects of counter-terrorism being jointly covered by the agency and the military facility. As soon as he vanished, both groups began investigating.'

'How soon after?'

'He was reported missing on Friday night after failing to turn up at a Russian supper club in Mayfair. One of his colleagues made the call that night.'

'So it was a business dinner.'

'It always is with that mob. Most of them have no friends and very little social life. Confidences aren't encouraged. MI5 sent their bods in to turn over his apartment in Muswell Hill, half expecting to find him zipped into a holdall, but they found nothing disturbed or out of the ordinary. It looks like he never reached home. They traced him here from phone records, CCTV and his travel card. There are no cameras in the park, on the common or in the woods – too many trees – but there's footage of him entering from the street and none of him coming back out the same way.'

'So the assumption is that he went missing inside the park,' said Bryant, fighting the ground with his stick.

'It looks that way. A team searched the entire area, but short of turning over every inch of turf with a spade there's no way of knowing what happened. Can a body be buried without leaving a mark? The agencies' internal investigators have no leads to speak of, but the biggest fear is that he was either murdered or kidnapped.'

'So what are *we* hoping to achieve in a rainy field in near-zero temperatures?' Bryant demanded to know.

'They've called us in. It's rather clutching at straws, but I went through Portheim's file this morning and found that he came from a military background. He'd been a keen sportsman at college, a free-runner, hiker, canoeist, skydiver, good athletic all-rounder. He studied medicine for a while, then joined the army – straight in at officer level – but as part of his training he also learned circus skills. And the only unusual contact anyone has been able to come up with is this.'

May pointed ahead through the sleeting gloom at what appeared to be a half-built stage set. As the pair approached, Bryant saw that it was a semi-circle of boarded-up sideshows, the old-fashioned kind consisting of tents fronted by tall painted flats, inset with strings of coloured light bulbs.

'Back when he was learning to tightrope-walk and swing from a trapeze, Portheim knew a man called Harry Mills. The chap was his mentor in competitive athletics, taught him a lot about physical prowess and showmanship. There's no evidence to suggest they had any further contact with each other after Portheim was headhunted by MI5. But here's the funny thing. This set-up appeared in the park the week Portheim went missing.'

He looked up at a rain-streaked board that read: 'Harry Mills' Incredible Arcade of Abnormalities!' Beneath the red and yellow lettering, set in a traditional circus typeface known as 'Coffee Tin', were posters painted on to linen and sealed beneath discoloured varnish, vignettes that had probably been produced in the 1930s, when such delights were popular at coastal resorts.

One painting showed a voluptuous young woman riveted into a steel bathing suit, holding a pair of terminals from which arced jagged streaks of blue lightning. Scrolled across the base of the picture was the legend: 'You'll Be Jolted by Electra the 30,000-Volt Girl!'

Another board showed a painfully thin young man, his ribcage visible under his pale translucent skin like the bars of a xylophone, a dozen lethal-looking steel rods piercing his chest: 'Nothing Can Prepare You for Lucio the Human Pin-Cushion!'

Beside him was an ethereally beautiful depiction of a woman clad in a diaphanous pink silk gown, with large furry wings sprouting from her shoulder blades. She was balanced on a perch, staring wistfully up at the sky through the bars of her cage. The picture was captioned: 'Witness the Heartbreaking Tragedy of Martitia the Moth Woman!'

The final vignette showed a green man with an elongated torso and no limbs, green antennae waving from his misshapen, beaked and bug-eyed head. The unfurled lettering beneath him read: 'Prepare to Be Horrified by Marvo the Caterpillar Boy!'

Bryant sniffed. 'Looks like he was painted by Francis Bacon.'

'I suppose it's what people did before television,' said May. 'Not much different from going to Bedlam to laugh at the insane.'

The sideshows themselves were surrounded by a six-foot-high steel-staved fence, which the detectives now circled, searching for an entrance. The rest of the funfair – the waltzers, rifle ranges and coconut shies – stood further back on open ground. Only the Arcade of Abnormalities was sealed.

'I remember these exhibits from when I was a nipper,' said Bryant. 'I knew they had to be illusions but they always gave me the creeps. Let's see if we can find any-one.'

'I guess they closed off this part to stop anyone from sneaking in.'

'Or out. Look over there.' Bryant pointed with his stick. They glimpsed a malformed figure hopping and running between the sideshows on the far side of the circle, and went after it.

Behind the show tents, the performers' caravans were arranged like a wagon train. 'Hey!' called May. 'You there!' But nobody came. Finally he rang his contact and the pair waited for someone to come and open the main gate.

'Sorry about that,' said a stooped elderly man with a shock of wild grey hair, unbolting the mesh gate and pulling it aside. He wore leather knee-boots, and the sides of a crimson-embroidered gypsy waistcoat struggled to meet over his stomach. 'I'm Harry, the owner of this place. Come on in.'

He clasped their hands with nervous gratitude and led

them to one of the caravans. 'We keep the gate locked tight to prevent the dogs from getting out,' he explained, ushering them in. 'There's been trouble in the past. One of the Alsatians bit a child after being teased.'

The trailer's streamlined exterior of blue and white steel was misleading; inside it was as cosy and over-crowded as a nineteenth-century Romany caravan, hung about with copper pots, vases, painted jugs and rugs. Mills made thick, dark Turkish coffee and served it in tiny steel cups. 'There, that'll keep the chill out,' he said. 'You said you want to know about Michael Portheim?'

'We'll come to that,' said Bryant, a luminosity in his eyes suggesting that, as usual, his primary interests lay elsewhere. 'Tell me about the sideshows – from the paint-ings they look like they're originals.'

'They are indeed, Mr Bryant,' said Mills, settling himself opposite them. A large man with mutton-chop whiskers and a bay-window belly, he seemed ill-suited to spending his life in such a cluttered interior. 'Most of these illusions date back to the early 1930s. They used to tour the seaside towns, Blackpool in the north, Margate in the south. I've become something of a custodian, and over the years I managed to save a lot of the original props and scripts from bonfires and dustcarts. I try to make sure that each act is performed exactly as it would have been in its heyday.'

'Do the illusions still hold up today?'

'You'd be surprised. We can still make the kiddies scream. Once in a while you get a few smart-aleck teenagers in who think they know how it's done, but we have ways of scaring them as well.'

'I think I saw something called The Girl Without a Head in Margate's Dreamland when I was about six,' said Bryant. 'I have a feeling I wet myself.'

'Can we get to the subject of Mr Portheim?' asked May, knowing that his partner would be quite capable of discussing the sideshows for hours if he didn't interrupt. 'When did you last speak to him?'

'We've stayed in touch over the years,' said Mills. 'He said he was having some kind of difficulty in his job. He didn't sound happy. Before he joined the agency he used to tell me everything, but of course that was no longer possible. I spoke to him about a month ago. He wanted to come and see the show.'

'And did he?' asked May.

'I believe so, but you'll have to speak to Andrei the Great about it,' said Mills. 'I was up north, arranging bookings. Andrei the Great is my general manager; he's in charge of the performances and the staff.'

'Could we see him?'

For the first time, Mills looked uncomfortable. 'I'm not sure if he's available.'

'It's very important,' May insisted. 'If we can't see him today, we'll have to keep coming back until we do. You understand.'

'All right, I'll see what I can work out. It's just that he's very, well . . . Wait here.' Mills lumbered to his feet, narrowly avoiding a collision with a ceiling lamp, and let himself out.

'Curious,' said Bryant.

'Why?'

'Something put the wind up him all of a sudden. It's almost as if—'

'Don't prejudge,' warned May. 'Let's hear them out first.'

After a few minutes, Mills reappeared. 'Come with me,'

he said. His earlier cheerful demeanour had vanished. The detectives followed him across the puddled grass, stepping between guy ropes, and found themselves in one of the sideshow tents. It comprised a series of battered wooden benches placed before a small blood-red stage that was framed in yellow satin curtains.

As Bryant and May seated themselves Mills stepped back into the shadows, as if he had been instructed to make himself scarce. The curtains opened to reveal a pastel-coloured 1960s Lambretta motor scooter with a slender girl seated side-saddle on it. She wore tight three-quarter-length jeans, rope espadrilles and a black halter top that exposed her pale neck and shoulders, but where her head should have been were half a dozen red rubber tubes. These extended up from the stump of her neck to four large glass jars set on the floor that appeared to contain her blood and organs. As they watched, the girl slowly unfolded her arms and waved to them.

From behind the scooter appeared a squat, broad-chested dwarf with a scarlet goatee and bright-red horns. This form of extreme body modification involved the insertion of cones under the skin on his forehead, and gave him the appearance of a miniature devil. His gypsy outfit of clashing indigo and violet silks was strung about with heavy silver chains, and made him appear even more garish and bizarre. Almost every inch of his exposed flesh was covered in piercings and dense black tattoos. He was carrying a black leather whip taller than himself.

But Andrei the Great was not dressed to amuse or entertain. He remained unsmiling and austere throughout the brief interview. 'Do you like the lovely Headless Dolores?' he asked in a thick Russian accent. 'Her mortification intrigues you? You would not be human if she did not excite.' He had a surprisingly rich and deep voice for a man of such diminutive stature.

'She does disturb me,' Bryant admitted.

'That is the intention. To arouse and upset.'

'How is it done?'

'I cannot tell you that.' Andrei wagged a fat index finger at them. 'We are just poor showmen. All we have in the way of currency is our secrets, and we will never give them up. But I can tell you these displays are a mixture of illusion and physical skill.'

'You mean there's something more to them than just a few well-placed mirrors,' Bryant said. 'Did you show Dolores to Michael Portheim?'

'Yes, indeed,' said Andrei unhesitatingly, as if he had been expecting the question. 'He was interested in all of the illusions.'

'Why did he come here?'

'For old times' sake,' said Mills, cutting across Andrei the Great before he had a chance to answer. 'To see me, I told you.'

'Harry, I will deal with this,' said Andrei, his voice soft with menace. 'There are always people who want to know secrets.'

'When was Michael Portheim here, exactly?'

'Just over three weeks ago. A Friday night. I'm sure Harry here will be able to give you a more accurate date.'

'I can check in the diary,' said Mills anxiously. 'I made the arrangement before I went north.'

'So he didn't come to see you,' said Bryant. He turned to the dwarf. 'If that's the case, you were the last one to see him before he disappeared.'

'Then I imagine he'll remember me when you find him,' said Andrei smoothly.

'What did he do here?'

'He watched some of the shows and was introduced to the performers. I imagine he left with the last audience at ten. I did not see him go.' Andrei pulled the curtains shut with a flick of his whip, presumably leaving the Headless Lady stranded onstage until they had concluded their business.

'How did Mr Portheim seem to you?'

'Perfectly normal, as much as anyone can be.' Andrei's sharp blue eyes slowly closed and he swayed slightly.

'You'd met him before?'

'No, but Harry had told me about him.' The dwarf's eyes remained closed. May noticed that he had tattoos of fish on his eyelids.

'If he sought you out, he must have had a reason for wanting to see you,' Bryant persisted. 'He didn't just come here to see the show, did he?'

When Andrei snapped back to attention the effect was startling. 'He spoke fluent Russian. He wanted to know if I still had connections in the Old Country.'

'Why do you think he wanted to know that?'

'I imagine he was looking to sell some secrets,' said Andrei with a leering wink. 'Isn't that what your British agents always want to do when they start to fail?'

'And did you buy them?'

'I told him what I've already told you. That all information is currency.'

'That's not answering my question.'

'No,' said Andrei, 'I did not buy them.'

'Well, that was creep-inducing,' said May as they walked away through the rain across the deserted park. 'I'll be happier when we're back under the street lights. There was something very unpleasant about that whole set-up, and particularly that little man.'

'Did you notice how scared Harry Mills was around him?' said Bryant. 'The poor devil was leaking sweat from every pore. He may be the owner and Andrei his manager, but it's the dwarf who's in charge. Why does Mills need him? You heard him say he's the custodian of the sideshows, the one with the passion. What's the general manager for? We need to do some digging on Andrei the Great. Something tells me he's got a lot to hide.'

'I don't know,' said May uncertainly. 'He certainly seems keen to project a disturbing image of himself. His self-assurance worries me.'

'I know what you mean. He's confident enough to admit that he was one of the last people to see Portheim before his disappearance,' Bryant replied. 'I have a feeling he thinks he's untouchable.'

'Don't take it as a challenge, Arthur,' May pleaded, 'at least until we know more about him. The Russian connection concerns me. What if he arranged for Portheim to defect?'

'He's a circus dwarf,' said Bryant, digging out his pipe. 'Not very likely, is it?'

Back at the headquarters of the Peculiar Crimes Unit in Caledonian Road, King's Cross, Detective Sergeant Janice Longbright had been put in the picture and was waiting for them with fresh information. 'You were right about Andrei Federov being dangerous,' she said, following them along the corridor. 'He spent twelve years in a maximum security jail in Irkutsk, Siberia.'

'What's on his charge sheet?' asked May, accepting the file as he headed to his office.

'Four murders that anyone could be sure of, possibly many more. The details were contradictory and pretty hard to come by.'

'Then what the hell is he doing out of jail?'

'He had his sentence slashed. No reason given.' Janice checked her notes. 'He was granted compensation by the Russian government.'

'They pardoned him?' said Bryant, shocked.

'It seems that way. So he was free to leave his homeland and enter the country. You know how that works, Mr Bryant. If you call someone a thief after they've served their time for theft, it's libel. He served his time and was discharged as being safe.'

Bryant was indignant. 'After four murders? He didn't exactly serve his time, did he? The compensation means he was either wrongfully accused or he did the government a favour of some kind.'

'He managed to escape on three separate occasions. Yet according to his records they still pardoned him.'

'Something's not right there. And why on earth would he end up working in an English sideshow?'

'He's a dwarf, for God's sake,' said Bryant, poking around for his pipe. 'It was that or panto.'

'That's not very politically correct of you,' said Longbright.

'It's very hard to be PC around dwarves, especially one who's chosen to transform himself into a carnival devil. I understand the term "midget" is considered offensive because it comes from the word "midge", but we're talking about someone who runs a sideshow of human oddities, even though they're mostly fake. Is it wrong to say "Headless Lady"? I mean, she has no head – what else are you going to say? If a boy has been made up to look like a caterpillar, you'd call him a Caterpillar Boy, wouldn't you?'

Longbright felt as if she had stepped into some kind of Pythonesque conversation to which she could not contribute. 'We've just received Federov's medical history,' she said instead. 'The murders were supposedly committed randomly, without motive.'

'Show me.' Bryant grabbed at Longbright's paperwork. 'Hm – looks like he exhibits the classic ego-signifiers of a psychopath. I was discussing it with Alma just today.'

'Oh, and what did she have to say about that?'

'I don't know, something about ironing. Goodness, whole batteries of tests were conducted by his doctors, and they all said the same thing.' He pointed to an immense list of attributes that ran down the page. 'Emotionless, detached, fearless, dissociated from reality, exhibits a grandiose manner, total lack of anxiety, attitude of entitlement, insatiable sexual appetite, tendency towards sadism. Has no normal responses to punishment, apprehension, stress or disapproval. A risk-taker and an uncontrollable liar.'

'You're telling me the last man to see our missing man alive is a clinically certified psychopathic Russian dwarf?' asked May.

'I see what you mean. It might be best not to let the *Daily Mail* get hold of this one.'

'We're going back to that sideshow tonight.'

'And put them on their guard?' exclaimed Bryant. 'What would be the point of that?'

'Why don't I go?' Longbright suggested. These days the detective sergeant found herself spending most of her life caged up in the office. 'You know I like getting out into the field.'

'This will get you out into *a* field.'

'I can tell them I'm after a job as an assistant, and while I'm there I'll take a look around.'

'All right, but for heaven's sake be careful. I don't like the sound of this one,' said May, somewhat understating the problem. 'You read the doctors' reports. He's duplicitous – an uncontrollable liar.'

'I'd be happier if I came along to protect you, Janice,' said Bryant, suddenly earnest. The sight of this shrunken, elderly gentleman with an arctic tonsure raised above his wrinkled ears and wide watery eyes swimming at her through bottle-thick glasses drew breath into her heart.

'I'll be careful, Mr Bryant, I promise,' Longbright told him gently.

The barkers and their charges, the Moth Girl, the Caterpillar Boy, the Headless Lady, the Mummified Princess, the Human Pin-Cushion, the Girl In the Goldfish Bowl and Electra the 30,000-Volt Girl were all on their second and third shows of the night. Most of the performances lasted only fifteen minutes, including the barker spiels, and on a good night the artistes would continue until most of the punters had seen most of the sideshows, paying separately for each in turn. But the driving rain had kept the attendance figures down for the fourth night in a row. Harry Mills paced fretfully in his caravan, no mean feat given his bulk and the doll's-house obstacle course of the interior. Finally he could stand it no longer, and stormed outside to find Michelle, the cashier. 'We should close it down,' he told her.

Michelle ran glittered nails through her frizz of dye-fried hair and puffed out over-rouged cheeks. 'It ain't as bad as all that. The rain's easing off. We might get a late turnout.'

'I don't care about the bloody attendance figures, we should just end this!' he shouted suddenly, frightening her. But of course he was in no position to explain his fear. He needed to see Andrei.

He found the Russian dwarf seated at the back of Electra's tent, watching as the bored girl stepped on to her steel plate once more and prepared to produce sparks from unlikely places. A third of the benches were taken with spectators, including some teenaged boys armed with cans of lager.

'Now can I have a brave young man from the audience?' called the barker, a disreputable drunk Cockney who had only joined the Arcade of Abnormalities on this leg of the tour. He worked for booze but, having spent his life in funfairs and circuses, was capable of memorizing his lines perfectly. 'You, sir, with the racy haircut, you look like you have an eye for the ladies – would you care to step up here?' The barker pointed so energetically and with such conviction that the boy could not refuse. His friends laughed and pushed him forward. The barker swung him up on the stage to make him look good in front of the crowd; the secret was to not show anyone up, to build expectations but then give them relief after a scare and show the volunteers how brave they'd just been, granting them a round of applause.

The barker produced a shiny metal salver and dropped a set of keys on to it. 'These keys', he said, 'are the keys to the lovely Miss Electra's hotel room. She's a very lonely lady and likes to have company on these long dark nights.'

He handed the salver to Electra, who raised up the tray

with a dazzling smile and a flourish for the audience. 'Now,' the barker instructed, 'if you can take these keys from the salver, I think Miss Electra will be prepared to reward your bravery with a night of pleasure.'

In the audience, a couple of families with small children looked awkward. The young man grinned out at his mates. To be honest, the arcade's latest Electra had seen better days, but a challenge was a challenge. He blew on his fingers like a safecracker, and prepared to reach out for the keys.

'But first,' said the barker, 'we must turn on Electra's own safety shield of thirty thousand volts, which she needs to protect herself from the attentions of her many admirers.' Someone in the audience gave a sarcastic laugh as the switch was thrown. There was a buzz and a crackle, and Electra was illuminated with tall, wavering spikes of blue-white static. The young man suddenly looked a little less confident. His friends egged him on. Stretching out his hand, he went to clasp the keys and received an electric shock. It was only a small one, but the anticipation had paid off and he yelped, jumping away as his mates roared with laughter.

Janice Longbright had seen enough. Some of the illusions were obvious. Electra was standing on a metal plate producing a low level of static discharge, capable of lighting a neon tube when she connected it to the terminal hidden in her palm, enough to scare a punter who had already been unnerved by the spinning dials and jolting needles of the standard Frankenstein-laboratory equipment behind Electra that included a spark regulator and a Wimshurst machine.

While she waited for Andrei Federov to finish overseeing the shows, Longbright wandered across to the other tents. The Half-Bodied Woman and the Moth Girl produced similar effects, one through judicious use of careful lighting and angled mirrors, the other via a rig that disguised her tightly contorted body beneath a framework simulacrum. The princess who turned into a mummy involved two performers with a glass scrim passing between them – although having the mummy break loose at the end was a nice touch. Lucio the Human Pin-Cushion clearly had a skin condition, and she knew that bleeding could be prevented by pinching the epidermis and folding it in such a way that it could be pierced without harm.

The only exhibits that still fooled her were Marvo the Human Caterpillar, effectively a writhing torso in green shag-haired monster make-up that was either a dressed-up amputee or a disturbing rubber-beaked prosthetic, and the Headless Lady, which she decided most likely involved someone putting their arms through a model of a woman's chest, although she still could not see how the trick really worked.

Longbright went in search of Harry Mills. She found the showman hiding away in his caravan, looking as if the weight of the world was on his broad shoulders. Introducing herself, she gave him her own barker's spiel.

'I was once a magician's assistant in Blackpool,' she explained, making sure that Mills got a good look at her infinite legs. 'Just during the summer holidays. But I'm very well rehearsed in the art of prestiges.' These were the gestures used by assistants to distract audience members from the magician's activities. The statuesque Longbright had arrived at the Arcade of Abnormalities dressed in a low-cut spangled red leotard she had borrowed from a costume shop in Camden. As much as she disliked using her sex appeal on Mills, she needed to get backstage access in a way that would never be granted to punters. Mills was clearly distracted by her voluptuous figure, but was tense and abrupt.

'If I could just have a meeting with your general manager, I feel sure I'd be able to persuade him to consider me,' she persisted.

'I'm afraid that's not possible, love,' said Mills. 'Andrei is very busy at the moment. Now if you'll excuse me, there's a lot of work to be done before we close up . . .' Rising, he began ushering her from his caravan.

Longbright was a police officer/showgirl who wouldn't take no for an answer. 'It's all right,' she said cheerfully, 'I can see myself out. Perhaps we'll run across each other.' Backing to the door, she pushed against the handle and slipped outside before he could stop her.

The audiences had gone home now, and the sideshows were in darkness. Moving between each of the tents in turn, she found that their entrance-flaps were held together with rope and were easily loosened. She checked the stages, but all were emptied and silent. Presumably the 'exhibits' had all returned to their caravans. Mingled scents of burned petrol, sawn wood, popcorn, electricity and stale sweat pervaded the canvas rooms, and beneath these lay an animal musk, the tang of something feral and corrupt. Two fat grey candles still burned behind tin shields in the Human Caterpillar's tent. Checking inside, she pulled back the yellow satin curtains and found the stage bare. She had just turned to leave when a dark, stunted figure blocked her path at the entrance. Longbright could see two cones of crimson skin sculpted like horns, broad bow legs set wide apart, a barrel chest topped with an abnormally large head.

'The show has ended. You should not be here.' The dwarf remained motionless beneath the flickering lights, watching her. A more bizarre apparition was impossible to imagine, not because Andrei was of diminutive stature but because he had exaggerated his unusual features as much as possible. As he spoke he kept his deep-set eyes fixed tightly on hers. In his right fist he trailed his whip. 'I thought you English know that it's rude to stare,' he said with soft menace.

'You encourage it,' she replied. 'The make-up, the piercings, the tattoos – I'd say you set out to deliberately provoke.'

'I am not as other people, so I have remade myself in order to increase the difference.'

'You mean because you're a dwarf.'

'I mean because I am of superior intellect,' Andrei replied.

'I was hoping to see you,' said Longbright. 'I'm trying to get a job.'

'You're trying no such thing. You're looking for Michael Portheim.'

There was no point in lying, she decided. 'What makes you think that?' Longbright assessed the situation, playing for time. Andrei was standing in the path of the only exit, and was armed.

'You're a police officer.' Andrei sniffed the air. 'It's like a scent you leave behind in a room. I suppose you want to know why he came to see me.'

'The information would be helpful, yes.'

'Let's just say it concerned the Seven Points.'

'The Seven Points? What does that mean?'

'You're the law; you tell me. Portheim works for the

secret service. You know most of their agents are psychologically disturbed. Their problems run very deep.'

'I guess you'd know about that. I've read your own medical evaluation.'

Andrei exhaled wearily, flicking the whip much as a bored tiger would twitch its tail. 'Doctors are hardly the best judges of character. Most of them are ill themselves. They lack a sense of vision.'

'Is that what Portheim lacked?'

'You know nothing about him other than what your bosses have told you. You've read a screenful of unreliable data posted in a document written by strangers half a world away.'

'How do you know that?'

'There is no other access to my medical records from here, only material which the state of my mother country allowed.'

'Then tell me what you know about Michael Portheim.'

'What do I get in return?'

'We don't make bargains,' said Longbright firmly.

Andrei smiled tightly. 'Then you get no information.'

'We're not supposed to tell you what we think when we're investigating . . . persons of interest,' said Longbright carefully. 'But these are unusual circumstances, and I'm speaking for myself, not my bosses. I think you killed him.'

Andrei's smile broadened, revealing filed teeth. 'Now why would I do that?'

'Going from your past record you don't need a reason. You're mad.'

The smile faded. Andrei suddenly raised his arm and cracked the whip in her direction, making her start. 'And you are trespassing on private property. Now get out of here before I set the dogs on you. They haven't been fed, and will tear you apart.'

'I'll be back with a warrant to take this place down,' Longbright warned. 'If we find any evidence against you, you won't avoid justice again.' She left, knowing that he was watching her every step of the way.

It was nearly 10.30 p.m. when the detective sergeant found Bryant and May in the Nun and Broken Compass, finishing their pints. 'I didn't let him see I was frightened,' she said, accepting a frothy pint of Camden Hells Lager from them. 'He's certainly arrogant. And there's a stillness about him that's incredibly threatening.'

'It still doesn't mean he knows anything about Portheim's disappearance,' said May.

'He was taunting me, John. He said Portheim went to see him, not Harry Mills.'

'That suggests he was ready to sell secrets. Federov may be a psychopath, but he's well connected.'

'He mentioned something called the Seven Points. What does that mean?'

'Well,' Bryant began, 'the only Seven Points I can think of are the key meditative stages of mind training. It's a system of behavioural modification and self-improvement conducted to awaken the senses, part of Mahayana Buddhism. We know Portheim studied a lot of Eastern belief systems because the contents of his flat list an awful lot of books on the subject, but why would he go to see Federov or Mills about them?'

'Mills may seem a rough-and-ready type, but he has a shared history with Portheim,' said May. 'They studied together. Maybe they shared other interests.'

'So he goes to see Mills about learning meditation and

instead Andrei Federov murders him?' scoffed Bryant. 'Forgive me, but that doesn't seem very likely. And where's he buried, under the common?'

'Federov is explosively unpredictable – anything could have happened,' said Longbright.

'There's something else to take into account,' said Bryant. 'I dug a little further into his background. Unfortunately most of his files are archived in St Petersburg and are only made available to authorized visitors who can arrange their appointments in person, but his academic records are online. It seems he was a brilliant student, specializing in codebreaking.'

'The same as Portheim,' said Longbright.

'I imagine his university achievements singled him out for attention by the Federal Security Service of the Russian Federation. After he leaves college, there's an eight-year gap in his file. The next time he appears is in court for murder – the case was heard *in camera*.'

'So you think he was released with help from his former colleagues?'

'I've no idea,' said Bryant. 'But you have to admit it's very suggestive.'

'So, what do we do now?'

'Crisps,' said Bryant. 'Worcester Sauce flavour. Three bags. And a sausage. I'll think more clearly then.'

'You won't be able to reason with him,' said May nervously as they pushed open the gate to the park and set off in the direction of the sideshows once more. It was past midnight, and the rainclouds had parted to reveal a sickly moon. 'Not that you've ever been able to reason. I mean, not properly. You're utterly illogical so maybe the two of you have something in common. And what if you're wrong? What if Michael Portheim left the arcade alive and just – I don't know – fled the country? Or lay down and died somewhere in the woods where no one has found him yet?'

'He didn't leave the park,' said Bryant. 'The CIA and MI5 couldn't find him.'

'And that means we can? Without back-up? I don't understand how.'

'The secret service agencies collate empirical data, but we operate on instinct and emotions,' said Bryant. 'We can't involve anyone else because we're not even supposed to be involved now. And my ears are tingling, which means I know he's killed again.'

'I don't trust your ears and we don't have a warrant yet,' May reminded him. 'And what do you mean, we're not meant to be involved? Did I miss a meeting?'

'Something like that, yes. I had a bit of an argument with MI5 earlier. But Harry Mills is closing the arcade after tonight,' said Bryant. 'If he does that, Andrei Federov will disappear and no one will ever know what happened to one of the country's top codebreakers. Slow down a bit, will you? You're very tense tonight.'

'Are you surprised?' said May. 'Trying to get the goods on a whip-wielding psychopath in the middle of the woods?'

'We're in a London park,' said Bryant. 'Honestly, I never took you for such a worryguts.'

'Do you really think he killed Portheim?'

'If he did, I'd pay good money to know what he did with the body.'

'He has an IQ of almost a hundred and thirty, not that I suppose intelligence translates into common sense, but I can't imagine he'd be so stupid as to bury it.'

'No,' said Bryant, thinking. 'The tents are pitched right in the middle of the park, which is bordered on all four sides by main roads, and they're all covered with traffic cameras. I suppose he could have fed Portheim to his dogs, but he's more likely to have hidden him somewhere.'

'Why do you say that?'

'Oh, you know,' said Bryant, waggling his fingers around his forehead, 'twisted mind, likes to play with people.'

'I can't get *my* mind around motiveless crimes at all,' said May. 'There are no reference points to work from.'

'Oh, I don't think it was motiveless,' said Bryant. 'Far from it.'

'Can you prove that?'

'I'm going to have a damned good try.'

They had reached the arcade entrance. The evening's customers had long been ushered from the area, but the main gate was unlocked. The burning flambeaux that lit the walkways around the edge of the tents were guttering in the rain, throwing odd angles of flamelight across the trodden, sodden grass.

And there he was, waiting for them, as dark and solid and mysterious as an ancient crow-filled oak.

'Mr Bryant, Mr May, thank you for sending me your showgirl. I returned her intact.'

'Ah, you met our Miss Longbright,' said Bryant cheerfully. 'Got a minute? Can we sit down somewhere? My legs are killing me.'

'Everything is killing you,' replied Andrei. 'Your air, your food, your water, but most of all, your beliefs.'

'Ah, you're in a philosophical frame of mind tonight, I see.' Bryant smiled indulgently as he eased his old bones on to the wooden bench. He was playing for high stakes now, and chose his words carefully. 'We find ourselves drawn back here, Mr Federov, because as you admitted yourself, Mr Portheim's story ends here with you.'

'That's not quite true. His story goes on.'

'We know he didn't leave your sight. We know you're the last person who saw him alive.'

'I'm afraid that's not true either.'

'Given your track record, it's not likely that we'll believe you, is it?'

'I don't know. I imagine your belief systems and mine are at variance. On my twelfth birthday I discovered a deep and powerful spirituality within me, and have acted according to its dictates ever since. It was like being touched on the cheek by a butterfly's wing.'

'Unfortunately you touched someone on the cheek with something a little sharper than a butterfly's wing,' said Bryant. 'You're a dab hand with a razor, by all accounts. Wasn't that why you were expelled from school? And didn't your father kill himself on your twelfth birthday, when he discovered what you were really like?'

For the first time, Andrei's still composure momentarily flickered, like a video transmission briefly losing its signal.

'This spiritual awakening of yours includes murder,' Bryant pressed.

'Not at all. I have never killed anyone.' The dwarf's features had recomposed themselves. He was in control once more. 'I would not presume to hold the power over life and death. That responsibility is not in the charge of mortals.'

'Interesting. Tell me, do you think you are mad?' Bryant favoured surprising his suspects with the kind of blunt questions few officers ever asked.

'Never. I know I'm not.'

'How do you know?'

'Because everything I do is for a reason.'

'Of course. The Seven Points,' said Bryant, realization dawning on him. Jumping to his feet, he made a dash – a slow one, as Mr Bryant is rather old – towards the yellow silk curtain that divided the stage from the public. Andrei spun himself around and raised his whip, cracking it so that the end wrapped itself around Bryant's wrist, but a moment later May was on him. The detectives never carried weapons but, knowing that Andrei was dangerous, May had borrowed Longbright's taser. He cracked it across Andrei's barrel chest, convulsing him.

'A bit more effective than Electra's thirty-thousand-volt static stunt,' he said as the dwarf fell to the floor. Bryant flicked back the curtain with his walking stick.

There, writhing and flopping on the crimson-painted dais in the centre of the stage, was the Caterpillar Boy. Its limbless emerald torso had an absurd rubber beak and bulbous articulated eyes. It emitted a mewling sound like a cat in pain.

'My God.'

Bryant began tearing at the plastic tapes holding the exhibit's mask tightly in place, but they proved hard to remove with bitten nails. The Caterpillar Boy's body had been painted in thick layers of green paint. His arms and legs had been severed and neatly sutured at their bases. He was held in place on the dais by a single broad plastic strap.

'Federov was a medical student for two years in St Petersburg,' said Bryant, looking for something with which to cut Portheim free. 'If that little fellow moves again, stick a few more volts up him.'

May looked at the Caterpillar Boy, aghast. 'Why would he do such a thing?' he asked.

'Because of the Seven Points. Give me a hand here.' Bryant found his Swiss Army knife and used the blade to sever the single strap. Then they set about removing the rest of his facial tapes. 'I knew there had to be a reason why Andrei Federov was released by the Russian Security Service. They wouldn't set a psychopath free and then allow him to leave the country without purpose. He was dangerous but knew exactly what he was doing, and he needed cover to operate as an agent. Portheim has a headful of counter-terrorist information that Federov needed to unearth and deliver, so he used a technique from the old country to get it. The immobilization of the prisoner by the removal of his limbs. He had to be kept alive until he'd been drained of information. He had everything taken away from him except the Seven Points.' Bryant indicated his ears, eyes, mouth and nostrils. 'Only one of the exhibits was reduced to relying on them.'

'My God, the poor devil,' exclaimed May.

'I imagine Mills is the only other person who knows the truth about what's been going on here since the night he arrived. I'm willing to bet that Federov perfected his interrogatory technique in Russia. The difference was that there his victims died before anyone could get to them. Technically you could argue that he didn't kill anyone – his countrymen let them die from their surgery.'

'All right, the FSB want information, but I can't imagine that they'd have asked Federov to put his victim on display in a sideshow, for God's sake,' said May.

'Well, that was a bit of an own goal on their behalf, I'm afraid.' Bryant looked back at the sutured man with sadness. 'They branded him a psychopath when it suited them, but he became one.'

The last of the plastic strips came away from Portheim's desiccated mouth, and he was able to croak a cry for help.

'He needs water,' said May. 'He's suffering from dehydration.' He handcuffed the dwarf to a tent pole with Portheim's strap, then called for an ambulance.

'They can do miracles with prosthetic limbs these days,' said Bryant, not very reassuringly. 'Of course, that will deprive the Caterpillar Boy of his career in show business.'

'Let's not use the term "Caterpillar Boy" in Mr Portheim's presence any more, Arthur,' May whispered.

'Tricky, isn't it?' mused Bryant. 'To define the exact point where sanity ends and madness begins.'

'In this job, yes,' agreed May, feeding the limbless spy from a water tumbler as his partner wondered how he could ever write up the case of a psychotic devil-headed dwarf found in a small South London park.

This tale began life as a challenge to write a short story that would allow readers to choose what happened next. Writers hate to throw anything away, and afterwards I thought it would make a perfect investigation for Bryant and May. The core idea came from the fact that I was sent a very glamorous credit card with a private concierge number on it – accidentally, as it turns out. The bank quickly took it back when they realized I wasn't a CEO, just a writer . . .

BRYANT & MAY ON THE CARDS

One of the lunchtime customers at the Over Easy Diner in Dalston High Street was driving Ian McFarland crazy. His beer was too warm, his burger too raw, his apple pie too chilled, his coffee too weak. It wasn't the Ritz; they sold battered saveloys, for God's sake.

Ian tried to maintain his cheerful demeanour through the increasingly fractious demands. He smiled, apologized, replaced the meal, served a free beer, to no effect. The customer, a raw-faced, stubble-headed bully with small dull eyes, a Liverpudlian accent and an unpleasantly suggestive T-shirt, eventually informed Ian that he would not pay for the meal at all.

That was when Ian lost his cool and tried to throw the

customer out of the door. Not acceptable behaviour, even in a dump like the Over Easy. Not only was it *not* the Ritz, it was one of the least classy dining spots in Dalston, an area which defied description in terms of class at all, accommodating a profusion of dubious social strata too numerous to name. Elsewhere in London you could see drunks fighting on the street at nine in the morning or desperately bartering their last few belongings at the edge of the kerb, but Dalston had that plus everything from artisanal bakeries to Turkish lap-dancing clubs. It was supposed to be up and coming, but never did.

The Over Easy had windows so greasy it was like looking out into a perpetual fog. One had been caved in and was covered in plywood. Inside, the pervasive fatty smell meant that you had to change your shirt after every shift, but it was a job. After his stint in prison Ian had needed something that paid him a bit of cash in hand to supplement the rubbish career opportunity his assistance officer had found for him: planting trees in an area where the kids tore them out of the ground before they'd had a chance to take root and stuffed them through their enemies' letter boxes.

Ian had handled two tours of duty in Afghanistan, only to return and find his wife and his home gone. Depressed, he'd started drinking a little hard, and had made the one small slip-up that had blotted his record and dumped him at the back of the queue. Before Afghanistan he had always considered himself a sanguine, balanced in-dividual; he knew that life wasn't fair, and that you had to face its depredations with resigned good humour, but losing his job on that Monday morning was the last straw, for the customer had called the manager over to complain about his waiter and demand that he be fired. Even in a dump like the Over Easy, the last thing the manager wanted was some Merseyside bruiser overturning tables and coming back to smash more windows, so he'd taken the cheaper option and let Ian go.

Now the lad found himself walking the mean, trash-filled streets with anger eating his heart and no prospects of any kind in sight. Worse, the Liverpudlian was waiting for him in the alley around the corner. In the fight that followed, Ian loosened one of his front teeth but retained his dignity, repeatedly slamming his antagonist into a dustbin until he was unconscious. It was a lousy way to start the week.

As he limped from the passageway, trying to see if his torn jacket could be repaired, he realized that the day ahead held absolutely nothing for him. It was a terrible thing to feel that you were no longer wanted or even noticed by the city in which you had grown up. He had always thought he would amount to something here. London was a tough climb, but if you could make it into a decent job you were set up for almost anywhere else.

He thought back to the moment when he realized that Mandy was seeing someone behind his back. He'd known it was serious, and that he'd lost her. The memory made him chew at the inside of his mouth until it was filled with blood. The worst part was, she hadn't even bothered to hide her infidelity. She had siphoned out their joint account, leaving him with nothing but debts and a note filled with such cruelty and venom that he had torn it to shreds before his eyes could finish blurring. No one had the right to call anyone else a loser. He was not a man of hatreds, but he hated his wife for that. The letter didn't feel as if it was written by her. He wondered if her new man had put her up to it.

Sooty rain had begun to sift down across the glistening grey streets. Checking his pockets, he found that he didn't even have enough for the bus fare. At the end of the high street he crossed the road to a graffiti-spattered ATM and inserted his debit card, already knowing what it was going to tell him: that he was nearly a thousand pounds overdrawn. The machine did exactly that and ate the card in the process, confiscating it as though he was a schoolboy caught with a stolen Batman comic.

That was it, then. His life, over at the ripe old age of twenty-nine. No skills, no future, no point in going on. He returned to his basement flat, to try and get his belongings out before the old cow who owned the house confiscated the lot in lieu of back-rent.

On the mat behind the door was another handful of bills that he resolved to put straight into the bin. Except that he felt the tell-tale rectangle of a credit card inside one slender white envelope bearing his name. Ripping it open, he found a letter which began:

Dear Valued Customer,
As a Priority Account holder your continued custom means a great deal to us. Please remember to sign the back of your new credit card before using it. Our 24-hour concierge service can be accessed by quoting the last four digits of your account number, and may be used for any service at all. Your new credit limit is:

£250,000.00

The card was black and silver, faintly sinister, attached to the letter with two tiny blobs of transparent rubber cement. Ian checked the name: 'Ian Charles McFarland'.

His name, his address, but clearly not his card. Unusually, there was no name of a holding company or financial institution attached. It was either a dodgy advertising tactic or a mistake, a ludicrous, wonderful error made by an outsourced computer in his favour.

What if he tried to use it? Would a fraud flag go up somewhere? Would he find the manager of the shop appearing with a pair of police officers, ready to charge him with theft?

He finished reading the letter.

To activate your card, call your concierge now and provide him with your account digits and the passcode we have sent you (mailed separately).

He dropped to his knees and tore open the rest of the envelopes – damn it all to hell! There was nothing. He'd been offered a final chance only to have it snatched away again.

But wait – there was one more envelope wedged between the mat and the door, behind the circus-coloured flyers for takeaway pizzas. The packet was so light that there seemed to be nothing in it at all. But as he tore it open, he saw the grey patch on one side that always came with pin-codes and passwords to prevent thieves from reading them.

There it was, a six-digit figure to be quoted to the concierge. Digging out his phone, he rang the number on the back of the card.

'Mr McFarland,' said an oddly accented voice. 'How can I help you today?'

'I'd like to activate my card.'

'Please give me the last four digits on the front of the card.'

'6823,' said Ian without hesitation.

'And now, your passcode.'

'908773.'

'That's fine. Would you like to change your code to something more memorable?'

'No.'

'Very well. How can I help you today?'

'I don't know what kind of service you offer,' he admitted hesitantly. 'I've not used this . . . particular service before.'

'I fully understand,' said the concierge. 'Well, there are the usual services, of course. Car hire, theatre and concert tickets, sporting events, dinner reservations, nightclub tables. We can book flights for you, or hire a yacht. I see you have the highest priority limit, which entitles you to use our special Platinum Service.'

'And what's that?'

'It's an exclusive private arrangement with our selected partners offering you a range of the more restricted personal needs.'

'Can you give me an example of something I would be able to buy?'

'Well, perhaps you are visiting a city you don't know and require companionship.'

'You mean a woman.'

'The gender is of course up to you.'

'And what do I get for £250,000?' he asked.

There was a pause at the other end of the line. He fancied he could hear the wind ticking in the wires but that was absurd; there were no wires any more. What he heard was the beating of his own heart.

'We could kill your wife,' came the reply.

*

The restaurant was filled to its stripped-oak rafters, as it had been every night since the glowing reviews first broke in the Sunday papers. Of course it helped that a Hollywood legend had been seen dining there with someone other than his wife, and had returned several times while he was filming in the city. Now the bookings were full until January, four months away, and those same Sunday papers were running articles containing instructions on how to beat the restaurant's obstructive booking system.

The Water House was an old converted municipal swimming pool in Marylebone which Jake Finnegan and his business partner had bought for an absurdly low figure from the town council on the condition that they restored its interior. Having done so, they hired a celebrity chef fresh out of rehab and set about turning it into one of the most exclusive restaurants in London. Almost too exclusive, it turned out, for the quiet backstreet which Jake and his team had colonized was now the subject of much furore in the press, as the residents were kept awake every night except Sunday by drunken soap stars and Russians revving gold Ferraris and swearing paparazzi.

Mandy loved every second of her new life. It was the one she had always dreamed of, but somehow she had been sidetracked into marrying a loser. Ian had survived his army years only to end up with a bad case of PTSD and a stint in jail for fencing stolen goods right across the road from a police surveillance spot. She had dumped him by text, and when that message bounced back, with a good old-fashioned letter. She had applied for the job of greeter long before Jake's restaurant hit the headlines, and was firmly installed behind her low-lit mahogany counter by the time the journalists arrived. She was good at her work, but found she had more respect from the staff now that they knew she also occupied Jake's art-filled bedroom overlooking the Thames, a few minutes' drive from the restaurant.

Tonight had been typically demanding. Nicole Kidman had lost her coat, and her minders were blocking the restaurant's entrance so that photographers couldn't get a direct shot of her waiting while Mandy searched the racks. She found the coat and handed it over, but not before the other diners had got a good look at the celebrity in their midst. Mandy brushed a long curl of blonde hair back behind her ear and gave Kidman the biggest, most sincere smile she could fake before the actress swept out to her waiting limo, every inch a star.

It was raining hard again, but nothing kept the paps at bay. They huddled in the doorway of the building opposite, grabbing shots as the vehicle sped past, yelling and following on foot, hoping to catch it at the traffic lights.

Mandy checked her watch: 11.45 p.m. *Thank God.* The kitchen had shut at eleven, and now all she had to do was divorce the diners from their credit cards and then ease them out into the storm-swept night.

The man in the hall must have slipped in after Kidman and her companions had departed. He was wearing a black suit and raincoat – virtually a uniform among the Water House's male diners – but it was topped with a black satin Venetian carnival mask. For a moment she wondered incredulously if he was part of a stag party looking for a late drink, but surely not – his shoes were far too expensive, and his left hand held a glove shucked from the right. He had removed it because it was hard to pull a pistol trigger with his fingers clad in leather.

The bullet passed through Mandy's brain and exited behind her left ear, smashing a crystal decanter presented by Ewan McGregor's PR team after a memorable night at the restaurant last month. As she fell, her Lucy Choi high heels slipped on the floor tiles, ensuring that her split skull connected with the floor before they did.

As the horrified waiting staff dropped to their knees around her, Mandy's grand dreams flashed away into darkness and the hallway of the Water House was empty once more. The entrance door swung closed, so that even the sound of falling rain faded to a respectful silence.

John May rested his chin on his fist as he watched his partner working. 'How much longer are you going to be with that thing?' he asked finally.

'I need two more flat bits with sky in them and a sailor's nose,' said Arthur Bryant without looking up. All of the files on his desk had been moved to make room for the jigsaw. May examined the picture on the lid and compared it to the partially finished article. Bits of it seemed entirely wrong. 'It's Hans Holbein's *The Ambassadors*,' he pointed out. 'It's an interior. You shouldn't have any bits of sky. Or a sailor's nose.'

'Well, that's the problem, you see,' said Bryant. 'I thought there was only one jigsaw in the box but there seem to be two. I think the other one is Géricault's *The Raft of the Medusa* but this sky is bright blue and Géricault's was a sort of orange. It might be from a Matisse.'

The Peculiar Crimes Unit had been quiet over Christmases past, but never this quiet. May had filed all of his outstanding reports (he was more meticulous than his partner), and had called the attractive blonde he had met in the Shoreditch Hotel on Christmas Eve to arrange dinner the following week. Now he had nothing to do, and watching Bryant fiddle with mismatched jigsaw pieces was as much fun, and weirdly similar to, a severe migraine.

Usually when Raymond Land stuck his head around the door, May inwardly groaned, expecting a sermon about excessive use of kitchen roll or tampering with stored evidence. What was it he had wanted to know last time? Ah yes, someone had broken into the confiscated packets of Old Mariners' Wartime Naval Rough-Cut Shag Bimsley had taken away from an illegal newsagent on the Caledonian Road. Looking over at Bryant's pipe on the mantelpiece, it wasn't hard to work out where the tobacco had gone.

'Blimey, is this what you get up to when there's a lull?' Land exclaimed, horrified. 'Why not hold a bloody cribbage tournament?'

'We did that. I won,' said Bryant, clipping the nodule off a piece of jigsaw and hammering it into place.

'Well, here's another game you can try your hand at,' said Land, checking the page in his hand. 'A young lady who used to work in a sandwich shop in High Holborn. I want you to go and see her.'

'If you're after a cheese and tomato bap, I'm sure we can send someone down to the shop on the corner,' said May.

'This person won't be serving you anything,' said Land. 'She's been shot through the head.'

Bryant immediately rose and reached for his hat.

'Not you,' said Land. 'I've got another job for you.'

'But we always work together,' pleaded Bryant, looking pitiful.

'Not this time,' Land warned. 'Let John handle it without your help. I need you to clean out all your rubbish. There's a stuffed moose blocking the fire door. We could be shut down.'

'Sorry, Arthur,' said May, heading for the door. 'I'll take Janice and keep you in the picture, I promise.'

It was the no man's land between Boxing Day and New Year's Eve, when London emptied out and even the Peculiar Crimes Unit was running a skeleton crew. Less than a fortnight after the Met had been forced to hold a placatory press conference about London's unexpected and unwelcome rise in seasonal crime, a shooting in its most ambitious new restaurant was not what anyone needed. John May had only seen its interior in magazines, all gilt columns and mosaics. Now, with the lights up and the revellers gone, you could see it had once been a municipal swimming baths. It was very different from the King's Cross trattoria where the unit's staff could be found carb-loading on spag-bogs after a long shift. The inside of the Water House was 'ironic', apparently, so it had kept its changing booths and shower cubicles as a reminder of its origins. But from the corpse near the entrance it appeared that someone had high-dived without checking the water level.

'Amanda McFarland,' he repeated, checking his notes and looking around. 'Either of the owners on their way?'

'Trying to get hold of them now,' Janice Longbright pointed out, studying the celebrity photographs lining the walls.

'The smarmy one who's always in the photos – remind me of his name?'

'Jake Finnegan,' Longbright said. 'The deceased was living with him.'

'I've got her down here as married. You, skinny lad, who's the husband?'

One of the waiters came forward. He looked very badly shaken. *As you would be,* thought May, *to find your boss gunned down at her reception desk.* 'I believe Mrs McFarland is separated,' he explained in an accent that confirmed his Eastern European origins.

May's interest was piqued. 'Ever seen the ex?'

'He came around once, making trouble.'

'What was he like?'

'An army type, and a – what you say? – *convict*. He'd been in jail.'

'How do you know?'

'She told me. She told everyone.'

'Who left who?'

'She left him. She said he was very angry when he came out.'

'Of prison or the army?' May looked around. 'Big man, running with the A-listers, you'd think the lover would have been the one to get shot.'

'You can't assume it was her ex,' said Longbright.

'I'm not assuming anything. Bring him in, will you?'

'Nice shoes,' said Longbright. She looked down at Mandy McFarland's feet, then up at her hands. 'Amazing nails, too. You can't blame her for trading up, although I imagine it came with a price.'

May frowned. 'What do you mean?'

'Jake Finnegan's business partner is a chap called Alessandro Ribisi. Ring any bells?'

'The commercial-property developer?' May asked.

Ribisi was well known to the PCU. His opponents had a mysterious way of dropping their objections when confronted. A couple of them had disappeared altogether. Nothing they could ever get on him would stick. 'We won't have anything more on her physical state until forensics have finished, but I'd say it was professional.'

'What makes you think that?' Longbright took a closer look at the body in the hallway.

'See how the bullet's placed?' May pointed to the oddly neat hole in Mandy McFarland's skull. 'Right between the eyes. It would have been perfect if she hadn't turned her head. The light's not good in here. Can you see what we've got in the way of CCTV?'

'I already looked,' said Longbright. 'Not a lot, as you'll see when you go outside.'

It was starting to snow. The only camera in the street was hanging off the wall, looking as if it had been shot as well. 'Bloody hell, what happened here?' May asked, staring up in annoyance.

'I don't know – maybe one of the paps climbed up there trying to get some snaps. They had a couple of celebs in tonight.'

'And maybe it was disabled before the attack.' May looked around. 'There's another one over that off-licence. Find me some decent footage, would you? Maybe there were fans waiting outside and someone put pictures on Instagram. You know how easily that can happen.' Longbright's ex-boyfriend had 'accidentally' posted a saucy picture of her to a friend, not realizing it was linked to his Facebook account; they'd all had a good laugh about that one.

May stepped out into the street, thinking. To walk

into a restaurant with a gun took some nerve. The obvious choice was to go after the husband, but first he ran a check. 'Wait,' he called to Longbright, 'before you do that, get Colin to go through her husband's charge sheet and find out what he was inside for.'

While May was waiting he talked to Keith Wallace, a cadaverous forensics expert who had been drafted in for handgun incidents while Dan Banbury was on holiday. Wallace was folded over the shattered decanter like a crane checking for fish.

'Mr May, always a pleasure,' he said, glancing up briefly before returning to the hole in the panelling where he had wedged his tweezers. 'Not interrupting your Christmas, I hope?'

'At least it's keeping me away from Morecambe and Wise reruns.'

'Get a good look at the lady, did you?' Wallace's knees cracked as he rose.

'Enough to stay with me for a couple of nights, thanks. She turned her head.'

'Oh, you noticed that? Yes, the bullet wouldn't have exited if she'd stayed still.'

'Maybe something distracted her at the last moment.' May turned his own head to the right of the reception desk. There was only a vase on a pedestal, a squiggly painting of a man on a diving board and a long Japanese sword mounted on a red wooden wall bracket. 'Or maybe she was already expecting something bad to happen.'

'Well, this is one for the books.' Wallace grunted and twisted and pulled at the splintered wood, finally removing a squashed piece of metal, raising it before him with a sigh of contentment. 'Feast your eyes on that – not many others will.'

May couldn't see anything to get excited about. 'What's so special?'

Wallace dropped it into a clear bag and twirled it before May's eyes. 'You get togged up for a posh restaurant, don't you?' he asked.

'I can't remember the last time I went to a posh restaurant,' May said pointedly. 'Why?'

'The shooter had a sense of occasion. This is fancy. A .45 ACP cartridge, one of the most successful cartridges ever, designed by John Browning. It doesn't over-penetrate.'

'What's your point?'

'That means if it enters head-on it's unlikely to injure anyone standing behind the original target. But she moved and it came out from behind her right ear with enough force to smash that decanter. It's one of the most powerful pistol calibres you can use with a suppressor. Subsonic, in fact. For that reason it's associated with a very particular weapon.' Wallace raised an eyebrow. 'Would you care to hazard a guess?'

'This isn't a quiz show, Keith, just tell me.'

'The .45 ACP Luger, the queen of handguns. Of the originals, only one, marked serial number 2, is known to have survived. Serial number 1 was scrapped after the initial trial. At least three more .45 ACP Lugers were made, one a carbine bearing serial number 21.'

May blew out a noisy breath. 'It's late, I'm knackered, just give me the bottom line.'

Wallace would not be rushed. 'The Luger is more correctly known as the Parabellum-Pistole, a semi-automatic patented in 1898. Originally designed for 7.65- by 22-mm Parabellum cartridges, but the army wanted a larger calibre.'

'Army.'

'That's right. It's an expert's field, this.'

'So it's rare, which makes it valuable.'

'You'd be hard-pressed to find one for under a million pounds,' said Wallace. 'Whoever shot Mrs McFarland was using the most expensive handgun in the world.'

'This wasn't somebody pissed off about being over-charged for the bread rolls, then.'

'Not very likely.'

'A bit over the top for the choice of target, wouldn't you say?'

'I wouldn't say,' said Wallace, still admiring the turning bullet. 'That's your department.'

Colin Bimsley was hopping about outside in the rain, waiting to talk to him. 'McFarland has a couple of strikes against him, Mr May, most recently serving eighteen months for a Section 18,' he said. 'Wounding with intent. See if you can guess who he shanked up.'

'To whom he took a knife,' said May. 'I thought you were a grammar-school boy. It wouldn't be a Mr Finnegan by any chance, would it?'

'Got it in one.'

'OK, don't bring him in, let's go and get him out of bed. Got an address for me?'

'Dalston,' said Gilmore.

'Ah, an area of intense ethnic diversity, as the social workers like to say.'

'That's not what my granddad calls it,' said Bimsley.

'I suppose we'll have to take my car. I'd like to come back with a full set of tyres.'

'Nearly half the area's total population is under the age of thirty,' Bimsley remarked.

May narrowed his eyes. 'Have you been reading books again?'

'It means the local lads either grow up with gang affiliations or get the hell out. I wonder which category McFarland falls into.'

'Army. Prison. I guess he knows how to look after himself,' said May. 'I just can't see him using the world's most expensive gun.' They set off towards May's BMW.

'Where's Mr Bryant?' Colin asked. 'He can't be on holiday, he never takes any time off.'

'He's on tidying-up duty,' said May. 'Apparently he found something in his old paperwork that needed investigating, and he's pursuing it on his own. Anyway, something like this calls for my specific skill-set, which includes a low sympathy threshold and the ability to appreciate that it's not 1963.'

'Mr Bryant has a different way of looking at things,' Colin agreed, dodging a sputtering downpipe. 'Couldn't that be useful?'

'Yes, if we were looking for a secret organization of devil-worshipping Zeppelin pilots,' said May, 'but in this case all that's needed is the copper's best tool: an incredibly suspicious nature. If a chap came over to me and said, "I was walking down Oxford Street just after midnight and some fellow came running up and snatched my phone," my instinct would be to ask, "What were you doing in Oxford Street after midnight?" Arthur's always happier when he's poking about in the basement of the British Museum uncovering the history of cursed Egyptian scarabs.'

Bimsley raised his eyebrows. 'You want to get backup?'

May bipped the door of the BMW and slid behind the wheel. 'What, for arrest on suspicion of murder with the world's rarest gun? And let someone else get that glory?'

May put his foot down hard and made the tarmac shriek before Bimsley had a chance to buckle up his safety belt.

Ian McFarland was having a nightmare. He was trapped on a fairground waltzer, and every time he tried to get off the damned thing sped up again, until he finally jumped. Moments later he was awake and standing at the bedroom window with sweat on his spine, looking down at the empty wet pavements, and right ahead of him was a patrol car with its lights turned off, creeping forward in silence to block the entrance to the flats.

He was naked. Grabbing a black T-shirt, his jeans and trainers, he tried to dress while hopping across the room, something no man has ever satisfactorily managed. With the car already outside, he knew there were only seconds to spare before they arrived at the first-floor door.

Ian had one advantage over the police. He knew about the new alleyway at the rear of the building; the builders had only opened it a couple of days ago as part of the block's renovation. He legged it out into the corridor, avoiding the main stairwell, staying back in the shadows. His clothes and trainers were still wrapped in a bundle under his arm. He needed to put some distance between them and himself, to give him time to think.

There was still rubble lying around on the darkened staircase. Darting between the scaffolding poles, he tried not to stub his toes or at least not cry out when he did, but on the way he dislodged a stack of tiles that crashed down the stairs, causing the footsteps behind him to suddenly change direction. As he fled into the narrow alleyway he found himself confronted by an elegantly suited man who looked nothing at all like an officer of the law.

'What, you think we didn't know about the alley?' May said, blocking the way. 'Do me a favour, pop your pants on before you get in my car. I don't want the lads thinking I've run in a strippergram.'

After they arrived at the King's Cross headquarters of the Peculiar Crimes Unit, John May headed down to the solitary holding cell that had been constructed in the basement and spent some more time with Ian McFarland. When he had finished, he went back upstairs and found Bimsley eating muesli from a plastic pot on the ground-floor terrace.

'I know you're on a diet but I can't adjust to not seeing you with a dripping fried-egg sandwich in one hand,' he said. 'Put down the bird-seed for a minute; I need to talk to you.'

Bimsley obediently followed his boss inside to the bank of computer terminals they were currently being forced to share in Raymond Land's misguided attempt to switch the staff to hot-desking. 'We're not going to keep him,' May warned.

'You're joking.'

'We can keep an eye on him easily enough. He's no money, no job, where's he going to go?'

'It's a murder investigation and he's the only—'

'He's not the only suspect and his story is solid,' May pointed out.

'You don't believe that guff about the concierge service, do you? Of all the rubbish I've heard from suspects that has to be the dumbest—'

'He was naked when we picked him up, Colin. What kind of guilty party is so confident that they sleep with no clothes on right after doing something like that?'

'Mr Bryant said he knew an axe murderer who cooked a pineapple soufflé in his victim's house right after killing him.'

'What you have to remember is that Mr Bryant sometimes confuses real-life investigations with what he's read in old horror comics. I can't believe that McFarland shot his wife in the face, went home, stripped off and went to sleep. Admittedly he might have changed if he thought there was residue on his clothes, but the clothes he had in a bundle were the ones he was wearing earlier.'

'How do you know that?'

'You mean apart from the fact that he told me? There were no other bloody clothes in or around the flat! And who'd make up a story as mad as his? Have you ever heard the like? A *credit card*? Why not come up with a normal alibi, or any alibi at all? At home, asleep? Really?'

'I know, but—'

'He says they offered to kill his wife for him, so does he tell us he said, "Are you crazy, don't do that?" No, he asks how they know about his wife, gets no answer and then agrees with them that yes, right now he'd pretty much like to strangle her with his own bare hands. And they ring off before he can say anything else. Now, if you think he was lying in bed waiting for us to call – knowing that he'd be first in line to get picked up – and plotting out that scenario as a foolproof alibi, then you're as daft as he is. And there's the bullet. Keith Wallace reckons it was specifically made for the most expensive gun in the world, which sort of fits with the concierge thing, don't you think? A high-end operation? Something a bit out of Ian McFarland's league?'

'What, are you going to tell me there's some kind of

new company offering this as a regular service?' Bimsley asked. 'I must have missed that episode of *Dragon's Den*.'

'I'm saying it's a set-up. You're not very thorough. Did you not read his charge sheet properly? Mr McFarland's first conviction was for fraud. He was caught selling fake antiques in Portobello Market, said he was trying to raise money for the kids of wounded soldiers.'

'That just proves he's an accomplished liar, doesn't it?'

'No, because he really *was* trying to raise money for them. What he didn't do was bother to check where the antiques were coming from. I think somebody sent him the card because they heard he was a bit of a mug. And where could they have found that out?'

'From the people he fenced the antiques for?'

'From his *wife*,' said May wearily. 'He was out of the country for two tours of duty, and she hooked up with this fellow Finnegan.'

'Then he had all the more reason to want her dead.'

'Let me guess, when you were at school you were the one at the back of the class mucking around with his mates instead of paying attention, weren't you?'

Bimsley picked a lump of muesli off his shirt. 'It's funny you should say that because—'

'It was a rhetorical question.' May sighed. 'McFarland has a gullible nature. He didn't realize he was being used to fence smuggled goods, he didn't notice that his wife was having an affair, and when he *did* find out, he was daft enough to walk into a pub and take a slice out of her lover's arm.'

'And that's why you think it was a set-up?' asked Colin, frowning again.

May rolled his eyes to the heavens. 'What more do you need?'

'The credit card,' Bimsley said.

'He says it freaked him out and he threw it away.'

'Yeah, right.'

'I can see I'm going to have to play my ace,' said May. 'I've got the phone call. It's true it might sound to an untutored ear – yours, for example – like an agreement to let someone kill his wife, but it proves he was talking to a third party.'

'They traced it?'

'To a chuckaway.'

'So what do we do now?'

May peered out of the dirty window and checked the sky. 'We pay a visit to the boyfriend, Jake Finnegan. A Jake, in the common underworld parlance of Glasgow, whence our Mr Finnegan hails, is a person addicted to class A substances who has a poor quality of life as a consequence. Mr Finnegan has a spectacular history of prosecution for drugs offences, yet he managed to raise the capital for one of London's most expensive restaurants, presumably by teaming up with Ribisi. Besides, when you've interviewed the cuckold, you owe it to them to do the same with the cuckolder.'

'I'm not sure I understand—' Colin began.

'I think the Water House started out as a money laundry. And now its owners are expanding, offering hitmen for hire. It's Ribisi. He's bringing the Mafia to London.' May pointed at the nearest keyboard. 'See if you can get your fat little fingers working on that and tell me how many unsolved gun crimes we've had this year. It'd be interesting if it turned out that Mr McFarland wasn't the only one enjoying the privileges of club membership.'

*

'Don't leave the city without telling us or I'll be chasing you naked down the street again,' John May had told him, but Ian knew they would be back as soon as their other leads failed. He had been conned again, and the possibility of going back to jail, this time for a much longer stretch, was starting to look like a probability. Unless he could find the card.

The whole thing was a mess. As he trudged miserably through the sodden *Metro* newspapers discarded on the Euston Road, he tried to recall the exact words of the phone call.

'We could kill your wife.'

An incredulous pause. And then him joking: 'I think I'll take you up on that, mate. I feel like strangling her myself.' And the line going dead.

The call had unsettled him. He'd have written it off as a prank set up by his army mates if it hadn't been for the fact that the service being offered chimed uncomfortably with his darkest thoughts. Mandy had ruined his life. He had trusted her implicitly, and she had taken advantage of him. And now she was dead.

He'd been set up. But unexpectedly, the set-up had failed. He'd been taken to some weird dump of a place that looked nothing like a regular police station, and they had decided, against all odds, to let him go. He knew he should have kept the credit card instead of chucking it into the river, but the damned thing had messed with his head. Now it was all that could prove his innocence.

He thought about Mandy. She had behaved appallingly, but he would never hurt a woman. What had she done to get herself killed? She'd always had a mouth on her. He'd heard rumours about the boyfriend's business partner, but he couldn't afford to get involved. Actually, right now he couldn't afford anything. He had no job and no savings, he owed back-rent and didn't have a penny left over for the utilities. He headed back to the Over Easy Diner to pick up his last day's wages.

Golden wasn't her real name, but nobody could pronounce that because she came from Vietnam and, in a moment of spectacular misjudgement, had married the café's owner after meeting him on his holiday in Hanoi. When she wasn't working as a manicurist she waitressed at the Over Easy, and made good tips from men who felt guilty about making a play for her.

'Ian, what are you doing back here?' she hissed as he walked in, looking alarmed.

'Came to collect my pay is all,' he said, taking a stack of dirty plates and setting them down behind the counter from force of habit.

'Someone's been looking for you. A man in expensive clothes. Kind of creepy-looking.' For Golden to think a man was creepy in this neighbourhood, he had to be very unpleasant indeed. 'You're not in any trouble, are you?'

Ian looked at her. She was as beautiful as her name, and the less she got involved, the better. She seemed so innocent that he couldn't help but worry. 'Why, did he say something?'

'He left a card. Hold on.' Wiping her hands on her apron, she ducked into the kitchen and came back with it.

'Alessandro Ribisi – LondonLink Direct Holdings'.

The card was black and silver, and exactly matched the credit card he had been sent. He knew at once it was Ribisi who had set him up, making him trot out a tall tale to incriminate himself. He knew a couple of other things about Ribisi, things his wife had told him: one, that he was a barely functioning crazy on anti-psychotic medication, two, that he was Mafia, over from Naples.

With nothing to lose now, he headed to the address on the card.

LondonLink Direct was up by Drayton Park and the new Arsenal football ground, in an anonymous two-floor 1970s office building that looked like the kind of place contractors pulled down after finding asbestos in the ceilings. He didn't call first; on this occasion, he decided that the element of surprise would work in his favour.

Except that it was lunchtime, and Ribisi was out. He wasn't expected back today.

Brilliant, Ian thought. *You should get a job as a private detective.*

There was one other place to try.

'Four unsolved deaths in the Dalston area this year,' said John May, tapping at the map on his screen with the end of a breadstick. Colin's diet required him to get through boxes of the things. 'Five if you count McFarland. Makes for quite interesting reading, this. Don't show it around; they'll all want to jump aboard.'

'Not if it turns out to be a complete waste of time,' said Bimsley gloomily.

'It won't. He's offering a proper bespoke service. There's been talk around town for a while now about something being set up called the Elimination Bureau. The Met treated it as a joke.' May scratched the back of his hand thoughtfully. 'What do you do when you want to set up a new business? Try to kill the competition. You can see the possibilities.'

'Finnegan's running a gold mine in that restaurant.

What would he want to jeopardize something like that for?'

'Who said anything about Finnegan?' he countered. 'I'm talking about Ribisi. Finnegan's no Stephen Hawking. He'll be doing the heavy lifting. Ribisi's the ideas man. Let's find out where they are. It's time we paid them a visit.'

Although the police had finished with the Water House, it was still shut for business. The gate was locked and a police sign read: 'Closed until further notice'. Already, a pile of flyers and newspapers had blown behind the grille across the entrance, giving the darkened building a derelict air.

Inside, the reservations hotline had been overloaded with unanswered complaints all morning, so Jake Finnegan had summoned his partner to discuss what to do. He was always wary of meeting up with Alessandro because you could never tell what might happen, but right now he needed the Italian. As he entered the cocktail-bar section of the ground floor, he flicked on the battery of lights behind the onyx-tiled serving counter and poured himself a rich Islay malt, leaving the bottle out.

He didn't realize that Ribisi had been sitting in the dark behind him, and jumped.

'You shouldn't be nervous,' said Ribisi, raising his glass. 'You should be worried.'

'What about?' Finnegan asked, waiting for his pulse to return to normal.

'Losing money every day this place is shut. Get it open tomorrow.' Even in the shadows of the lounge, his crocodile smile glowed.

'I have no control over that,' Finnegan replied.

'You know your problem? You worry too much. Let me take care of business.' Ribisi shook his head, tutting. 'This unit, the one that arrested McFarland. A couple of old men hanging on for their pensions and a bunch of misfits. They're not Met, they're not City of London, they're an outsource. They can be compromised. They can probably be bought. I've got an idea.'

'No,' said Finnegan, feeling the ever-present acid in his stomach starting to bubble. 'If you do anything like that, you're going to start a war.'

'I'm not interested in preserving the status quo; I want to overthrow it.' He released an explosion of laughter that made Finnegan jump again. Ribisi's eyes radiated madness.

There was a peculiar scraping sound behind them.

'Did you leave the back door open?' Ribisi asked, slowly rising.

'For you. I didn't know you were already here,' said Finnegan.

Ian McFarland walked forward into the light and stood before them. The source of the noise became apparent. He was dragging the forty-inch hand-forged *Shirasaya* sword that should have been on the wall in the hallway. A shadow moved behind him. 'What did my wife do?' he asked.

Finnegan stared at him in amazement. Ribisi started laughing again.

'*What did she do?*' Ian asked again, cocking his head on one side.

'You were married to her,' said Finnegan. 'You should know what she was like.'

'I know that if Mandy had found out something bad

about you, she would have told someone else. What, are you going to kill them as well?'

'That's the easy part,' said Ribisi. 'Expanding our operations base, that's harder. You've tried the service, you know it works. I thought you might like to help us.'

Ian stood there with the sword trailing on the concrete floor, staring at them. 'What's in it for me?'

Ribisi flicked a finger between himself and his partner. 'We get you off the hook.'

Ian thought it over. It was the first decent job offer he'd had all year.

'Of course, there would have to be a trial period,' Ribisi continued. 'You could do something for us, to prove your worth.'

'Like what?'

'We've sent a new credit card to the person your wife talked to. As soon as she calls us, she'll need to be taken care of.'

Finnegan proffered a glass of whisky, but Ian shook his head. 'She? Who is it?'

Finnegan's reply proved a step too far. A moment later the sword was hoisted high, and a slender scarlet arc appeared on one of the walls. There was the noise like a football filled with sand thudding to the floor and lolloping to a stop . . .

May and Bimsley were on the threshold of the curtained area leading to the Water House's cocktail bar when they heard something that sounded like a melon being chopped open. Colin wanted to haul May back and warn him, but before he could May flicked aside the curtain and stepped in.

As his eyes adjusted to the gloom, he began to pick out

details. 'Colin,' he called finally. 'Come in here. We've got a situation.'

The DC stepped into the room and looked down, dreading what he'd find.

'So,' said May, 'Jake Finnegan won't be buying any more hats. His head's over there by the ice machine, staring at you. On the counter, two whisky glasses. Ribisi can't be far away. You'd better call this in.'

The search for Ribisi was unsuccessful.

May stood on his balcony watching the snow sifting over the black waters of the Thames. He hated operating without his partner, but Arthur had specifically asked to be left alone for a couple of days. He finished his glass of amontillado and went back inside.

He heard the man in the corridor outside his Shad Thames apartment and held his breath as the envelope was slipped underneath the front door. As the man walked off, May picked it up from the mat and turned it over in his hand. Inside the envelope was a brand-new black and gold credit card.

He stared at the name on it.

'John Hougham May'.

'That's not possible,' he said aloud, tilting it to the light and reading the name again. He told no one about his hated middle name, which was pronounced 'Huffam'. The only other person who knew about it was Arthur Bryant, with whom he had struck a deal: *If you ever tell anyone about my middle name, I'll tell them about you and Princess Margaret.*

It was the sheer effrontery of the Elimination Bureau that shook him; the fact that they thought he was for sale. The courier had driven up by motorbike. There was no sign of it now, of course. It could have gone anywhere.

He took stock of the situation. He tried to put the events in order. If Mandy McFarland had discovered the truth about the Water House it meant she had become a liability, and there she was meeting and greeting journalists and celebrities at a high-profile restaurant where she could keep shooting her mouth off to all and sundry. She had to be silenced, so Ian McFarland had received the card from the Elimination Bureau which would frame him.

Jake Finnegan was no longer needed either, because his role in setting up the restaurant was over and done with. Which just left whomever Mrs McFarland had talked to, and as soon as that person had been taken care of things could return to normal. The police investigation would be buried once the Met realized that the streets were suddenly quieter. It was too bad that a few innocents had got caught in the crossfire, but nobody wanted to start a war with Ribisi. Why risk drafting in more foot soldiers from the Camorra? So a few nondescript civilians would have disappeared, and officers would shake their heads and mutter about moths getting too close to flames, and all would be right with the world once more.

Except, thought May, *that if the cops allow scum like Ribisi to strut about with guns and swords treating the city as their killing grounds, they'll think they've become invincible.*

Taking out his phone, he balanced it in his hand.

He decided to call his partner.

As the line opened he heard a gurgling sound like a bath being emptied out. 'Arthur?' he said. 'What on earth is that? Are you there?'

'I'm making punch,' Bryant bellowed back. 'I'm at the British Museum Egyptology department's Christmas party. We couldn't find a punch bowl big enough so I'm using a burial tank. I thought you promised to keep me in the picture.'

'I did, but – Listen, I've got a problem and I need your help,' May began, swallowing his pride.

'Yes, I thought you might,' said Bryant annoyingly.

May outlined the situation, adding all the details he could recall.

'I've already had quite a bit to drink but let me see if I can get this right,' Bryant answered. There was the sound of an Egyptian sistrum jangling in the background, and someone shrieking with laughter. 'Let me ask you something. How do you know it was McFarland who chopped off his wife's lover's head?'

May sighed. As usual, Bryant was asking the wrong question. 'Well, who else could it be?'

'I would have thought that was fairly clear,' he replied. 'You saw Wallace's photos of Mrs McFarland—'

'And you saw them too? I thought you were sticking to your own case this week.'

'Yes, but I like to know what's going on, obviously. I asked him to keep me in the loop, and I noticed something straight away.'

'Well?'

'The wife's nails.'

'*What?*'

'A very specific design. Only the Vietnamese do them like that. Mrs McFarland wouldn't have talked to anyone in the restaurant, but she'd have talked to her manicurist. There's a girl everyone calls Golden. She was close to the wife *and* works with the husband.'

'Wait a minute, you've formed a theory about this case *and it isn't even your case?*'

'I made a couple of phone calls, just to keep my hand in. Now, this girl Golden is tougher than she looks. If she cared for Ian McFarland she'd watch out for him and stop him from making any further stupid mistakes. She'd have gone to the restaurant.'

'My God – you think *she* killed Finnegan?'

'If she was a horse I'd put twenty nicker on her. And now she's gone on the run with McFarland. Either that or Ribisi has taken her. McFarland's no killer. Whatever the situation is now, he's not the one you have to worry about. Ribisi will want to know if the girl talked to anyone else before he gets rid of her,' said Bryant.

'I don't know where to start looking for them,' May admitted.

'He owns a lot of commercial buildings, doesn't he? He'll have a place that would drown out the noise of anyone screaming.'

'Ribisi owns a printing plant on the old Lee Valley Industrial Estate,' said May.

'I think you'd better head over there,' said Bryant. 'I have to go, I'm being asked to join a conga line through the Byzantine reliquaries.'

The road to the east was quiet in the evening's sudden squall of rain, and the slick tarmac forced him to keep his speed down. May knew he was running out of time, but decided to run no more reds after he'd done it three times and nearly ended up beneath the wheels of an artic.

It was dark by the time he pulled into the rear of the car park beside the factory, but lights showed in the great paper sheds. As May climbed gratefully out of his BMW he could feel the hammer of machinery vibrating through the soles of his shoes.

'I'd be a lot happier if we had a nice show of blues and twos sliding around in the gravel here,' said Meera Mangeshkar, joining him as he walked.

'How did you get here before me?' May asked. Meera pointed back to her Kawasaki, cooling near the main gate.

She looked up at the plant. 'You seriously want us to go in there alone?'

'We'll take a side entrance, talk to the workers, keep it all as safe as we can,' said May, heading towards the entrance.

'If this is about you not wanting to split credit with the Met—'

'It has nothing to do with credit,' May called back. 'I don't want to call it in because I don't know whom to trust.'

'What do you mean?'

'I mean that Ribisi might have sent more cards out. If he sent one to me, he's probably targeted others.'

He reached the steel entrance door and tried the handle. It swung open on a vast, brightly lit chamber filled with the smell of hot newsprint. He walked further in, beckoning to Meera. The place was big enough to induce a sense of agoraphobia when they looked up. On either side rose towering steel struts from which were suspended three floors of printing equipment. The machinery took up the entire length of the factory. Newspapers wound around and down through the system on curving steel ramps like a hellish roller coaster.

The noise was tremendous. At the base a great swathe of paper roared beneath the rollers, under a row of red and yellow lights.

The pair looked about for signs of human life.

'Where is everyone?' Meera asked.

'It's fully automated,' May replied. 'I hadn't thought of that. The offices. They must be upstairs. Those stairs. One way up – easier to monitor who's coming in. They've probably already seen us.'

'So how are we going to get to them?'

'I don't suppose we'll have the element of surprise, whatever we do. But even they might not act up with a couple of officers on the premises. Are you wearing a camera?'

'Yeah, but I never use it.'

'Leave it on. We'll need proof of this.' He began to climb the steel staircase to the first level office.

At the top of the staircase, a broad metal landing led to offices that looked like steel Portakabins, their blinds drawn across their lit windows. May turned to his DC and shrugged, an in-for-a-penny-in-for-a-pound gesture as he tried the door handle and pushed in.

As he feared, they were expected.

The opening door placed the room's two occupants in an awkward tableau. McFarland was attached to his chair with thick plastic ties. He looked like he'd had a few teeth knocked out. Opposite him, under the strip lighting, Ribisi appeared paler and more gaunt than ever. For a moment, nobody moved. Ribisi's men were nowhere in sight. Something was off with the whole scene, which was as stiff and unnatural as a set of Madame Tussaud's waxworks.

'We were beginning to wonder when you'd get here,' said Ribisi. 'Did you have a good journey?' He might have been a hotelier speaking to an arriving guest.

'You know we're not leaving here without you,' said May, trying to sound confident. 'We're looking for the Vietnamese girl.'

Ribisi ignored him. 'Do you still have the credit card, Mr May?' He rolled one finger over the other. 'Turn it over and call the number.'

'I think we've had enough of your games, sir,' said May. 'What have you done with Golden?'

'Call the number and you'll find out,' said Ribisi.

'What is it with gangsters and melodrama?' May asked. Pulling the card from his pocket, he held it high between thumb and forefinger.

'It's a company formality,' said Ribisi, setting down his whisky tumbler. 'We like to do things by the book.'

Playing for time, May took out his phone. 'Meera, you'll have to read out the numbers,' he said. 'The type's too small for me.'

Mangeshkar stepped forward, her frown deepening, but she did as she was instructed. May punched out the number and waited.

'Mr John May,' said a very British voice. 'How can we help you today?'

'Tell them you want to activate the card,' said Ribisi.

'I'd like to activate my card.'

'Please give me the last four digits on the front of your card.'

'6859.'

'And now the passcode.'

'908724'

'That's fine. Would you like to change your code to something more memorable?'

'No.'

'Very well. Your credit limit is five hundred thousand pounds.'

May drew a sharp breath. 'What do I get for that?'

'If you'd care to speak to Mr Ribisi, I'm sure he'll be

happy to take you through the procedure.' The line went dead.

'You see, Mr May, I have a problem,' said Ribisi, walking around the desk. 'We need people like you on the ground. Respectable gentlemen. There's a lot of work to be done in this city.'

'So you put a price on everyone, is that it?' said May. 'I think you've misunderstood the basic principles of policing. I want to see the girl. I know she's here.'

Ribisi studied his opponent in some puzzlement. 'You do understand what we're offering you, do you, Mr May? You see what the Elimination Bureau does.'

'I think so. You send out the cards and get others who are more easily tempted to carry out your dirty work for you.'

'They're well paid. The privilege of membership. At first we thought we might try crowdsourcing illegal activity, but we decided that involved too many unstable elements. Cardholders are checked out for creditworthiness. This is a better system.'

'So what do you expect me to do?'

'We want you to help run the legitimate side of things for us. We'll take care of the rest.'

'What exactly would be my duties?' asked May, playing for time.

'Think of it as a marketing problem. We're working in the interests of London. You just have to make sure that nothing gets in our way.'

'And if I don't?'

'Your partner is a liability,' said Ribisi. 'He's an outsider. Not the kind of person any company would actively seek out as a potential member. We'd need to get rid of him.'

May flicked the credit card back at him. 'I formally refuse your offer and I'm taking you in, so you can stay away from my partner.'

He threw Mangeshkar an urgent glance. She needed to pick up the look and interpret it. Ribisi wouldn't let either of them go now.

'Let's go downstairs,' said Ribisi, rising and heading over to the barely conscious McFarland with a penknife in his hand. 'It's time for you to join Golden.' He cut the ties holding McFarland to the chair and forced him to his feet.

They might have been visiting dignitaries getting a tour of the plant, heading in single file down the staircase, although they were at the point of the world's most expensive pistol.

As they reached the first of the printing presses, May stalled for time. He had to shout to be heard. 'So what happens now?'

'Look over there.'

He followed Ribisi's eyeline and saw to his horror that the far side of the press was coated in crimson gore. 'Golden made the evening edition,' he explained.

May realized that Ribisi wanted him to keep moving until he reached the metal steps on the other side of the last machine press, which was not for printing at all but for cutting the quad sheets into double pages. The great guillotine blades rose and fell with a terrible zinging sound, separating the paper stock into crisp clean stacks. The papers rolled off around a corner and were collected by steel arms. The thundering sound of the presses was unbearable.

'It's your turn. Get in.'

Ribisi punched a red mushroom-shaped button that

raised the mesh guard in front of the slithering blades. An alarm added to the cacophony somewhere above them, and yellow lights began to rotate, warning employees that the safety bar was raised while the machine was still in operation. He prodded May in the kidneys and forced him up the steps.

The detective understood the Elimination Bureau's thinking; they had never expected him to take up their offer. Wiping out the only investigating officers sent a very clear message to the underworld. *There's a new empire in place, and we're bigger than the law.* There was nothing he could say or do that would make any difference now. He stopped on the top step and looked back at Mangeshkar, his eyes desperately locked to hers.

May was out of ideas.

The alarm siren was so loud that he couldn't think. The lights strobed the walls, but nobody came.

The alarm . . .

It should be connected to the emergency services. Wouldn't the emergency response unit call to ensure that everything was all right at the plant? May's question was answered when the alarm suddenly cut out.

Assailed by the smell of hot paper, he looked down at the racing beltway below and knew he could only stall for a few more moments.

Ribisi reached out and gripped May's arm. 'Do it,' he instructed.

Back at the party in the British Museum, Arthur Bryant felt inexplicably bereft. Then he realized why; it just wasn't the same without John being there. True, his partner would only stand around complaining about the poor quality of the wine and the academics' inadequate social skills, but he had the common touch and saw through nonsense, something that Bryant never managed to do.

I suppose I'd better invite him, he decided, digging out his phone.

Unbeknown to May, Bryant had borrowed his partner's mobile a few days earlier and had asked Dan Banbury to add his own special ringtone to it. To make sure that he got his partner's full attention, he had Dan remove the volume limiter from the ringtone.

The sudden shriek of a girls' chorus singing 'Fair Is Rose as Bright May-Day' from Gilbert and Sullivan's *Ruddigore* could be heard above the presses and made everyone start.

McFarland brought Ribisi down so suddenly that in the noise and pulse of the emergency system, it was a moment before anyone realized what had happened. Ribisi lost his balance and the pair of them went over the edge on to the papers.

McFarland darted forward and hit the safety stop, but Ribisi landed ahead of him, and the momentum of the paper track was still carrying on too fast to prevent him from going underneath the blades.

Ribisi screamed as his legs were neatly sliced off by the guillotine. He tried to claw at the pulp beneath him but was drawn into the belly of the machine. A great spray of crimson blasted over the edges of the steel trough, blinding them all. Moments later he disappeared from view, and the machine crunched to a halt. In the ensuing silence they could still hear him crying out from inside.

McFarland stumbled to his feet and climbed back on to the steps. He grabbed May around the throat as he descended, holding the detective in front of him.

Their clinch suddenly ended as McFarland dropped back with a cry. May realized that Mangeshkar had been able to grab Ribisi's gun before it disappeared into the machine with him. She was still looking at the weapon with some amazement.

'Be careful with that thing, it's worth a fortune,' May said, freeing himself as McFarland slid to the floor. He had been clipped through the shoulder.

'Wallace reckoned the bullet wouldn't injure anyone standing behind the original target,' said May. 'Looks like he was right.'

'I didn't know that when I fired,' said Meera.

May knelt down beside McFarland, who was more surprised than in pain.

The detective rose and looked over the side of the trough. 'What's black and white and red all over?' he asked.

'I can still hear him,' said Meera. 'Don't you think we should see if we can get him out?'

'No,' said May, 'I don't want to get newsprint on my hands.'

McFarland gave each of them a long, hard frown of a stare, then passed out.

Meera shrugged. 'Lightweight.' She went to the door, where a squad car was arriving at the same time as the first ambulance.

May looked over Bryant's shoulder at his typed-up version of the investigation and read a few paragraphs. Bryant was adding the case to his second volume of memoirs. 'That's not how it happened at all,' said May.

'The arrest was a bit boring in the original version so I pepped it up a bit,' Bryant explained.

'Perhaps, but you need to stick to the facts,' May suggested.

'Oh, *facts*,' said Bryant dismissively, 'I always think they're terribly overrated, don't you?'

My favourite filmed murder mystery is the superb but neglected The Last of Sheila, *written by Stephen Sondheim and Anthony Perkins, directed by Herbert Ross. It's a brilliantly conceived (and very starry) puzzler set on a yacht going along the coastline of the Côte d'Azur. I love so-called 'precinct' stories which keep their characters all marooned together – Christie was brilliant with them – and one day I'll tackle my own version of a country house murder mystery. Until then, here's one set on a boat.*

BRYANT & MAY AHOY!

Arthur Bryant and John May only ever took one holiday together. They never did it again because it didn't turn out at all the way they'd expected. It began when they had an argument about sailing.

'There are only two things I know about boats, and they're that you can't wear shoes on board and you can't put toilet paper down the loo, instructions that seem positively uncivilized,' said Bryant testily.

'I take it you're not one for going to sea?' May ventured as they sat in their office looking out at a septic September morning comprising equal parts grey clouds, rain and dirt.

'My father loved water, of course, but only because it gave him a chance to shoot at Germans.'

'Sorry, not with you.'

'Royal Navy.- I had an unusual experience on the Woolwich Ferry and have stayed off water ever since. It's not natural, all that bobbing about. Even Horatio Hornblower used to get seasick. Of course he was a fictional character, but you get my point.'

'You haven't had a holiday for donkey's years,' said May. 'Why do people say that? Why a donkey?'

'Rhyming slang, 1923, "donkey's ears" – "years",' said Bryant, not bothering to look up.

'Well, it's a chance to get away and we shouldn't look a gift horse in the mouth – Hey, that's another odd one.'

'You can tell the age of a horse by checking to see how far its gums have receded,' muttered Bryant. 'From St Jerome's "Letter to the Ephesians", around AD 400: "Equi donati dentes non inspiciuntur." Who gives a holiday as a gift? I smell a rat. And before you ask, I have absolutely no idea where that expression comes from.'

The senior detectives of the Peculiar Crimes Unit had been offered a week's holiday on a grateful client's yacht moored somewhere off the Turkish coast, but Bryant was unconvinced. 'Why don't we offer it to Raymondo?' he suggested. 'He's always moaning about having his holidays cancelled.'

'That's because he goes to the Isle of Wight. Cancellation is a blessing. No,' said May. 'Just think, there's no internet so there'll be no emails.'

'I don't do emails now,' Bryant pointed out.

'The change will do us both good. I'm putting my foot down. We'll go.'

'But I have nothing to wear.'

'It's a holiday in Southern Turkey, not a dinner party in Finchley.'

'Fair point. I suppose dressing up in hot countries simply involves putting on shoes. A bit like Wales.'

'You can't say that.'

'I can say whatever I like. I'm a police officer – institutional racism is our stock-in-trade.' That was the thing about Bryant; you could never entirely tell if he was joking, although May had worked out that if you had to wonder, he probably was.

'The yacht has its own gourmet chef,' said May by way of temptation. 'Fresh fish every day, and Turkish salads are amazing.'

Bryant considered the thought for so long that his stomach rumbled. He saw a steamed sea bass served against a crystalline seascape. 'I suppose it would be quite nice to go somewhere without a scarf,' he conceded. 'Seven days feels like a bit long, though. Maybe four?'

'Trust me,' said May, sensing a win, 'you won't want to come home.'

Bryant glanced out of the window, where the thick grey drizzle pattered on litter-strewn pavements. Below the trees, a tramp finished eating something out of a rubbish bin and sucked his fingers clean. 'Perhaps I could manage a week,' he said.

They flew to Bodrum and were met by a freshly waxed chauffeur-driven Bentley. The outside temperature was 28 degrees centigrade.

'I can't even remember what we did for this chap that would make him so grateful,' said Bryant as they headed over to the mooring.

'In a roundabout way we saved his daughter,' said

May. 'She had a boyfriend who was importing Turkish antiquities into London.'

'Oh, *that* case,' said Bryant as the memory returned. 'The dodgy dealer in Anatolian kilims. We got him on drugs offences in the end, didn't we?'

'That's right. Away from his influence, she returned to her father and now helps him run his business.'

Demir Kahraman was waiting to meet them on the deck of the gleaming white Azimut yacht. The little round-bellied businessman wore a blue and gold blazer, a spectacular black beard and a broad white grin, and welcomed them with arms thrown wide. 'My dear friends!' he said. 'What a pleasure it is to have you on board. I hope your stay will be a most relaxing one. You remember my lovely daughter Nevriye?'

A stunningly beautiful girl of some nineteen summers rose to greet them from the cabins below. Her lustrous dark mane lifted in the light breeze as she shook their hands. She was dressed in a fluttering tunic of embroidered white muslin, and wore a fine gold chain around her waist. Even without glancing over, Bryant knew that his partner would have just drawn in his stomach, the silly old fool.

'You have not met my wife, Yosun,' said Kahraman, formally presenting the elegantly coiffured, jewel-bedecked lady who swept imperiously on to the deck with a hulking attendant in tow.

'Enchanted,' said May, kissing her hand. 'Forgive me, but your face seems familiar.'

'But of course,' said Kahraman, beaming with delight. 'Yosun is one of Turkey's most famous actresses. Come, you must be in need of refreshment after your trip. Ymir will show you to your cabins, and we will await you on deck with chilled champagne.'

Below, the detectives found themselves in a corridor of highly polished inlaid teak, with spacious facing rooms.

'Blimey,' said Bryant, peering across the hallway from his cabin door, 'I could get used to this.'

'I told you it would do you a world of good to get away from work for a few days.' May had already changed into beachwear, and now took note of his partner's attire. 'What – what on earth are you wearing?'

Bryant looked down. 'This? I didn't have any beachwear so Alma ran it up for me from old Windsor Safari Park souvenir tea towels.' He was in bright yellow shorts and a matching baggy shirt covered in lions, tigers and baboons. 'How do I look?'

'Like the circle of life just stopped. Come on, let's get a drink.'

Up on deck were two more guests: an ovoid Englishwoman in an iron-grey hair-helmet and a long, pleated Laura Ashley skirt; and a slender, wet-looking young man with a prominent Adam's apple, wearing what looked to be a very hot woollen blazer and baggy black shorts.

'This is Jane Beaumont,' said Yosun Kahraman. 'Mrs Beaumont is an antiques dealer.'

The Englishwoman stiffly proffered a hand. 'Yosun and her husband have kindly offered to take me down to Yali to examine an Ottoman tapestry,' she explained.

'And this is the Reverend Charles Parsley. He's visiting the Christian mission at Yali.'

The vicar finished vigorously cleaning his wire-framed spectacles and shook hands with the detectives, burbling greetings. Everyone seated themselves around the deck's great dining table as champagne was popped and the yacht cast off.

*

'We're a motley mix, I must say.' Bryant scrunched up his eyes and blasted himself in the face with mosquito spray. 'You can't complain about my shorts after seeing the vicar's knobbly white knees. Of course we only have Kahraman's word for it that he's a man of the cloth. I didn't see a dog collar.'

'Arthur, you might try keeping your voice down. It's too hot on deck to dress formally,' said May from across the hall. 'The chef's preparing freshly caught octopus for dinner.'

'We've almost got a full Cluedo set. All we need to do now is find someone hanging from the yard-arm. But who would it be, eh? The millionaire industrialist? His actress wife? The dazzling daughter? The dry-as-dust antiques dealer? Or the bony bible-basher?'

'You're forgetting the staff,' said May. 'I didn't catch the captain's name, but I think the chef was called Raci, and then there's Ymir.'

'What, the butler did it? That idea was old a century ago. Seriously, though, I wonder why we've been asked.'

'I told you, he's grateful for the service we provided.'

'You honestly believe that?' Bryant shook his head. 'No, there's a hidden agenda at work here. We're the odd ones out. The vicar was very kind to Nevriye, Demir's daughter, when she was living in London. Demir is an old friend of the tapestry dealer Mrs Beaumont is visiting; he asked Demir if he wouldn't mind bringing his client down. The rest are family – and then there's us.'

'Wait, how did you find out all that?' May asked.

'We're on a boat,' said Bryant as if it was obvious. 'My hearing aid flattens out all sound, so I can hear several conversations at once. Mrs Beaumont is broke.

She needs to get her hands on the tapestry because she has a buyer lined up in London. The vicar is probably on the scrounge for a donation to his mission. If Demir Kahraman had simply wanted to thank us he could have sent us a hamper or something. Instead he gets to put up a couple of old farts—'

'Speak for yourself!'

'—on his nice boat for a week. And I don't trust that Ymir, either; he's got the build of a bodyguard.' Bryant packed away his mosquito spray. 'Right, let's go up to dinner. The last thing I ate was an easyJet sandwich. It was so bland I ate part of the cardboard wrapper without noticing.'

With the setting of the sun, the sea had deepened to sumptuous, glowing shades of emerald. A few other yachts were moored nearby, dotting the edges of the lush coastline. No lights showed in the hills and cliffs. The night was so still that the stars were reflected in the ocean. It was impossible not to relax in such an atmosphere of placidity.

The chef prepared dinner on a wood-fired barbecue clipped to the side of the yacht's railing. On the table were courgette flowers stuffed with minted halloumi, pilafs and koftas, dolmades, baked sardines, tabbouleh, hummus and chicken skewers. The centrepiece was a grilled octopus, its tentacles separated.

Bryant whistled. 'It looks like everybody gets a leg.'

Demir Kahraman was the perfect host, making sure that his wife and daughter were split among the other guests around the table. Nevriye and Yosun were natural conversationalists, and May loved being seated between two such charming women.

Alcohol loosened everyone's tongues. The Rev. Charles

Parsley had already caught the sun and was turning blotchy. He was the only one the mosquitos seemed to bother with, and irritably batted them away from his face.

'This isn't your natural habitat, then?' Bryant ventured.

The reverend brushed at his right ear, distracted. 'What? No, not at all. I have a parish in Winchester. But we're required to visit outposts from time to time. I'll only be staying for a few weeks.' He looked as if he was already thinking about his trip home.

Mrs Beaumont seemed on edge and uncomfortable. 'We're making a stop tomorrow morning, is that correct?' she asked the captain.

'That's so, madam. We always stop there.'

'It's a funny little place,' said Yosun Kahraman, 'so small that it has no name. We'll be making several stops over the next few days. It's easier to collect mail and fresh vegetables from these little landing points than in Bodrum.'

As his partner joked easily with the ladies, Bryant narrowed his eyes and studied the group. The guests helped themselves to food and wine, and the atmosphere grew more relaxed. There was so little breeze that the candles on the table burned in perfect unflickering tear-drops.

But Bryant was puzzled. There was a tension at work he could not see, only sense. Something felt out of kilter. Occasionally he caught what he thought was a strange look, a covert glance, a quickly changed expression – and then it was gone.

The chef served pastries, and a tray of after-dinner liqueurs appeared. Nevriye played the guitar, singing sweetly and softly. Demir talked admiringly of his wife's recent appearance in a Turkish romantic comedy, then moved on to discussing the worsening political situation in his homeland. He talked about the difficulty of doing business in a country of increasingly authoritarian excesses, and seemed genuinely worried until his daughter stroked his shoulder, calming him.

As the others prepared for bed, Bryant and May sat at the bow drinking thick Turkish coffee. 'You know why I think we've been invited?' said Bryant. 'To keep an eye on things. Yes, Mr Kahraman wanted to thank us, but we're his insurance.'

'Insurance against what?' asked May.

'Not what, whom,' Bryant replied, rising unsteadily. 'Well, they're safely off to bed and so am I. I just hope I'm wrong.'

The next two days passed in a haze of sun, swimming and seafood as the Kahramans' yacht docked at tiny coastal towns and deserted beaches along the rocky coast. At one stop the ladies went ashore to look at fabrics and jewellery while the men found a blue and white bar overlooking the sea. Ymir collected mail for his boss. Bryant bought a wholly preposterous hat. May tanned and read a week-old copy of *The Times*. The Reverend Parsley flapped a handkerchief around his scarlet face and complained about being hot, as if it was the last thing he had expected from a country like Turkey. Demir Kahraman strode along the jetty barking into his phone. The ladies arrived laden with bags and ordered lemonades.

Nevriye tipped back her chair and dozed. Her mother read mail, started a book and slowly fell asleep. Mrs Beaumont wrote letters home and stared out to sea, lost in thought. Bryant marvelled at the effect of the sun on everyone. He did not fall asleep.

Ymir arrived with the tender and they headed back to the boat for lunch. The chef had laid out a dazzling meze with a whole glazed salmon as its centrepiece. The desserts were just being cleared away when Yosun Kahraman clutched her forehead and called her daughter over.

'I'll take Mum down to her cabin,' said Nevriye, 'she's not feeling well.'

'It's probably just the heat,' said Mrs Kahraman as she was helped to her feet. 'I'll be fine after a nap.'

The captain turned on the air conditioning below deck, and the yacht drifted in the hazy heat of the afternoon.

An hour later, Demir Kahraman went to check on his wife, and found her seriously ill.

His initial shock was followed by an urgent demand to fetch a doctor, who arrived by tender and diagnosed a very bad case of food poisoning. Mrs Kahraman would have to be taken to hospital at once. Luckily there was a well-equipped clinic just over the next hill.

Demir went with his wife. When he returned two hours later, he was able to announce that his beloved Yosun's condition was serious but stable. She would have to stay in hospital until the cause of the illness could be ascertained and reversed. Demir summoned the chef and asked him to explain himself. Raci described the ingredients of the lunchtime feast in great detail, and insisted that there was nothing unusual in any of the dishes. 'Besides, you all ate everything that Mrs Kahraman ate,' he pointed out with great indignation.

'Then why is my wife now in a hospital bed?' shouted Demir.

'I say, look here, making accusations won't solve anything,' said Parsley. As the recriminations continued, the detectives shot each other a look and slipped below deck to Mrs Kahraman's cabin.

'What do you think you're doing?' asked May as his partner began ransacking drawers.

'I'm taking a quick shufti,' said Bryant. 'Have a look around for pills or anything else she could have swallowed.'

'The doctor said food poisoning.' May snatched a bottle of aspirin out of his partner's hand and set it down.

'Poison is poison. It just means she ingested something,' Bryant insisted. 'What are these?' He opened a packet of pills and pulled out several silver foil sheets so that May could inspect them.

'They're statins, for high cholesterol. Tamper-proof packs. Put them back.'

'You heard the chef. She ate the same as everyone else. Now, either she took something that acted in combination with her food, or she was fed something separate and harmful, either knowingly or unknowingly.'

'Are you suggesting that someone on this boat deliberately set out to poison her?' asked May. 'Because that would be the most preposterous—'

But Bryant wasn't listening. 'They went ashore and separated. We need to question everyone.'

'You can't do that, Arthur! We're guests on a yacht, not working out of King's Cross. If we do we'll upset Demir.'

'And if we don't his wife could die,' said Bryant.

They started with Raci the chef, who enumerated every ingredient in his cooking and presented every unwashed wine glass for inspection.

'She drank some iced water,' May pointed out. 'Is it possible she contracted a bug that way?'

'All of our ice is made with bottled water,' the chef explained, 'but in general Turkish tap water is fine to drink – it just doesn't taste very nice.'

The captain and Ymir also tried to help as best they could, but no new light was shed on how Yosun Kahraman had become so seriously ill.

The Reverend Charles Parsley was uninterested in the whole affair. Several times he mentioned that he urgently needed to reach his mission and would probably have to take a taxi now, which would prove ruinously expensive. He was obviously regretting having persuaded Demir to take him along the coast. As for Demir's wife, it was a terrible shame, of course, but he would pray for her recovery.

Jane Beaumont was more solicitous, in her unyielding county way. She had been seated opposite Yosun during her meal and had not seen her eat or drink anything unusual.

'What about on your shopping expedition?' asked Bryant.

'Ymir went to collect mail from the post office, Mrs Kahraman and I went to look at cushions and some supposedly antique brassware that turned out to be nothing of the sort, and her daughter went to a T-shirt shop. Then we met up again and all came back on board.'

'And lunch was called when?'

'About half an hour after that.'

'Hghm,' Bryant grunted.

May knew that sound and it worried him. It meant that his partner had just stored some information away, but he could not imagine what it was.

Nevriye and her father sat together. 'I know it seems rather impertinent to ask questions while you're worrying about Mrs Kahraman,' May began, 'but the more you can tell us about your wife, the more we may be able to help her. She's a highly respected actress, which means that certain obsessive fans may regard her as public property. Has she ever had any trouble from them?'

Demir looked at his daughter, who shook her head. 'No, we don't think so. She adores her fans. She always says she couldn't live without them. Nobody has any reason to hate her, nobody in the world. This has to be an accident or a terrible mistake.'

'And in your business, have you any enemies?'

'I export furniture, Mr May,' said Demir. 'It is not the kind of profession that makes enemies of people.'

In the evening, the family headed to Yosun Kahraman's bedside and spoke to the doctor. They returned with heavy hearts. Mrs Kahraman's condition had worsened. The doctor warned that if he could not find out the cause of her ailment he would not be able to treat her properly.

Once again the detectives sat on the deck after everyone else had gone to bed, and discussed the problem. 'Well, it looks like you were wrong,' said May. 'Ymir isn't here as a bodyguard, and we weren't invited in a professional capacity. You don't suppose this has anything to do with the daughter, do you? After all, we did get her boyfriend jailed.'

'The dealer in fake Anatolian kilims?' Bryant considered the point. 'I wonder if he's out of Wandsworth yet.'

'It would help if I could get a Wi-Fi signal,' said May, checking his phone for the zillionth time.

'If it was the boyfriend, surely he'd have gone after

Nevriye?' said Bryant. 'After all, it was she who came to us for help and told us of her suspicions. He must know that.'

'He would have had no reason to go after the mother,' said May.

'I suppose not.' Bryant took a ruminative sip of his coffee. 'Unless this wasn't about motive.'

'What do you mean?'

'What if it was about opportunity?'

'*What* opportunity? We're on a boat, Arthur. We're miles from anywhere and anyone.'

'The ladies went ashore yesterday.'

'Yes, to a town that consisted of five shops, a general store, a bar run by a man with industrial-strength body odour, and several unattractive donkeys.'

'Exactly. Don't you see?' Even in the moonlight, May could catch the gleam in his partner's eye.

'Have you got something in mind?'

'Yes, but it involves a conversation with someone down there.' He pointed his finger at the deck as he rose to his feet and headed off.

'Why do you have to make a mystery out of everything?' May shouted in his loudest whisper. 'Just for once, couldn't you confide in me?'

'I will, as soon as Ymir has answered one simple question,' Bryant called back. 'It's just a precaution in case I'm wrong. Wait here for me.'

A few minutes later he returned not just with Ymir but with everyone following him on to the deck in various hasty states of dress. The vicar, somewhat surprisingly, was in a heavy metal T-shirt.

'They were all awake,' said Bryant apologetically. 'I hated to disturb them but perhaps it's for the best.'

Oh sure, thought May, knowing how dearly his partner loved an audience.

Bryant turned to Nevriye. 'What did you do when you went ashore, Nevriye?'

'I walked with my mother and Mrs Beaumont for a while,' the girl replied, yawning. 'Then I saw a T-shirt I liked in a shop window and went in to see if I could try it on, but they didn't have my size.'

'And meanwhile, your mother and Mrs Beaumont looked at antiques?'

'That's right,' said Jane Beaumont, unhappy to be roused from her bed but curious all the same. 'They were mostly locally produced bits of junk. There was nothing worth buying.'

'And Ymir, you went to the general store, is that correct?'

'Yes, sir,' replied the Kahramans' assistant.

'Would you say it's an old-fashioned place?'

'Yes, sir, it's a simple country store.'

'Why did you go there?'

'To collect the mail.'

'Why would you have mail waiting there? Doesn't it just go to the post office in Bodrum?'

'Mrs Kahraman knows she has fans all over the country, and likes to keep in touch with them,' said Ymir. 'There's a bedridden lady who always sends letters to a *poste restante* here.'

'Does Mrs Kahraman keep all her fan mail?'

'Yes. I look after the correspondence for her.'

Bryant turned to the captain. 'You keep a guest book on the bridge, don't you?'

'You know I do, Mr Bryant, you asked to see it five minutes ago and tore a page out of it.'

'So, if I lay down *these* signatures . . .' Bryant set the

torn page on the deck table with a theatrical flourish. 'And add this one from Mrs Kahraman's fan letter, you can see—'

'I'm glad,' said Jane Beaumont loudly and suddenly, pointing at Nevriye. 'You deserve to lose your mother, just as I lost my son! You deserve to suffer as I suffered!'

'Mrs Beaumont is the mother of the boy we jailed on your evidence,' Bryant explained. 'He was running drugs out of a counterfeit carpet shop. Unfortunately, it appears that while he was in jail, he got into a fight and died of a knife wound.'

'He was a good boy,' Mrs Beaumont cried. 'But he went to London and kept bad company. He probably met his friends through *you*!' She stabbed an accusing finger at Nevriye.

'Mrs Beaumont concocted a very simple plan,' said Bryant. 'She decided to poison your mother using a completely undetectable method. She started writing to her over the course of a year, telling her what a big fan she was, making sure that Mrs Kahraman regularly received a flattering note or gift from her. It got so that your mother looked forward to the letters, and got Ymir to pick them up for her. The latest one was filled with all the usual flattery, and Mrs Beaumont asked for one thing back: an autograph. She even included a stamped addressed envelope, but not one of the new kind that stick themselves, an old-fashioned one you have to lick to seal. You see the beauty of her method? She not only got Mrs Kahraman to poison herself; she mailed the sole piece of evidence back to the killer!'

In the silence that followed, you could have heard a sea anemone flowering on the ocean bed.

'Except that Ymir hasn't had time to post the letter

yet.' Bryant produced it from his pocket with the flair of a master magician. 'Captain, can you make sure this is taken to Mrs Kahraman's doctor at once for analysis? Unless you'd care to do the decent thing, Mrs Beaumont, and tell us what you used?'

'It's wheatear,' said Mrs Beaumont, deflated and defeated. 'It grows in my garden. The stems contain oenanthotoxin. Hemlock. It's lethal if it goes untreated.'

'I didn't know he was your son, Jane,' said Nevriye. 'We never stayed in contact with each other. I hadn't heard—'

'The fact remains,' Bryant interrupted, 'that he would not have died if he hadn't first broken the law. It's a tragedy, but another death doesn't make it right. Mrs Beaumont, thank you for telling us the truth. Captain, can you radio the hospital at once?'

Mrs Beaumont fell to her knees and cried, her rigid county demeanour finally shattered.

The next morning, after a conversation with the doctor, who said that they had been able to successfully administer an antidote to Mrs Kahraman, the detectives discussed the matter with Demir Kahraman and his daughter, and it was decided that Mrs Beaumont should escape prosecution.

When John May went to her cabin to tell her the news, he discovered that tragedy had not been averted. Mrs Beaumont was lying half out of her bed, staring blankly at the ceiling. In her right hand was an empty plastic bottle of sleeping pills. On her chest was a photograph of her dead son. Unlike her victim, she could not be saved.

'And that was the end of my holiday,' Bryant told the staff at the PCU, when asked to explain his early return. 'I thought I'd get some nice grub and a suntan, instead of which I got attempted murder, revenge and suicide. You won't catch me mucking about on boats again. Things are quieter here in King's Cross. Here.' He threw Janice Longbright a bottle of mosquito repellent. 'I won't be needing this again.'

I thought it would be nice to include a tale told from a different perspective, so here's a first-person account from the old boys' detective sergeant and long-time friend, Janice Longbright. I'd already touched on her years as a nightclub hostess in the graphic novel The Casebook of Bryant & May, *but here she is on secondment to another unit. I worked out everyone's back-stories many years ago, and now I'm getting to reveal them little by little. If this book of cases goes well I hope to produce another volume in the future.*

BRYANT & MAY AND THE BLIND SPOT

'No fuss,' I'd told them. 'Don't make it obvious.' Instead, the whole street was a sea of red and white plastic ribbons.

They were all over the road, coming loose from orange traffic cones, sagging and snapping in the rain, wrapping themselves around people's legs, tangling and trailing across the wet pavements. The cordon sealed off the entire centre section of Oxford Street. Shoppers tried to climb over them but were turned back by uniformed cops. There was a sale at Selfridges department store but nobody could reach the main entrance.

This was in November, on the sort of miserable, barely

visible London day where you think it won't bother to get light at all. I had taken a break from the Peculiar Crimes Unit and was working on a public-security detail, which wasn't what I'd planned to be doing at all.

What had happened was this: I'd been dating a married DS on and off and he'd finally decided to go back to his wife, which was the last straw, and when John May found me clearing up my office in a sort of frenzy at nearly midnight, he had told me to take some time off. 'I've been looking at the files,' he said. 'You haven't had a holiday in years.'

'I'm fine,' I told him, emptying more redundant paper-work into a bin bag. 'I don't need to take time off. I had a full medical earlier this year. I'm in perfect health. Good BMI, low heart rate.' I didn't tell him that my optometrist had failed me on several counts and wanted me to start wearing reading glasses. After all, Colin Bimsley was still working on the street despite suffering from DSA.*

'I agree there's nothing actually wrong with you,' John said. 'But you should take a month off. Go and lie by a pool in a Moroccan riad, and come back refreshed.'

I'd explained that I couldn't just sit frying in the sun without some kind of work, and I'd prefer to remain in the UK in case I was required for active duty, so he let it be known that I was available for a one-month second-ment to another unit. Which is how a man called Adrian Dunwoody found me and suggested I start working in his security detail.

'He's a control freak and a miserable excuse for a human being,' John told me, 'but it'll be easy, well-paid work, which should prove a novelty for you, plus you'll

*Diminished Spatial Awareness

be able to run rings around him if he gets difficult.' So that was what I did.

The first thing Dunwoody had told me on my third morning was that I shouldn't have joined his detail at all. He said, 'You don't need to be here. You've already helped us enough by going over the scenarios for today's visit. There's nothing else to do. Wait a minute. Turn around.'

'What?'

'What are you – Are you wearing a Kevlar vest?' He flicked a hand at my untucked shirt.

'I got it out of stores,' I explained. 'I thought I might have to, you know, go down there into the street at some point. In case of trouble.' I liked to be prepared. I decided not to tell him I still keep a house brick in my handbag for bouncing off difficult customers.

The first task of the week should have been easy. The French Ambassador's wife had decided to do a little shopping in London. She travelled over on the 1.30 p.m. Eurostar from Paris to St Pancras International, and was on her way to Selfridges without her entourage. With the exception of the American Embassy, which always makes its own arrangements, most embassies use security logistics provided by the Home Office, working with the Met. The cost of covering Madame's little retail expedition was charged to the taxpayer.

'She's going shopping,' said Dunwoody. 'There's not going to be a firefight. You won't need to dive behind a bollard and bang off a few rounds.'

'I was told to be ready for anything,' I said, sensing that nothing would induce Dunwoody to leave his surveillance post. 'I enjoy field work.'

Dunwoody snorted, then was forced to blow his nose.

He always seemed to have a cold. He said, '*Field work?* This isn't the CIA, Longbright, it's one step above being a shopping-mall guard. It's easy money. That's why your boss was happy to let you come here – it's a paid holiday.'

It had already become clear that Dunwoody was a natural moaner. Weather, staff, transport, workload, I'd already learned to screen out most of his conversation. Apart from the fuss and mess, I saw something down on the pavement that bothered me.

'Why have the Met got so involved?' I asked him. 'They've made the area look like a murder scene. I thought the point was not to draw anyone's attention to the visit.'

He said the instruction came from their side, not ours. Dunwoody's official title was Senior Security Liaison Officer, which basically meant that he passed his problems over to the techs and took all the credit. The surveillance room had no heat but he was sweating. It seemed he could produce sweat in a meat locker. I told him they shouldn't have closed the street.

'Well,' he said, 'one day when you've given up playing silly buggers at the PCU and you're in charge of operations at the Met, you'll be able to tell everyone what to do. Meanwhile you sit here and do as you're told.' He looked around for something to wipe his forehead with, and for one horrible moment I thought he was going to use the end of his tie. 'I don't know why there are so many people milling around down there. She's the wife of the personal envoy of the President of the Republic to the Court of St James, not some footballer's tart.'

Protecting London is a complicated business. The Parliamentary Under-Secretary of State for Security and Counter-Terrorism reviews public places, working out how they can be better protected from attack. Co-ordinating everything means analysing the routes of all state visits and reducing risk without disrupting normal services. I'd attended a seminar on the subject and it amounted to a single rule: *Don't let the great unwashed disturb the privileged*.

I told Dunwoody that the new wife was a liability. Her political opinions had turned her into a target for extremist groups. Madame Natalie Desmarais had a habit of opening her mouth in public without thinking and had received death threats from a number of officially recognized organizations. During the briefing, I'd suggested that the best way to protect her would be to downgrade the visibility of her visit. Instead we turned it into a circus.

People are like dogs before earthquakes; they always know when something's about to happen. Shoppers were hanging around on the off chance of seeing Tom Cruise turn up. Foot traffic had slowed to a crawl around the store. A much bigger risk. I complained about it.

Dunwoody stood at the window, wiping his forehead with a tissue and starting on his pet subject: bombs. He said, 'You could drop an IED from any one of those buildings and catch her between the car door and the store entrance.'

I dismissed the idea. Improvised explosive devices range in size from pedestrian-borne rucksacks to large goods vehicles. I know what explosions can do. There are six main effects: the blast wave, the fireball, the *brisance* or shattering effect, the primary and secondary fragments, and ground shock. But no amount of scientific analysis could account for the sheer sense of chaos, disorientation and confusion created by a bomb.

An official group would send a coded call first. The worry was that a lone nutcase might decide to try his luck.

When I looked across the street I saw a misshapen grey lump near the top of the opposite building. I pointed up at it. Whatever it was, it made the frontage look wrong.

'That's a curtain,' Dunwoody said. 'Someone didn't shut a window.'

I hate untidiness. I prefer everything to be neat and square. Ideally I'd place London in a grid and rearrange it borough by borough until all the roads had right angles and the buildings were correctly aligned. Straighten the river out, drop in the offices like Tetris blocks. And get rid of all the litter. How hard can it be to keep the streets clean? They manage in other European countries. John May and I are similar in that respect. We'd like to rearrange the world. The difference is that I'm naturally untidy. I spill nail polish on my keyboard and leave tights in my office drawers. But I looked at Dunwoody and knew he was *sloppy*. He couldn't even keep his sideburns level.

I went back to my laptop and studied the plan. Actually I'm not great with technology, just the planning. I knew I could highlight all the key risk points between Oxford Circus and Marble Arch tube stations, and check the street closures via their CCTVs. Red dots pinpointed the police positions. The Met was handling the job with minimal personnel, trying to meet their seasonal budget figures. Which would have been fine if they'd been in the right places. The surveillance team had a couple of their own people in place, identifiable to us by a discreet stripe on their hooded jackets.

We were stationed in a storage room above a Miss

Sixty clothes shop opposite the department store, so we could remain in visual contact with the ground crew. I'd requested an observation post at ground level near the store entrance, but the Met refused to let us come any closer. I had every reason to be angry. I don't like opportunities for error. I didn't care about Desmarais – it was the fact that Dunwoody hadn't taken into account all the families in the street that bothered me.

Dunwoody dug a handkerchief out of his pocket and blew his nose again. 'You're wasting your time even bothering to look.'

I told him it never hurt to double-check. Before coming here I'd read Dunwoody's profile; his military years had left him with a disconnect from civilian life. By contrast, I'd spent my spare time away from the PCU at endless evening classes, taking courses in everything from crowd control to first aid.

Madame Desmarais had changed her itinerary three hours earlier. It didn't give an extremist group enough time to react. I thought if there was any kind of situation it would definitely come from a lone operative, and that meant close contact.

I checked my watch, then looked at Dunwoody's monitor. The French Embassy's chauffeured vehicle was turning from Wigmore Street into Duke Street, prior to entering Oxford Street. It meant that Desmarais was going to step on to the pavement in less than three minutes. Dunwoody had allowed the French Embassy to arrange for a black stretch Mercedes 450SL with diplomatic flags, the kind of vehicle that was only used at state funerals and coronations. It would have drawn attention to itself in a Pride parade.

I rose and looked down from the window, then checked

my laptop map again. A red flarepath flashed along the street grid, marking the route.

How easy is it to say now that something felt wrong? But it did. When I looked at a street plan it was like studying a video game. Dimension, flow, bottlenecks, exposures, at-risk players, potential threats, the GIS tech neatly tagged and flagged in my head.

Geographic Information Systems. I had checked the Met's positioning plan. Each officer operated in a triangle of observation that could be overlapped with the position of a team-mate. There was nothing immediately obvious, not the usual sense of disparity that pointed to a breach in the line, but something was still amiss.

I'm an old-fashioned policewoman through to the marrow of my bones, as my mother had been before me. We were all the same in our family. If you wanted to convince us of your innocence, you had to work at it. I think if you know your rights you should also know your responsibilities. I don't want to hear lies from members of the public. I looked down at the street and studied each person I saw in turn.

My private life, such as it was, hadn't been good for a while, which was why John had wanted me to take a break. When I was young I had looked after my little brother, so I'd had to grow up fast. He was killed on his motorbike when he was seventeen. Life became very precious to me. I always felt like an outsider until I followed my mother's path and joined the PCU.

Some nights I'd be the last one left in the office – this was when we were still based in Mornington Crescent, before Mr Bryant managed to blow it up – and I'd sit there fantasizing about a big plate of fish and chips with vinegar and pickled onions. I'd look out of the window and see a single tall, icy lamplight on a blue-grey street, lifeless and melancholy, hardly a soul around. All the lads and lasses up at Camden Lock would be tipping out of bars and getting into fights, not venturing as far as the residential streets around our office, where there was only the scuttle of rats in the bins and frightened thoughts in cold bedrooms. And I remember feeling so alone. Which was why when Ian Hargreave announced he was leaving me and returning to his missus, not because he loved her but for the sake of the kids, I just lost it a bit.

John had been right. Working for Dunwoody and his team was like working with idiots. It was rather relaxing.

I studied the real-time footage on Dunwoody's monitor, then went to the window and watched the scene below again. It was like one of those 'Spot the Difference' competitions that showed two photographs with mismatched elements. Except that everything was as it should be. Too much so.

'The kiosk at the edge of the pavement,' I said. 'Is it still open?'

'Shouldn't be.' Dunwoody checked the image. The green wooden stall sold tourist crap: Union Jacks, teddy bears, pillar boxes and plastic police helmets.

But it didn't look shut. It should have had flaps that closed over it and were padlocked. He said, 'You can't have everything looking shut. Things are meant to look normal.'

'Why has he still got a customer?'

Dunwoody looked again. 'I don't know. He's beyond the cordon, he's just looking at stuff.'

'It's three fifteen p.m. now,' I said. 'Rewind to three oh five p.m.' Dunwoody sped the footage back. He slowed the image at 3.05 p.m. The same skinny young man was standing in exactly the same place.

There were children milling around, grandmothers, pregnant women, a huge family of tall Somalians, their kids playing on the concrete bus benches. I saw the skinny guy turn to face the diplomatic vehicle as it drew into Oxford Street, and knew he was cupping the palm of his right hand over something in his jacket pocket. He was counting the number of police officers inside the cordon. I could see him actually counting, moving his lips.

I got a lock on his face and to my amazement a database profile came up, courtesy of the system Dan Banbury had installed on my phone. The guy's name was Carlo 'Loco' Fabrizi. Three lines of text appeared beneath his mug shot. Later I got the rest of the details. Four years ago Fabrizi had emerged from Poggioreale Prison in Naples where he'd finished a three-year sentence for stabbing a student in the leg at a climate change protest rally. He'd been released into psychiatric care, but I guessed the Italian system was so disorganized that he was easily able to leave and make his way here. The last time I'd seen someone like him hanging around near a police cordon, he'd turned out to be a crazed fan of Kristen Stewart, who'd gone to the Odeon Leicester Square, where she was attending a film premiere. He tried to threaten her with a knife, and later told interrogators that he had been instructed to kill her by a secret society of vampires. Elated by the thought that he was carrying out Satan's work, he was pronounced unfit to stand trial. I couldn't take any chances with this one, in case he was cut from the same cloth.

I looked back at Fabrizi and saw him duck his head, staring intently at Desmarais in the back of her car. He made a movement that I instantly recognized; his left hand was cradling the underside of a gun while he used his right to slip the safety catch off. Dunwoody hadn't noticed a thing. Before he could stop me, I went for it. I had no choice.

I took the stairs three at a time and slammed open the shop's side entrance door. A knot of rubbernecking tourists blocked my path. Everyone was trying to see who was getting out of the car.

I was slipping and sliding on the rain-slick pavement, trying to tear my way through the cordon of plastic tape, but a beat copper stuck his arm across my chest. I suddenly realized that he thought I was a member of the public. At the PCU we wear black jackets with unit logos, but today I was in civvies. There was no time to explain. I backed around him and ran straight through the cordon.

The ambassador's wife made most English politicians' partners look like sacks of potatoes. She waited for the chauffeur to open the door before stepping out of the Mercedes in a low-cut fawn trouser suit and huge Sophia Loren sunglasses, despite the fact that it was dark and raining. Very 1960s. I liked her style.

By this time, the skinny guy at the tourist stand was on the move. His eyes were locked on the movement of the vehicle.

I watched the distance closing between them and knew I wasn't going to make it in time. The crowds had been alerted by the cordon and the car. They stopped to watch and take pictures on their mobiles. There were umbrellas up everywhere, obscuring the scene. The police were looking in the wrong direction; I followed their attention and saw a cluster of teenagers drifting about, just being young and annoying and in the way.

The assailant was closing in. The ambassador's wife

slowly looked around. It felt as if the moment was stretched out to breaking point. Everything got slower and slower.

There are times when I change gear without first engaging my brain. This was one of those moments.

Without even being aware of what I was about to do, I stepped up on to the black metal bollard beside the kiosk and used the leverage to throw myself forward. I'm a strong woman, and it was a big leap. I hit the would-be attacker in the small of his back and brought him down. Heard his knees hit the pavement with a crack. His gun clattered to the pavement undischarged, and the screaming began.

What a mess. The surveillance team went bananas. There was me thinking I'd saved a life.

Later that day Dunwoody asked me if I was expecting a commendation. This was when we were alone in his ugly office with photos of his fat kids funereally arranged around his laptop. I'd twisted my left ankle and torn a thigh ligament performing my flying leap, and wasn't in the mood for a fight.

It turned out that when I intervened, the Italian's arm had struck Desmarais in the face, knocking her against the car. She suffered a wardrobe malfunction that made the front pages and brought a spectacular loss of dignity down on her, which was far worse than being shot, from a diplomatic point of view. She had been humiliated – and on British soil.

To my horror, it turned out that Carlo Fabrizi was one of the surveillance team's own undercover men. He an-nounced that he would be trying to sue me because I'd fractured his collarbone. The Met internal investigator lodged a formal complaint against me for failing to communicate my plan of action. Dunwoody was furious and told me he'd got it in the neck for not keeping me under control.

The Met team said they would testify against me. I complained about Dunwoody's inappropriate handling of the event, including his request for the ambassadorial limo. I was immediately removed from active duty. That was when I knew I wasn't going to last out the month. Dunwoody said, 'We can put you on gardening leave, with one difference. You'll be expected to go and bury yourself in the garden.'

I explained that my brief had been to see things others couldn't. I asked him: 'You didn't recognize one of your own team. I couldn't take the risk. Do you honestly think what I did was wrong?' I was hoping, just this once, for a straight answer.

'That's not for me to say,' Dunwoody replied primly.

'Did you know Fabrizi had done time in jail?'

'It wasn't my job to know.'

There's a lot in our business that goes unsaid. I knew I should never have acted on impulse. I left Dunwoody's depressing office, returned to my own and even though I was only on temporary secondment it felt like I'd been fired from the force. I put my stuff in one of those cardboard boxes the company specifically kept to give dumped personnel, and was out on the street without an office key fob or a job, having earned Dunwoody's ridicule and hatred.

I went back to the PCU with my tail between my legs, a miserable failure. I bumped into Mr Bryant, bumbling along the hall with his hands in his pockets, looking as if he hadn't a care in the world.

'Do I smell amber oil?' he asked, sniffing the air. I

must have looked confused because he said, 'I thought you went to Marrakech.'

'No,' I told him, 'that was John's suggestion. I just got chucked out of Adrian Dunwoody's security detail.' I explained the circumstances.

'Oh dear, that doesn't sound right,' he said, fishing in his top pocket for his pipe stem, which he'd lately taken to noisily chewing as Raymond wasn't allowing him to smoke it. 'He'll try to mark your record, and it could affect your career. Luckily you don't have much of a career as you're with the PCU. I'll have to sort this out. Something isn't right. Give me a minute, will you?' He wandered off in the direction of his office, then stopped and came back. 'Dunwoody approached you, yes?' I nodded and he left.

I wondered what he meant. A few minutes later I found out when Mr Bryant appeared in my doorway. 'Can you spare a moment?' he asked vaguely. I ushered him in.

He unfolded a creased sheet of paper and held it up before me. 'Tell me, what can you see?' he asked.

It looked like a child's art class scribble. 'Just some grey crayon strokes,' I told him.

'Ah, well, there we have it.' From his jacket pocket he pulled an old-fashioned pair of cardboard 3D glasses, the kind with red and green lenses, and handed them to me. 'Look at it again through each lens in turn, covering the other one up.'

I did as I was instructed. When I looked through the red side some lettering jumped out.

'It says, "We're out of tea,"' I told him, mystified.

Bryant gave a happy laugh. 'You see?'

'What, that you're out of tea?'

'Oh, that's just the first coded phrase I ever sent

to John. You could see it through the red lens but not through the green one.'

'I don't understand.'

'You're colour-blind,' he said. 'You should have been able to tell that Carlo Fabrizi was a member of Dunwoody's team by the green diagonal stripe he wore on his blue hooded jacket, but you couldn't read it, so you thought he was a member of the public. They say Americans always tell you too much and Europeans never tell you enough. Dunwoody deliberately withheld information from you. He knew about Fabrizi's prior history and wanted him out to spare himself embarrassment, and he also wanted to humiliate the French Ambassador's wife.'

'But why?' I asked.

'Because she had bad-mouthed British surveillance details on previous visits to London. Dunwoody didn't want to have his own team blamed, so he approached you for the secondment. There was a game being played at another level that you could only glimpse, Janice. He hired you after looking at your records. He knew you were colour-blind and told Fabrizi to behave as he did. True to form, you took care of the rest.'

'How did you know?' I asked, amazed.

Mr Bryant waved the thought aside. 'Oh, as soon as I checked up on Fabrizi I realized that Dunwoody had made a mistake hiring him. When I saw his name scathingly singled out in a despatch from Madame Desmarais it became a little clearer. But the clincher was realizing that Dunwoody had requested your medical records. He hired you because your colour-blindness was right there on the page. He was out to kill two birds with one stone.'

'I never mentioned my medical result to you,' I said.

'You didn't need to,' Mr Bryant replied. 'When you came to work wearing that hideous green sweater with a bright purple shirt last month, I jokingly asked if you were colour-blind and you fudged your answer, so I checked your records. The most common type of colour-blindness muddles greens, reds, purples and blues. The only question that remains is, how do we get rid of Dunwoody?'

Luckily, that problem took care of itself. In the course of the investigation the internal security team discovered that Dunwoody had been single-handedly supporting the Colombian export industry, which explained his perpetual cold. Realizing that his chances of promotion had suddenly become less likely than having a sophisticated night out in Blackpool, he took himself off on gardening leave. And I hoped that while he was at it, he would bury himself in the garden.

To celebrate, I treated the whole of the PCU to a night at the pictures. We went to see a loud, stupid Hollywood space movie in 3D. The modern kind – without the red and green lenses.

This title was suggested by a reader in a competition I held on my website. I thought it was very suggestive of political shenanigans, and set about writing a story to go with it. It was also my second stab at a period Bryant & May tale. I find the old cases work very well in the short format, and plan to write others set in specific time periods. I'm particularly drawn to the idea of using 1960s swinging London as a backdrop – a vibrant time I managed to entirely miss out on, as I was still at school. Damn!

BRYANT & MAY AND THE BELLS OF WESTMINSTER

I.

It was one of the only cases they failed to crack. Not only that, they failed twice, and there was nothing they could do about it.

The year was 1969. It was the year that Richard Nixon was made President of the United States, the year a man walked on the moon, the year Concorde and the hovercraft took off, Mick Jagger performed in what appeared to be a Victorian nightdress and Queen Elizabeth II caught an underground train on the new Victoria Line, which had just three stations. It was also the year Arthur Bryant bought his yellow Mini Minor, Victor, and John May grew unfeasible sideburns, a look he compounded by purchasing an astoundingly ugly patch-pocket wide lapel electric-blue suit from the outfitter Lord John in a fit of trendiness that his partner referred to as being indicative of an early middle-aged nervous collapse.

And it was the year that Bryant and May met Mia.

Her name was Mia Waleska. She was twenty-three, originally from Tallinn, of Estonian–Polish parentage, and she had the astonishing beauty of so many women from her country, where Swedish and Baltic blood mingled to produce tall, ice-eyed blondes. She was studying early-twentieth-century European history, and to augment the meagre income she received from a trust fund left by her uncle, she modelled for glamour photographs that appeared in the kind of magazines newsagents had once sold from under their counters in the Charing Cross Road.

Mia told everyone she lived at the Howard Hotel, but she was actually broke and sleeping in the hotel's beauty spa after it shut, thanks to the kindness of a male benefactor who worked there. Her magazine work was getting harder to find because she refused to appear in pornography, and the changing times demanded something more than a few coy naked poses.

One Saturday night in August, a murder occurred in Bayham Abbey, a grand old 'Georgian Gothick' mansion on the Kent–Sussex border, set in grounds designed by the famous landscape gardener Humphry Repton, who also planned the grounds of Kenwood House in London. Simon Montfleury had been found stabbed to death there.

He was the last of its original inheritors and unmarried, and therefore the family line stopped with him.

At the time of which we speak, the Peculiar Crimes Unit was stationed in Bow Street, this being before the period when they occupied offices above Mornington Crescent tube station (a fondly remembered workplace which Arthur Bryant unfortunately blew up). The reason why they were invited to the countryside to investigate the case only became apparent when they arrived at the mansion.

'He's got a load of sensitive papers scattered about,' said Inspector Ian Hargreave, who was handling the investigation for the Met. 'Friends in high places and all that, so we thought we'd better call you in.'

'You did a wise thing,' said Arthur Bryant, handing the inspector his chewing gum. 'I'm trying to give up the pipe.'

'Er, the body's in the library,' said Hargreave, passing the wet, pink gum to his constable. 'We've got ourselves a suspect but there's a problem.'

The library was like the library of every country house Bryant had ever glimpsed on a National Trust tour. It had a hideous chandelier, two grand windows overlooking the gardens and tall bookcases filled with green and orange leather-bound volumes no one had opened in years, mainly because they were all so boring.

'Skelton's *Arms and Armour*,' Bryant read out, checking the shelves. '*European Scenery*, *A Tour in Greece*, *The Architecture of British Cottages*, *Landowners of Great Britain Volume 1: Bedford to Norfolk*. Stone me, I wouldn't pay a rag-and-bone man to get rid of this lot.'

'There's a body over here, if you'd care to come and look at it,' said May drily.

'I'm not sure I want to stand near you in that suit,' said Bryant, sidling over nevertheless. A pair of gunshots sounded which were in fact Bryant's knees clicking as he bent over. Simon Montfleury lay face down on the floor with a deep cut at the height of his kidneys. His blood had soaked into the carpet, and he was cold. 'When did this happen?' asked Bryant.

'Last night. He was having a bit of a party, and we think he was killed just before the guests arrived.'

'What, nobody moved him or bothered to call an ambulance?'

'Nobody knew where he was. He wasn't missed because he very often failed to attend his own bashes, and the servants were instructed never to disturb him. Our idea – as much as we have one – is that one of the guests killed him and slipped back into the party afterwards. Funny thing, though. I can't see how it was done. Apparently the old man was paranoid about being attacked. He had some outrageous political views and quite a few enemies.' Hargreave knelt beside the body. 'We think the wound was caused by some kind of exotic dagger. It had a long, scalloped blade. We searched the guests, the room and grounds, and found nothing at all.'

John May pointed back at the library door. 'Is that the only way into the room?'

'Apart from the French windows, you mean? Well, there's that thing, but yes, I suppose so.' He was referring to the huge, dark, iron-grated fireplace. 'It hasn't been used for years. The chimney's closed up. The windows are bolted shut. The library door closes by itself and can't be opened from the outside. It was eventually broken open by the servants. They didn't come into the room, just stuck their heads in, saw he was dead and called the police.'

'So you're saying Mr Montfleury was found stabbed to death in a locked room?' said Bryant. 'We've never had a locked-room mystery before, have we, John?'

'It's not a parlour game, Arthur,' said May. 'I've read about Mr Montfleury in the papers. "Send the blacks home", "Bring back hanging" and so on. How long has it been since the death penalty was suspended?'

'Nearly five years,' said Bryant without thinking. 'The last hangings were Evans and Allen, twenty-four and twenty-one, Strangeways, Manchester.'

'So there were plenty of reasons to kill him,' said Hargreave.

'You say you searched the guests as well as the house? Who were they?'

'Mostly high Tories, a couple of MPs and their dolly birds.'

'So they didn't come with their wives,' said Bryant, returning to the bookcase. 'Have you had this lot out?'

'Every single damned one. It took half the night,' said Hargreave wearily. 'I've got tickets for the Rolling Stones tonight and I haven't slept in twenty hours.'

'Well, you won't get any sleep while they're on,' said Bryant. 'What about the caterers?'

'Just the family chef and two footmen, a couple of jungle-bunnies they brought in for the bash.'

'Can you not call them that?' asked Bryant, annoyed. 'Did you talk to them?'

'Yeah. They didn't even know who they were working for. Clean as a whistle.'

The detectives left with the names and addresses of everyone who had attended the party the night before. There were twenty-eight people in all, most of whom were such household names that they had to be placed entirely above suspicion. Bryant wandered about his office in Bow Street with fistfuls of paper, periodically tearing pieces off and scribbling notes.

'I don't know the women's names,' he admitted. 'They're nearly all wives. I find it incredible that in this day and age there are so few female politicians. Can you imagine what England could be like if we got a woman prime minister? We might finally get a few things done.'

'Who are you missing on that list?' asked May, peering over his shoulder.

'Six ladies. This one, Eudoria Fanning, she's an old Tory benefactor, twenty stone if she's a day,' said Bryant. 'They probably had to put a gangplank on the stairs for her. And Maureen Lippincot, she's eighty-five, in a wheelchair and nearly blind. They bung the old guard pots of dosh whenever the campaign funds are running low. But none of the other names are familiar. They're young, though; they have young names. Mia, Jackie, Sandra, Lisa – ring any bells? No one you've dated there, for example?'

'Very funny. No, no one familiar. I'll have to go and see them.'

'*We'll* have to go and see them,' Bryant corrected him. 'I don't trust you around young ladies at the moment, what with your hot flushes.'

They all knew each other, it turned out. They perched demurely around the table in the tearoom of the Howard Hotel. They spoke in the softest of tones and were mindful of each other's opinions. They were attired in miniskirts and kinky boots, and two wore hairpieces of the kind that were popular in the late 1960s. They had large plastic earrings and Alice bands. Their eye shadow was black, their lips and nails were pink. They had attended the party at Bayham Abbey because they were friends with two MPs who were friends of Simon Montfleury. They were all students, and all had part-time jobs.

Mia caught John May staring at her. She had the greenest eyes he had ever seen. They were enough to trip the most absurd comparisons in his head. He was entranced, and phrased his questions with exaggerated politeness. Bryant's view was somewhat more jaundiced. The girls wore good watches and expensive clothes. They did not bear any resemblance to typical students. More intriguingly, they seemed to speak as if they were a single organism, listening and agreeing in low murmurs with one another. They had each been the guest of a single male invitee, the names of whom they willingly surrendered. They were terribly upset about the tragedy. They wanted to do anything that could help the investigation.

They seemed to be sharing some secret joke.

Mia enchanted John May. Bryant could see that his partner was utterly smitten. The more he tried to feign disinterest, the more he gave himself away.

'Did any of you see Mr Montfleury that evening?' Bryant asked, checking his notebook for timings.

'I saw him,' said Mia. 'He asked me to meet him in the library, soon after we arrived. He sent word by way of a servant.'

'Did he know you?'

'No, he'd never met me before.'

'Isn't that rather an extraordinary thing to do?'

'I gather that my escort for the evening had spoken of me,' Mia explained.

'And he was . . . ?' Bryant searched his notes but couldn't lay his hands on the name.

'David Stuart-Holmesby, the MP.'

'Right. So why did Montfleury want to see you?'

'I won't lie to you, Mr Bryant. I think David – Mr Stuart-Holmesby – had told him that I was studying European history and that I was pretty. He showed me some of his books, making me climb one of those library ladders to bring down a particular volume, and when his hand wandered a little too close to my leg I made an excuse and left.'

'Where was Mr Montfleury's wife while all of this was happening?'

'She was greeting the guests in the main hall.'

'So it's likely that you were the last to see him alive. Where did you go then?'

'I came into the main hall and accepted a drink from Mr Stuart-Holmesby. A few minutes later I believe the servants went to fetch Mr Montfleury and found him dead. We were all told to stay where we were. The police arrived and searched us. It was all terribly upsetting.'

'How awful for you,' said May, 'I can't imagine how you must have felt.'

Bryant shot him a desiccating look. He didn't hold with sympathy.

'It had to be one of the staff,' said May as they left the Howard. 'It's terrible what sweet girls like that have to go through these days, getting mauled by creepy old politicians.'

'It beats policemen,' said Bryant.

May was mortified. 'Good heavens, you don't think that I would – I'd never—'

'I'm joking, I know you're a gentleman. Mia Waleska arrived with Stuart-Holmesby, who is old enough to be her grandfather. Now what do you suppose first made him decide to take a twenty-three-year-old girl on a trip into the English countryside? He'd booked a room for them in the nearby village of Trant at a pub called the Globe. One room, John. She's not nearly as innocent as she looks.'

'You've a very cynical nature, Arthur.'

'So have you, when your suspect's not wearing a mini-skirt and kinky boots. She wasn't planning on taking any long walks.'

Back at their office, John May received a stack of photographs that had been taken at the party by a freelance newspaperman who had managed to worm his way into the event.

'Wait a minute,' said May. 'Did Coatsleeve Charlie take these?'

'He thought he'd sell them to one of the Sundays,' said Bryant, shuffling through the photographs.

'I thought it looked like his work. Why would he be trying to flog pictures of a boring old Tory fundraiser?'

'I asked him that. He said he had an idea to do a follow-up to the Christine Keeler scandal. I suppose he managed to get his mitts on a list of those in attendance and saw our four young ladies in amongst the mouldies. You can imagine how these chaps' minds work. Did you know that Mia Waleska used to do glamour photography on the side? So did Keeler. And, like Keeler, Mia wouldn't do anything too hard core.'

'What are you saying? That the girls are involved in pornography?'

'No, not at all, but Mia is a very beautiful companion for somebody's arm. Perhaps she's paid to brighten up otherwise drab public events. Keeler kept bad company but did not make money from immoral earnings. The problem with her was that she and her friend Dr Stephen Ward provided the link between two very different worlds. She had relations with a West Indian thug and the Secretary of State for War. By the time the former was running around firing shots into the wall of Ward's mews house, the government decided to make an example of them.'

'Surely girls are more careful now, in the light of what's gone before?' asked May. His desire to protect Mia and the others was touching, but didn't wash with Bryant.

'I imagine so,' Bryant agreed. 'I thought they were being very careful today, don't you? That's odd.' He picked up one of the photographs and held it an inch from his snub nose, staring hard at it. 'I have to get some reading glasses. Take a look at that.' He threw the photo at May.

'I can't see anything,' said May.

'Mia Waleska's outfit.'

'What of it?'

'She's in a dark trouser suit. It was a hot night. The other three were in miniskirts, as she was today. It's what all the girls do now. Don't you think she'd have worn a short skirt to a party like that?'

May shrugged. 'Only if she was seeking to meet more men like Stuart-Holmesby.'

'Which is exactly why I imagine she went.'

'She wasn't hiding a dagger down her knickers, if that's what you're wondering. She was searched like everyone else.'

'Would she have had any reason to want to kill him?'

Bryant asked. 'Could they have met before somewhere?'

'His secretary says absolutely not.'

'What about this fellow she came with? He clearly said something to Montfleury to make him ask to see her.'

'We've had a stroke of luck there. The secretary heard him make the phone call to Stuart-Holmesby two days before the party. Montfleury was always issuing doom-laden warnings about the government. He said that "the time had come to ring the bells of Westminster". She wonders if it might have been some kind of warning.'

Bryant dragged out his Bradshaw and began checking train times. 'As much as I hate the thought of venturing back into so much greenery, I think we need to have another look at the house. The murder weapon has to still be there. Without it we have nothing.'

Algie Forshaw was at the abbey to greet them, just packing up his forensics case. 'Her dabs are all over the library shelves,' he said, climbing to his feet. 'If Waleska did it, she certainly wasn't too worried about leaving marks.'

'She's never been in trouble with the law before,' said May defensively. 'Are her paw-prints consistent with her story?'

'What, that she was asked to get a book down from the top shelf and he used it as an excuse to maul her? Pretty much so.'

'Algie, you're married, aren't you?' asked Bryant.

'Yes,' sighed Algie. 'She's still alive.'

'What kind of clothes does your wife wear in the summer?'

'I don't know, I've never looked.'

'Well, would she wear black?'

'Only if someone's died. Or if it's formal. We went to

the embalming industry dinner-dance last summer and she wore something that looked like a shroud. It's better that she keeps her legs to herself.'

Back at Bayham Abbey later that afternoon, Simon Montfleury's secretary reluctantly admitted them again. 'You people have already stamped your way through the house,' she said. 'I don't know what more you expect to find.'

'Your boss, he was often photographed for the press, wasn't he?' asked Bryant, baring his pegs in what he thought to be a friendly smile, but which looked more like a dog with rabies.

'He was a public figure,' said the secretary, folding her arms.

'Was he photographed here?'

'Always in his library.'

'Do you have any of the pictures?'

'Of course. I keep a press file.'

'Could I see them?' He turned to his partner. 'God, it's like pulling teeth.'

They went to the secretary's office and waited while she pulled open various drawers and located the press clippings. Bryant removed a handful and headed back to the library. May was mystified, but followed in his wake.

The only sign that a murder had taken place was the dark stain on the Indian carpet. Bryant held up a *Times* photograph of Montfleury leaning against his desk with a book in his hand. He grunted, holding the picture at different angles. 'Does the photographer bring his own lighting?' he asked.

'There's no need,' said the secretary. 'It's bright enough in here, provided we turn the lights on.'

'What are you doing?' asked May finally.

'Turn the lights on, will you?' Bryant waved his free hand behind him. May did as he was told. Bryant looked up, raising the photograph in comparison. He looked around, found the library steps and rolled them to the far end of the bookcase. Climbing up, then down, he paced back across the carpet and reached a baroque brass grating in the floor. 'Where does this lead?'

'To the boiler,' said the secretary, unimpressed. 'It's the heating system. Your inspector already looked down there.'

'He's not my inspector,' Bryant remarked. 'Did he remove the grille? These screws don't look like they've ever seen a screwdriver.'

'No, he shone his torch down.'

Bryant had a poke around in his pockets and produced several conkers, a yo-yo, half a cheese and beetroot sandwich, and a scout's penknife. Settling on his knees, he unscrewed the grille and lifted it off, reaching inside.

'Well, well,' he said, sitting up with something held in his fingertips. 'The question now is whether Mr Mont-fleury's murder was a premeditated act. The decision to wear the trouser suit rather suggests it was.' He rose and bounced over to the library steps. 'When she came in, he asked her to use the steps, yes? When she got to the top, he slipped his hand – well, we don't need to know exactly what he did with his hand but let's imagine he either gave her a fright or she had been expecting something like it. She turned, found herself level with the chandelier and pulled off one of these.' He held up a scalloped glass dagger. 'There are, let me see, nineteen of them on the chandelier. And this one, I think, made twenty. After stabbing him with the only weapon at hand, she wiped it clean on her trousers. She could have then left the room and stood over the nearest drain or grating to let it fall down her trouser leg into the drain. But then she saw the heating grille and it fitted perfectly. And of course when Ian Hargreave shone a torch down there, his torch beam just went straight through it.'

'OK, we've got the murder weapon but this is still circumstantial evidence,' said May. 'It would never stand up in a court of law.'

'Then we search for the trouser suit and have it analysed for bloodstains,' said Bryant.

Mia Waleska had a perfectly plausible excuse, of course. She said that she had only borrowed the suit for the evening, from Lisa. She had been planning to wear a summer dress but found that she no longer fitted it. She had washed the trousers because she had spilled a glass of red wine down them.

There was nothing else to be done. With the discovery of DNA forensics still two decades away, the case against Mia Waleska collapsed. One year later, something happened to open it again.

2.

The Howard Hotel had once occupied an elegant Gothic building overlooking the Thames near Temple Gardens, but it had been replaced by an ugly sixties block of magnolia-coloured concrete. On a sunny morning in late summer, David Stuart-Holmesby, MP for Rotherhithe, was sitting in his usual armchair in the perpetually deserted foyer bar, sipping a coffee into which he had slipped a large vodka, a Scandinavian cocktail known as Karsk. The name derived from an old Norse word meaning 'agile' and 'vigorous'. Stuart-Holmesby was feeling neither, having been out on the town rather too late the night before, and was thinking about giving his luncheon a miss when he heard the ticking of heels on marble.

Looking up, he saw a familiar face approaching across the expanse of green stone. Even wearing huge sunglasses, a little black dress and a large black silk hat, he could tell that Mia Waleska had somehow grown even more beautiful. He had not laid eyes on her since the scandal at Bayham Abbey. He couldn't risk the contamination of association by being seen anywhere near her.

Now, though, a year later, and in the setting of the empty hotel, where only the bartender stood cleaning a glass, it was an entirely different matter. 'My dear,' he said, making half an effort to rise from his extremely comfortable chair. 'What a pleasure it is to see you. I feel I must thank you for all the hard work you—'

But she had stopped before him and removed a silver pistol from her purse. The bartender ducked down behind his bar. Mia Waleska's face was a porcelain mask, her lips as frosted and frozen as a Dali brooch. She checked the dainty gold timepiece on her wrist, then aimed and fired once. A single bullet pierced David Stuart-Holmesby's heart, passing out of the back of the armchair and embedding itself in the wainscoting.

Mia dropped the pistol on the floor with a clatter, then turned and tapped through the marble foyer of the Howard Hotel. She walked out into the sunlight and down to the Victoria Embankment, where she threw her hat into the river and shook out her hair, and left her old life behind for good.

'Nobody saw her,' said John May, striding across their

Bow Street office and throwing down the morning news-paper. 'The barman threw himself on the floor and only has the vaguest recollection of a backlit woman in black looking at her watch.'

'Hardly anyone ever stays in the Howard,' said Bryant, chewing on his pipe stem. 'And there's never anyone behind the counter. You have to wait ages to get served.'

'Are you taking this seriously?' May barked. 'We couldn't pin her down last time but we're damned well going to do it this time.'

'You've changed your tune,' said Bryant. 'Lovely Mia could do no wrong until she made a laughing stock of you.'

'Us, Arthur, us! She waved two fingers in our faces and walked away, and I'm not letting her do it again. It doesn't matter that there was no one else in the reception area, she was seen walking into the hotel and heading in the direction of the Strand afterwards. We've got her. I can place her at the scene and I have the murder weapon, hopefully with her prints all over it.'

'When is that forensics-wallah getting back to us?'

'Any minute now, I hope,' said May, willing the tele-phone to ring.

DS Gladys Forthright stuck her head around the door jamb. 'I'm popping over to the stationer's for some fresh typewriter ribbons. Can I get you anything?' she asked.

'Yes, twenty Senior Service,' said May, digging in his pocket for change. 'If I give you five bob you can give me sixpence back.'

'Don't I get to keep the change for going?'

'You're going anyway.'

'Cheapskate,' said Forthright. 'There are men out there who know the value of a lady.'

'"The value of a lady."' Bryant rolled the phrase around his mouth. 'Gladys is right, of course. To some men, young ladies have a very special value.' He turned to look at his partner. 'You know, something that Simon Montfleury said still sticks in my brain. It was when he called Stuart-Holmesby. The secretary thought it was a warning. What if it wasn't?'

May stopped staring at the telephone. 'What do you mean?'

'What if it was an instruction? *It's time to ring the Belles of Westminster.*'

'You mean—'

'They had their own club. They were a call-girl ring, John. And if Montfleury wanted them rung, it meant that both he and Stuart-Holmesby had access to them. What if the girls no longer wanted to be controlled by a pair of sleazy old politicians – wouldn't they do something about it?'

The phone rang, making them both jump.

'John, is that you?' said Algie Forshaw. 'I've got a bit of bad news for you. The gun that young lady dropped on the floor of the Howard Hotel, it has her fingerprints on it.'

'Well, that's good, surely,' said May.

'It would be, except that the bullet we dug out of the wall behind Stuart-Holmesby didn't come from it. It's a completely different gauge. She fired a blank.'

May put his hand over the receiver. 'You're not going to like this,' he told Arthur.

They arrived at the Howard Hotel to find that a sleepy concierge had finally been posted at the reception desk. Bryant paced across the green marble floor. The armchair in which Stuart-Holmesby had been sitting when he was shot had been replaced, but it sat at the exact same angle as before. Bryant paced backwards from it, stopping at the approximate point where Mia Waleska had stood.

He nimbly turned on one foot and stared out of the door. 'The bullet had lost more power than Algie expected it to,' he told May. 'I think I know why. Somebody else fired from the street. The Belles of Westminster. They'd have looked out for one another, wouldn't they?'

'If they'd formed a club, as you suggested,' said May, 'I imagine they would.'

'One of the other girls,' said Bryant, pointing. 'She stood there and fired at exactly the same time. That's why Mia looked at her watch. They'd synchronized watches. They were all in it together.'

'That's ridiculous,' said May. 'It's far too elaborate.'

'Is it any more absurd and elaborate than using a chandelier pendant to stab a man?' asked Bryant. 'Unless we find the other gun and girl, we'll have nothing again.'

The detectives didn't find either. All four girls had seemingly vanished from the face of the earth. All John May had left was the memory of Mia's emerald-green eyes, lingering for one all-too-brief moment on his.

Five years later, Bryant and May's paths once more crossed with the Belles of Westminster – but that's another story with a very different outcome.

This was the first short case history I wrote up, and it must have showed that I had a lot of fun with it, because my publishers asked if they could release it as a single e-mystery. So to anyone who finds they already have this story, may I just say that I added it to the finished book as an extra for those who hadn't read it, therefore you're still getting your money's worth! It's another 'precinct' tale – this time set on that most iconic of London landmarks: a double-decker bus.

BRYANT & MAY'S MYSTERY TOUR

Early on Christmas Eve the Home Office called Arthur Bryant of London's Peculiar Crimes Unit with an urgent request to attend the scene of a crime in King's Cross. Bryant did so, then called his partner John May with instructions to meet him at 10.15 a.m. beside a bus stop in Marble Arch, but with no explanation as to why. It was muggy, grey and wet, not at all appropriate to the festive season, and May resented being dragged away from the PCU's offices.

'Ah, you got my message, good.' The elderly detective hailed his partner with a wild whip of his walking stick, and nearly pruned a passing tourist. Bryant resembled a beady-eyed tramp more than an officer of the law. He had misbuttoned his shapeless brown cardigan and dragged a moth-eaten Harris tweed coat over the top of it. A sprig of holly protruded from his battered trilby, looking less like seasonal decoration than a sign that he had lately been trapped in a bush. 'I got here ahead of time and had a potter through the German Christmas market in Hyde Park. Four pounds fifty for a knockwurst. They're getting their own back for the war.'

'You had your mobile with you?' asked May, surprised. Arthur was three years his senior but several decades behind the rest of the world when it came to technology.

'I did have, yes,' Bryant admitted, tugging his trilby further on to his head. 'Here's our bus.' He indicated the old open-topped Routemaster that was pulling up beside them.

May was suspicious. 'Then where is it now?'

'I think I dropped it in the Princess Diana Memorial Drain. Don't worry, it'll just keep going around. I'll get it when I come back. Well' – he threw out a hand so that May could haul him on board – 'you're probably wondering what this is all about.'

'And why we need to meet on a sightseeing bus, yes,' said May, leading his partner inside the idling vehicle. The portly driver looked back over his shoulder, watching them through the glass. 'I've seen the Regent Street lights already.'

'It won't do you any harm to see them again. I think Christmas gets better as you get older,' Bryant remarked somewhat unexpectedly.

'Do you?'

'Oh yes. You have to buy fewer presents because most of your friends are dead. Let's go inside; I can't face the stairs. Let me fill you in. There was a rather sad little murder in King's Cross during the night. A fifty-four-year-old cleaning lady named Joan McKay was strangled to death in her third-floor flat in Hastings Street. The HO felt the case warranted our involvement.'

'But this bus doesn't go anywhere near King's Cross.' May checked the route on the wall and saw that it tacked through central London on a loop.

'Oh, we're not going to the murder site. I've already been there.' Bryant seated himself on the arrow-patterned seat at the front of the bus, next to a gingery young man who was standing in the aisle with a microphone. His badge read: 'Hi! I'm Martin!' 'I wanted you here so that you could help me apprehend the murderer.'

The Routemaster pulled away from the stop at Speakers' Corner, heading into Oxford Street. Shoppers were out early, but many had already left the city to spend Christmas with their families. 'My Uncle Jack used to get up on his soapbox over there, just after the war,' said Bryant, tapping the rain-spattered window. 'He was used to telling people what they shouldn't do, like that man who used to wander the length of Oxford Street with the board that said 'Less Passion From Less Protein'. Uncle Jack would pick a different subject every week: ban licentious theatre, hang Sir Anthony Eden, shoot the Welsh; he'd rant about anything so long as it involved getting rid of something or someone. Not a terribly positive attitude, I suppose, but at least Speakers' Corner still gives us some semblance of free speech.'

'Now, does anyone know the name of the great b-i-i-i-g department store on our right?' Martin the tour guide was as proud and patronizing as a first-time father. There were no takers. 'Anyone?'

Bryant listlessly raised his hand. 'Selfridges, opened in 1909 by Harry Gordon Selfridge. He coined the phrase "The customer is always right", and was the first salesman to put products out on display where they could be touched.'

'Well, I don't know about that,' said Martin.

'No, but luckily I do,' Bryant countered.

'We're catching a murderer on a bus?' whispered May in disbelief.

'We are now heading towards Oxford Circus, which was once described by Noël Coward as the Hub of the Universe,' announced the guide.

'This boy's a dunderhead.' Bryant jerked a wrinkled thumb at Martin, who overheard him. 'It was John Wyndham, and he was describing Piccadilly Circus.'

Bryant occasionally worked as a tour guide in his spare time, but his revolutionary methods of involving the general public in his talks tended to frighten off casual tourists. He forgot most things, but never the facts he had painstakingly gathered about his city.

'I don't understand,' May persisted. 'It sounds very straightforward. Why did we get the case?' The PCU only handled investigations the Home Office found detrimental to government policy. A death of the kind his partner had described would usually fall under the local jurisdiction of the Metropolitan Police.

'There are three oddities.' Bryant ticked them off on his fingers. 'One, after strangling Mrs McKay the murderer ordered two pizzas and calmly ate both of them. B, he slept overnight in the apartment. And three, his victim was killed after he left.'

May considered the matter as the bus turned into Regent Street. 'I'm sorry, Arthur, you've utterly lost me.'

'Do try to pay attention. The murderer left the flat at seven fifteen this morning, not realizing that his victim was still alive. Mrs McKay struggled to the window to raise the alarm, but the effort of opening it was too much for her. She lost consciousness while sitting on the sill and fell out into the street, landing on a gentleman called Sir Ian Lowry—'

'The MoD bigwig?'

'The very same. Sir Ian was leaving a call girl's flat on the ground floor, where he had apparently stayed the night. Mrs McKay broke her neck and his leg. And that's why the HO called us in. Obviously, it's a serious security breach because Sir Ian is privy to all kinds of military secrets. It doesn't help that he was putting the call girl's services down on his expenses. Private secretary, if you please. The girl has already been brought in, the coroner has certified that Mrs McKay bore the bruises of strangulation around her neck, and all that's left is the apprehension of her killer.'

'So I'm here to help you identify him,' said May, still a little confused.

'Oh, I know who the murderer is.' Bryant cheerily flashed his oversized false teeth. 'You were complaining about getting old the other day, so I thought this would be a chance for you to test your fading faculties.'

The old-fashioned Routemaster bus stopped outside Hamleys toy store and the driver stared impassively ahead as a single Japanese tourist came on board. May looked around. There were now eight passengers seated downstairs. The rain was falling too heavily for anyone to remain on the upper open deck. Bryant checked his ancient Timex. It was 10.44 a.m.

'You already know the murderer's identity?' asked May.

'Better than that,' replied Bryant smugly, 'I can tell you the precise time he'll be arrested. At 11.26 a.m.'

'Are you saying we're looking for somebody on board this bus?'

The tour guide was attempting to deliver a potted history of the Haymarket, and was not happy about being distracted by these chatting elderly men. 'There are seats further back,' he pointed out.

'We're quite happy here,' insisted Bryant. He withdrew his pipe from his top pocket and absently struck a match to it. A hefty woman in an LA Dodgers baseball cap, an oversized sweatshirt and huge baggy shorts reacted with horror behind him. 'Oh-my-Gahd, that's disgusting,' she complained. 'Hey, it's illegal to smoke that thing.'

'Yet it's apparently not illegal to dress like a gigantic toddler, madam, which I find most curious.'

'Listen, buddy, if you'd take my advice—'

'I'm not your buddy, and if I took your advice I'd be enormous.' Bryant turned back to his partner. 'So take a look around and tell me who you suspect. Give me the benefit of your observational skills.'

The ancient bus was now chuntering towards the rain-swept plain of Trafalgar Square. 'On your left, Nelson's Column, finished in 1843, with four bronze panels at the base depicting his naval victories,' said Martin the guide.

'His left arm was struck by lightning in the 1880s and he only just got it X-rayed a couple of years ago,' said Bryant. 'That's the NHS for you.'

'So you know exactly where the murderer will get on this bus, how long he'll stay on and where he'll get off?' asked May.

'Indeed I do.' Bryant could be supremely annoying when he was the only one holding privileged information.

At 11.02 a.m., the bus stopped near the corner of Craig's Court. 'Pall Mall derives its name from a seventeenth-century mallet and ball game played here by, er, members of royalty,' Martin the tour guide stated with a hint of uncertainty.

'Everyone knows that,' said Bryant, fidgeting in his seat. 'Tell them something new. Alleys of shops are called malls because they're shaped like the game's playing sites. Did you know that Pall Mall is only worth £140 on the Monopoly board?'

'I don't think he cares too much for your interruptions, accurate though they may be,' whispered May. 'You're unsettling him.'

'Some people deserve to be unsettled,' Bryant replied. 'When a man is tired of London he should clear off. Oh dear, he's wearing a clip-on tie.' Coming from a man as sartorially challenged as Bryant, this was a bit rich.

When the bus stopped halfway along Whitehall, May surveyed the new arrivals. One of them was a murderer, but which one? There were now eleven passengers on the lower deck: two Americans, two Italians, two Chinese, one Japanese boy in a mad hat and two couples of indeterminate origins. He decided that the murderer had yet to put in an appearance.

'Was this woman McKay in her own apartment?' he asked.

'Correct.'

May thought of the call girl living on the ground floor. 'Did she look after the other girls? Was her killer a client?'

'No, she had nothing to do with them.' Bryant sat back, trying not to listen to the tour guide's incorrect description of the Cabinet War Rooms.

'But the killer left behind a clue to his identity.'

'No, it was something he took away with him that gave me the lead.'

'Well, I don't see how you could possibly know what he took.'

The bus continued along Whitehall, picking up three more passengers, and lumbered towards Parliament Square through thickening traffic. May eyed the new-comers with suspicion. A German couple – he over-heard their conversation – were taking pictures behind a fiftyish man with unmistakably Russian features and anxious, flitting eyes. May studied the Russian's loud Italian jacket, his unshaven chin. A sad little murder, Bryant had said. This man had dressed in a hurry, with-out stopping to shave, and looked around every time the bus came to a halt. But if he was the killer, why would he make his escape aboard a slow-moving tour bus, on a trip that ended back where it began?

'Who can tell me the name of this building?' asked Martin the tour guide.

'Houses of Parliament,' the assembly muttered faintly, as if being asked to recite a prayer in church.

'Now, many people think Big Ben is the name of the tower . . .'

'Dear God no.' Bryant sighed loudly. 'Can't he come up with anything more original than that?'

Martin shot him a filthy look. 'But it is actually the name of the single bell housed inside—'

'Absolute rubbish.' Bryant thumped the guide on the arm with his walking stick. 'There are five bells in the Elizabeth Tower, young man. The other four play the Westminster Quarters, variations of "I know that my Redeemer liveth" from Handel's *Messiah*.'

'Your information is not correct?' the German husband asked the guide, puzzled.

'Look, who's giving this bloody tour?' Martin's cheeks were turning as red as his hair.

'It could be him,' said May, pointing to the Russian. 'He's got a shifty look about him. Oh – that doesn't sound very scientific, does it?'

'I'll take over if you like,' Bryant snapped back at the guide. 'These people aren't getting their money's worth.'

'But, Arthur, how do you know when he was due on the bus? That just leaves—'

'Listen, mate, I don't have to put up with this. My shift ends here, anyway.' As the bus stopped in the corner of the square, Martin threw down his microphone and tapped on the glass, signalling to the driver.

As he made his way along the aisle, May said, 'The guide, it's the guide. And he's getting away!'

Bryant did not move a muscle as a moon-faced young woman with scraped-back hair and a ponytail took over from the departing Martin.

'Hello, my name is Debbie, and I'm your guide on the last part of this tour,' she told them. The bus pulled into the traffic and made its way around the square.

'Why didn't you stop him?' asked May with growing incredulity. The ginger-headed tour guide was walking quickly away along the crowded pavement with his hands in his pockets.

Bryant pulled back his sleeve and held up his watch so that his partner could read it: 11.19 a.m. There were still another seven minutes to go.

'Who can tell me the name of this building?' asked Debbie, pointing to Westminster Abbey and cupping her hand around her ear.

'Is there some special nursery school where they're trained to speak in this fashion, I wonder?' said Bryant. The bus headed back on to Victoria Embankment.

'Where does the tour go from here?' asked May, keeping an eye on the Russian, who seemed to be sweating.

'Around Covent Garden, where the lovely Debbie will probably regale us with selections from *My Fair Lady*, then back towards Oxford Street,' said Bryant.

'You said it was something he took with him that gave you a clue,' May repeated, checking out the Japanese boy's strange headgear.

Bryant rested his chin on his knuckles and regarded the stippled thread of the Thames that could be glimpsed between buildings. 'The lovely Debbie will ask them to name the river next,' he muttered.

'He was so unfazed by the thought of murdering Mrs McKay that he stayed all night . . .' mused May.

'I wonder if anyone knows where the lion on Westminster Bridge comes from?' asked Debbie.

'Because he was used to her . . .' May followed the thought.

'Good Lord, an intelligent question,' Bryant beamed delightedly at the new guide.

'It stood on the parapet of the Lion Brewery until 1966, near Hungerford Bridge . . .' said Debbie.

'. . . Because he was married to her,' said May.

'Yet we have come to regard it as a symbol of London . . .'

'. . . And he stuck to his routine, ordering pizza for them both, sleeping beside her and getting up the next morning . . .'

'. . . So when we photograph the lion standing proudly beside Big Ben, we recreate the traditional link between

Members of Parliament – and alcohol.' Debbie flourished a smile.

'Oh, bravo!' exclaimed Bryant. 'I like her!'

'. . . And he came to work just as he always did, because he couldn't think of what else to do. He had to stick to the schedule. Not the tour guide at all, but the bus driver,' said May as the truth dawned.

'Correct. His timetable was still on the kitchen counter, but his jacket, cap and badge were all missing from the flat.' Bryant rose unsteadily to his feet and pressed the stop bell. 'That took you long enough,' he sniffed. 'I'm sorry, Debbie. I'm afraid the tour will have to terminate here.'

May looked out of the window. The bus stop faced New Scotland Yard. It was exactly 11. 26 a.m.

'He won't run off,' said Bryant. 'He wants to be taken in for the murder of his wife. He loved her. But the neighbours said she never stopped nagging him about his weight.'

The Japanese tourist and the Russian took some very nice photographs of the two detectives leading the devastated driver down from his cabin. 'Arrest ye merry gentlemen,' said Bryant with a grin as the flashes went off.

'You've got holly in your hat,' May pointed out.

'Yes,' said Bryant, 'I like the smell.'

'Holly hasn't got a smell.'

'It does, actually. The bright, spiky appearance is all bravado. If you gently break the stem, you'll smell it – there's a bitter tang inside,' he explained. 'Like some people.'

BRYANT & MAY: THE CASES SO FAR

New readers start here: Arthur Bryant and John May head up the Peculiar Crimes Unit, London's most venerable specialist police team, now based in King's Cross. It's a division that was founded during the Second World War to investigate cases that could cause national scandal or public unrest.

Previously based above Mornington Crescent tube station, the technophobic, irascible and vaguely revolting Bryant and his smooth-talking modernist partner John May head a team of equally unusual misfits who are just as likely to commit crimes as solve them.

Arthur Bryant has been writing up his strangest cases as memoirs, but they're as unreliable as he is, because he couldn't possibly have tackled his first case during the Second World War – could he? The memoirs were turned into novels by a hack writer employed by Mr Bryant's publishers to present them to the world. Here are the twelve cases covered so far.

FULL DARK HOUSE

In Which Mr May Gets Stage Fright
And Mr Bryant Gets Blown to Kingdom Come

When Arthur Bryant got blown up in his office and all that was left of him were his false teeth, his partner John May looked for clues to his death. The hunt took him back through the decades to the unit's foundation, the worst day of the Blitz and a murder investigation in the Palace Theatre, where an outrageous production of *Orpheus in the Underworld* was being staged, and where the principal dancer was found without her feet.

Everyone in the Palace Theatre became a suspect. Soon there were more bizarre deaths, including a gruesome on-stage spearing from a lightning bolt, and as the argumentative young detectives tracked their elusive quarry through the blackouts, the fog and the falling bombs, they found themselves unwittingly following the pattern of the play, chasing Orpheus down to Hades. It seemed that the killer they sought was 'some kind of giant dwarf', which made about as much sense as anything else in the investigation.

BRYANT You must be Mr May. What should I call you?
MAY John, sir.
BRYANT Don't call me 'sir', I've not been knighted yet. And at this rate I never will be.

Backstory

My father was a scientist who worked in an experimental wartime communications unit. He and his colleagues were very young, and could not have realized that they were working towards a discovery that later changed the world. The full story is told in my memoir *Paperboy,* which he sadly didn't live long enough to read. This series starter was created in the memory of the stories he told me about his job, one of which was about the way he and his colleagues used to blow each other up with exploding paint as a joke.

THE WATER ROOM

In Which Mr Bryant Goes under the Street And Mr May Hunts a Killer above It

Bryant and May's investigation of a secret world beneath London began when a woman was found dead in a dry basement with her throat full of river-water. In the quiet London street where she lived, the residents were unsettled by the ghostly sound of rushing water and some particularly unpleasant spiders. Further impossible deaths, including a man suffocated by soil, revealed a connection to the lost underground rivers of London and a disgraced academic who hunted an ancient secret that might soon be lost within the forgotten canals.

Meanwhile it refused to stop raining, the weatherman warned of a coming flood, and nobody's house was safe as Bryant and May headed beneath the city to stop a murderer from striking again. What was the connection between the victims, an old lady, a builder, a TV producer and a homeless alcoholic? And what did forgotten artworks and the four elements have to do with it?

MAY You cannot act against the law, Arthur!
BRYANT You can when the law is an ass.

Backstory

Bryant and May's investigation of the world beneath the London streets came from the fact that the North London house in which I used to live had a room exactly like this, built with a break-panel in the floor over an underground river. For years I had trouble with crayfish jumping out of my drains, which overflowed from the Fleet during storms. I sent one to the Natural History Museum, whose experts told me that Turkish crayfish were forcing British crayfish out of the sewage systems. Who knew there was a war going on beneath our feet? The map in the front of the book was an exact copy of my street.

SEVENTY-SEVEN CLOCKS

In Which Mr Bryant Runs into Evil And Mr May Runs out of Time

Arthur Bryant, writing his memoirs, recalled a case from 1973. As strikes and blackouts ravaged the country, a rare painting in the National Gallery had acid thrown over it by a man in a stovepipe hat. Soon, the members of a high-born Whitstable family were being knocked off in a variety of lunatic ways – by escaped tiger, by clockwork bomb and by demon barber . . . Bryant and May set out to investigate the family.

As the hours of daylight started to diminish towards winter's shortest day, the detectives discovered that a forgotten Victorian legacy held the key to the strange deaths. It was a mystery that would lead behind the sealed doors of London's most ancient and secret guilds – and to the murderous legacy of British imperialism. Time was running out for the detectives, unless they could find seventy-seven clocks. It was when Bryant uncovered the mystery of 'Chandler's Wobble' and had to babysit a horribly rich family that all hell broke loose . . .

PC How long have you been a policeman, Mr Bryant?
BRYANT Longer than you've been alive, mate.
PC That must make you the oldest team on the force.
BRYANT Not if we keep lying about our ages.

Backstory

This book came about because I stumbled upon an amazing snippet of London history, an event that occurred in the late nineteenth century. It was a moment well documented at the time, a source of great wonder and excitement, but then utterly forgotten. Obviously, it would make the basis of a great B&M adventure. Also, Robert Louis Stevenson's *The Wrong Box* had a bit to do with it. This is by far the most outrageous of all the cases, yet there really is a nugget of truth at its heart.

TEN-SECOND STAIRCASE

In Which Mr Bryant Suffers for Art
And Mr May Hunts a Highwayman

When a controversial artist was found dead, floating face down in her own art installation inside a riverside gallery with locked doors and windows, the only witness turned out to be a small boy who insisted that the murderer was a masked man in a tricorn hat riding a stallion.

Then a television presenter was struck by lightning while indoors, and another victim was immolated in a public swimming bath . . . clearly, they were the kind of impossible crimes that only Bryant and May could solve. But Bryant had lost his nerve following a disastrous public appearance, and May was busy fighting to keep the unit from closure.

With a sinister modern-day highwayman bringing terror to the London streets, the detectives tracked their suspects to an exclusive school and a deprived housing estate. But then the highwayman started to become a national hero, and the public turned against the policemen.

Exploring the dark side of celebrity, the conflicts of youth and class, and the peculiar myths of old London and its cut-throat highwaymen, Bryant and May dived into the case with a vengeance . . .

BRYANT That's what happens when you get older. You become irritated by the views of others for the simple reason that you know better, and they're being ridiculous . . . Some silly man will start complaining about police brutality until I want to beat him to death with my stick.

Backstory

It was a time when the public started to venerate vacuous celebrity over anything controversial or demanding to think about. I wanted to write about the subject in the context of an enjoyable novel, and this was the result. Celebrity fever has waned to a point where we can understand its implications and be a little more wary of its effect on the young.

The opening murder occurred at an event equivalent to that of Charles Saatchi's innovative 'Sensation' exhibition in London. A number of statements made by the killer came from actual press reports, but the novel is still preposterous in places. After this, the more outlandish elements in the series were toned down.

WHITE CORRIDOR

In Which Mr Bryant Gets in a Jam
And Mr May Goes below Zero

One day the unthinkable happened at London's Peculiar Crimes Unit. A key member of staff, the coroner Oswald Finch, was found brutally murdered in his own mortuary, and everyone who worked there was suddenly a suspect. But Arthur Bryant and John May weren't on hand to solve the crime. They had become stranded on a desolate snowbound section of country road. As the blizzard grew more severe, they attempted to solve the crime long distance using only their mobile phones.

Unfortunately, their situation quickly worsened. Unknown to the stranded detectives, an obsessed killer had travelled from the French Riviera to Dartmoor, and was stalking the stranded vehicles, searching for one particular victim, coming closer to them with each passing minute.

As if it didn't have enough trouble, the Peculiar Crimes Unit received a demanding royal visitor, and the Home Office prepared to shut the PCU down when the visit inevitably started to go wrong.

Two murderers, two incapacitated detectives, just six hours to solve two crimes and save the unit. Armed only with their wits, woolly coats and a stack of dubious veal and ham pies, Bryant and May braced themselves for a day trapped inside the white corridor . . .

BRYANT Look at the snow falling in the trees. It's so postcard-pretty out there. I'd forgotten how much I hate the countryside.

MAY That's because you never spend any time there.

BRYANT Why would I? Rural folk think they're so superior just because they have a village pub and a duck pond.

Backstory

This was my take on the traditional Christie-style whodunnit. I wanted to limit my detectives' abilities by imprisoning them somewhere without their staff. Then I recalled the snowdrifts that had often cut off drivers in Devon (people die; it seems surprisingly extreme considering the English countryside is thought of as tame and safe) and the traffic jam seemed like the perfect place in which to hide a killer.

One of the biggest problems I had was finding a legitimate way to introduce other characters, when most of them wouldn't want to get out of their vehicles and risk the elements. I had a lot of fun with the concluding royal visit, and based the visiting dignitary on a well-known and famously disliked minor regal personality.

THE VICTORIA VANISHES

In Which Mr May Goes after a Killer And Mr Bryant Goes for a Beer

It began with a life lost on a London street; an ordinary woman collapsed outside a public house called the Victoria Cross in Bloomsbury. Yet it became one of the most disturbing cases the Peculiar Crimes Unit ever undertook . . .

Arthur Bryant passed the woman on the way back from his coroner's wake just before she died. But when he returned to the scene a few hours later, nothing was how he remembered it. For a start, the busy nineteenth-century pub had turned into an Indian supermarket. The elderly detective's greatest fear was that he might be suddenly losing his mind. After all, he had already managed to mislay the coroner's funeral urn on the same night.

While Bryant faced some home truths about perception and memory, his partner John May investigated a similar death occurring in another busy London pub. It seemed that a killer was taking lives in the city's safest and most convivial places, but how was he doing it, and why?

The detectives' search came to involve arcane mysteries, secret societies, line-dancing, speed-dating, hidden insanity, and the solution to a forgotten London conundrum.

BRYANT I wish I remember what I did with Oswald's ashes, because that was really where it all began – oh my God.
MAY What's the matter?
BRYANT I just remembered what I did with them!

Backstory

This was the sixth book, and in it were planted the seeds of the next six. One of my favourite Golden Age mystery writers was Edmund Crispin, whose academic-detective Gervase Fen solved crimes in Oxford, and I wanted to make this book a direct homage to his novel *The Moving Toyshop*, one of his best. 'Homage' would just be a polite word for stealing if you didn't bring something else to the tribute. In this case I wanted to take the idea further and explore the strange world of pub societies. Many London pubs have private rooms in which all sorts of odd clubs meet. I quickly came to the realization that many of the quirkiest pubs were vanishing, falling victim to rapacious property developers by nature of their sheer size, so the book turned into a testament and the title became ironic. A list of all the pubs I visited for research (drinking) went into the back, and became a sort of requiem as they vanished in real life.

BRYANT & MAY ON THE LOOSE

In Which Mr Bryant Hunts a Headsman
And Mr May Digs Up Something Ugly

In rush-hour King's Cross, one of the busiest crossing points in Britain, finding a murderer would have been a nightmare for any force. But when a decapitated body was discovered in a kebab-shop freezer, London's Peculiar Crimes Unit was *not* summoned – because the unit had just been disbanded, and elderly detectives Bryant and May had no access to evidence that could help them find a killer.

With the team dispersed and Arthur Bryant retiring to his bed, depressed and determined never to work again, it seemed like the end of the line for the PCU. But then something began disturbing the area's property developers. Half-man, half-beast, a terrifying figure with a head of knives appeared at night on building sites, his pagan horns the mystical image of a forgotten legend.

It was time to gather the gang once more, even though they had no resources and could not be paid. With the appearance of a second headless body, the detectives uncovered the pre-Christian secrets of the historic streets and found a pattern to the deaths. But the sinister solution led them back to the heart of the city's oldest mystery: who really owns the London landscape? As they got closer to the truth, Bryant and May made a very bad enemy. A man known only as Mr Fox, who could seemingly change his identity and vanish at will . . .

RAYMOND LAND You can't tell me what to do. I'm your superior officer.

BRYANT Oh, that's just a title, like labelling a tin of peaches 'Superior Quality'. It doesn't mean anything.

Backstory

This book was born from two ideas. First, I moved to King's Cross, an inner-city spot I'd hung around as a child, now one of the most manic areas in London, and I'd watched as public housing developments were torn down and replaced with luxury private apartments for overseas investors, just as the neighbourhood's slums and child-labour factories had been torn down before them.

Also, I wondered, who really owns the London landscape? Extraordinary stories emerged from various archives about lost deeds, stolen properties and outrageous government dishonesty. In fact some of the cases proved too upsetting to be added to the book, and with so much ground to cover I was in danger of packing too much research material into the novel. Even after trimming it back, I realized that some of it would spill over into a sequel.

BRYANT & MAY OFF THE RAILS

In Which Mr Bryant Goes Underground And Mr May Leads the Chase for a Fox

London's Peculiar Crimes Unit was given a week to clear its backlog of investigations. But the only mystery on their books looked like a mundane accident: a young mother had fallen down the escalator in a rush-hour tube station, in full view of commuters and cameras. Still, Arthur Bryant and John May were nagged by the suspicion that a wicked deed had occurred. There was something strange about the way she fell . . .

When a young student went missing on the last train home one night – impossibly vanishing between stops on the train – the detectives headed into the London Underground. Bryant needed no excuse to start investigating the strange history of forgotten stations, ghosts and suicides, as a seemingly trivial clue sent him searching for a clever killer who always covered his tracks. With the suspect list spreading to include an entire household of students, it seemed that everyone had secrets to hide. And who was the sinister Night Crawler spotted in the tunnels after the last train had pulled out?

With the Peculiar Crimes Unit roaring back into business in new premises, the detectives headed down on to the darkened platforms of the world's oldest underground railway to hunt the murderer. To solve the puzzle they explored an unseen world, uncovering hidden histories in order to stop the ruthless, invisible Mr Fox from striking again. But the biggest surprise was discovering that nothing is ever quite as it appears . . .

BANBURY A serial killer. That's what I reckon we've got here. We've not had many of them at the PCU, have we?

BRYANT Not proper saw-off-the-arms-and-legs-boil-the-innards-put-the-head-in-a-handbag-and-throw-it-from-a-bridge jobs, no.

Backstory

I'd long wanted to write in detail about the London Underground system, and this picked up on themes that were explored in the previous book, but now I decided to take my detectives below the level of the streets, into the strange new world.

It was also a chance to confront the urban crime writer's greatest problem: how do you hide a criminal in the world's most spied-upon city? Saying that mobiles and CCTV aren't working is a cop-out. I decided to confront the problem head-on and create an impossible crime occurring in plain sight, dependent on your point of view and the assumptions you make.

The ending was a risky challenge. It even took me by surprise, and I grew quite upset writing it because so much of it was true, culled from news reports and my own experience.

THE MEMORY OF BLOOD

In Which Mr May Pulls the Strings
And Mr Bryant Performs an Illusion

On a rainswept London night, the wealthy unscrupulous theatre impresario Robert Kramer hosted a party in his penthouse just off Trafalgar Square. But something was wrong. The atmosphere was uncomfortable; the guests were on edge. And when Kramer's new young wife went to check on their baby boy, she found the nursery door locked from the inside.

Breaking in, the Kramers were faced with an open window, an empty cot, and a grotesque antique puppet of Mr Punch lying on the floor. It seemed that the baby had been thrown from the building, but it had been strangled, and the marks of the puppet's hands were clearly on his throat . . . What's more, there was a witness to tell them that the puppet killed the baby.

As Bryant and May's team interrogated the guests, Arthur investigated the secret world of automata and stagecraft, illusions and effects. His suspicions fell on the staff of Kramer's company, who had been employed to stage a gruesome new thriller in the West End. As a second impossible death occurred, the detectives uncovered forgotten museums and London eccentrics, and took a trip to a seaside Punch and Judy show.

Then Bryant's biographer suddenly died. Was it a tragic accident, or could the circumstances of her death be related to the case? With just one hour left to solve the crime, Bryant buried himself away with his esoteric books. The stage was set for a race against time with a murderous twist . . .

RAYMOND LAND This office is starting to look like your old room in Mornington Crescent.

BRYANT Of course. It's the contents of my head.

RAYMOND LAND It certainly contains the contents of *a* head, unless you've had the brainpan of that stinking Tibetan skull cleaned out.

Backstory

This book was born from my discovery that London had its own Grand Guignol theatre like the one in Paris – I located the scripts for the sinister plays that were performed there, and thought it would make a great basis for a novel. At the time of writing the book I was rehearsing a play on the same stage where the Grand Guignol scenes had been tried out.

The British versions of the plays were different from their French counterparts because the Lord Chamberlain wouldn't allow explicit violence, so we did something typically British – we made the plays about mental cruelty, which was far worse than seeing a rubber hand chopped off.

Also, after the dark realities of the previous two books I needed to write something lighter and funnier, so this is one of Bryant and May's 'sorbet stories' – something refreshing after a big meal.

THE INVISIBLE CODE

In Which Mr May Breaks the Law And Mr Bryant Cracks the Code

As Arthur Bryant's memoirs were published, he started to feel his age. But a case came in that changed his life. A young woman called Amy sat in the quiet London church of St Bride's, off Fleet Street, and was found dead in her pew after the service. But no one had been near her. She had no marks on her body and the cause of death was unknown. The only odd thing was that she had a red cord tied around her left wrist.

Then, at a government dinner party to welcome heads of state, the wife of businessman Oskar Kasavian got drunk and insulted the gathering. She believed she had been made a social outcast by her husband's friends because she was a foreigner from a lower class. Angered at being affected by the invisible code governing British behaviour, she continued to behave so badly that she was eventually locked up in a private clinic in Hampstead.

Her husband's circle closed ranks against her. 'Women of our social standing remain by our men,' one politician's wife reminded her. But Bryant suspected that the wife was being victimized. Especially when she told him that she was the victim of witchcraft. The detectives started investigating Hellfire clubs, secret codes and the history of London's oldest madhouse.

DOCTOR You need to start acting your age, Mr Bryant.
BRYANT If I did that, I'd be dead.

Backstory

There are certain places in London that remain relatively unchanged, even now. I had long wanted to write something partly set in a London church, and here I had the perfect setting of St Bride's, which proved to have a fascinating history (lead coffins! bombings!) that I could use. Soon I had Bryant and May investigating the strange story of Bedlam.

The trick, I suppose, was not to overload the narrative with history but to balance the fun with genuinely intriguing facts. The idea of codes had a double meaning: the Bletchley Park kind and the more secretive code of 'fitting in' in London, a device used by the upper classes to keep foreigners in their place.

THE CASEBOOK OF BRYANT & MAY
(Graphic novel)

Two illustrated untold cases for Bryant and May, 'The Soho Devil', which sees them coming face-to-face with a clown cult and a runaway rhino, and 'The Severed Claw', in which they go up the Telecom Tower to search for a celebrity's missing hand.

BRYANT Why do women always do that thing with you?
MAY What thing?
BRYANT The gooey-eyes.
MAY They sense my charisma.
BRYANT Smell your aftershave, more like.

Backstory

I'm a huge comics fan, and had always wanted to create a comic version of the *Bryant & May* stories. Artist Keith Page was ideal for the job and the finished artwork was sumptuous. Keith modelled Arthur Bryant on photographs of my deceased business partner, so looking at the panels was rather eerie. The result was an artistic triumph and a marketing disaster. Crime readers don't buy graphic novels. The *British* don't really buy graphic novels. The rare slip-cased edition was a delight and is now fetching high enough prices to make me wish I'd hung on to a couple.

THE BLEEDING HEART

In Which Mr May Faces Premature Burial And Mr Bryant Confronts His Childhood Fears

It was a fresh start for Bryant and May and the Peculiar Crimes Unit. Teenager Romain Curtis saw a dead man rising from his grave in a London park and heard him speak. The next night, Romain was killed in a hit-and-run accident. Stranger still, in the minutes between when he was last seen alive and found dead on the pavement, someone changed the boy's shirt.

But Arthur Bryant was not allowed to investigate. Instead, he was sent off to find out how someone could have stolen the ravens from the Tower of London. It appeared that all seven birds had been snatched from one of the most secure buildings in the city. And legend says that when the ravens leave, the nation falls.

Meanwhile, the PCU uncovered a group of latter-day bodysnatchers, visited a strange funeral home and went to Bleeding Heart Yard, where a gruesome London legend involving a heart pierced with arrows seemed connected to the crime . . .

Death was all around. More graves were desecrated, there was another bizarre murder and the symbol of the Bleeding Heart started turning up everywhere. It was even discovered hidden in the detectives' offices. It seemed as if the Grim Reaper was stalking Bryant, playing on his fears of premature burial . . .

BRYANT I must take this call. If anyone wants me I shall be in my boudoir.

RAYMOND LAND You haven't got a boudoir, you've got an office!

Backstory

Some of the tiniest London parks have gravestones in them that go unnoticed. Tie that fact to the city's true history of bodysnatching, and you have a really creepy case. Then I had lunch with my publisher at Bleeding

Heart Yard and heard the truth about Dickens and the legendary ghost said to haunt the area. At the same time I had dinner with the warders in the Tower of London, and they told me something about the ravens that would not have occurred to most people. Suddenly I had the makings of two impossible crimes: how could seven ravens vanish? They're huge! And how could a corpse walk and talk? The solution to the latter came to me after visiting a very unusual vault . . . the finished novel ended up being full of surprises, even involving the staff cat.

THE BURNING MAN

In Which Mr May Finds a Firestarter And Mr Bryant Misplaces His Mind

London fell under a very modern siege. A banking scandal filled the city with violent protests, and as the anger in the streets detonated, a young homeless man burned to death after being caught in the crossfire between rioters and the police.

But all was not as it seemed; an opportunistic killer used the chaos to exact revenge, but his intended victims were so mysteriously chosen that the Peculiar Crimes Unit had to be called in to find a way of stopping him.

Using their network of eccentric contacts, Arthur Bryant and John May hunted down a murderer who adopted incendiary methods of execution. But they found their investigation taking an apocalyptic turn as the case came to involve the history of mob rule, corruption, rebellion, punishment and the legend of Guy Fawkes.

At the same time, several members of the PCU team

reached dramatic turning points in their lives – but the most personal tragedy was yet to come, for as the race to bring down a cunning killer reached its climax, Arthur Bryant faced his own devastating day of reckoning.

BRYANT People are sick of being treated as if they're invisible, fit only to be used up and cast aside like any other exhausted commodity. The uprising is coming from something deep inside us, all of us.

MAY Funny how upset you got when someone knifed the tyres on your Mini.

BRYANT That's different. One should never confuse legitimate protest with vandalism.

Backstory

'Torn from today's headlines' just about covers it. While I was thinking about a Bryant & May story that would be relevant to what was happening on the streets of London, I headed to a theatre matinée one Saturday afternoon and found the building engulfed in fire. Outside, police and protestors were clashing over the latest banking scandal, Occupy London was involved in the ensuing riot and shops were being smashed and set alight. Inside, the oblivious audience were watching a restoration comedy of English manners, *She Stoops to Conquer*. The scene was too bizarre to be believed, and from it I got the basics of *The Burning Man*. There was one plot casualty: I cut a new character who was terrific fun in order to improve the pace of the book. I'm saving him for a later date.

Bankers prove an irresistible target; the story of King Mob and the history of London rioting fitted neatly with press articles about the downfall of a prominent banker, and also tied together with a once-ubiquitous calendar event: Guy Fawkes' Night, which survives in the shires but is vanishing from London, except for large council-organized displays. No longer do children ask for a 'Penny for the guy' on street corners, and backyard bonfires are largely forbidden.

But I wanted something more from this twelfth volume. It was a chance to dig a little deeper into the lives of the characters and spend as much time with them as I did with the mechanics of the plot. I'm addicted to change, and felt it was time to burn a few bridges. What ended up getting burned this time was London itself. And so the twelve volumes came full circle with another conflagration, and two carefully planned six-volume story arcs dovetailed. The first story arc had involved a Ministry of Defence conspiracy based on a number of real incidents involving the suicides of several MoD workers. By this time I realized I had created a weird sub-genre of my own, not as comfortable as 'cosy', fanciful but within the realms of possibility.

The individual novels are designed to stand alone and be read in just about any order except for *On the Loose* and *Off the Rails*, which I think benefit from being read one after the other. What will happen next? Well, I've given you all the clues . . .

ARTHUR BRYANT'S SECRET LIBRARY

Arthur Bryant uses his collection of rare, abstruse and deeply peculiar books to help him solve cases. Here are some of the bizarre volumes to be found on his shelves. (NB: Not all of these titles are imaginary; I'll leave you to work out which ones are real.)

Bats of the British Isles
The Everyman Book of Wartime First Aid (with haddock bone bookmark)
Common Folk Remedies of the Onka-Wooka Tribe
How to Perform Occult Rites Using Everyday Kitchen Items
Incurable & Unnatural Vices of the Third Sex
Fifty Thrifty Cheese Recipes
Nachtkultur and Metatropism
How to Spot German and Italian Aircraft
Whither Wicca? The Future of Pagan Cults
The Apocryphal Books of the Dead
Tibetan Skulls and Their Supernatural Uses
Mystical Diagrams of Solomon's Temple (Colouring-in edition)
Criminal Records from Newgate Gaol (32 volumes)
Kabalistic Pentagrams of the Absolute

Seymour's *British Witchcraft and Demonology* (Rare, limited edition)
RAF Slang Made Easy (Uncensored paperback edition)
The East Anglican Book of Civil Magicke
Gardening Secrets of Curates' Wives (Privately circulated volume)
The Oxford Handbook of Criminology (First edition)
Mayhew's *London Characters and Crooks*
J. R. Hanslet's *All of Them Witches*
Deitleff's *Psychic Experience in the Weimar Republic*
Another Fifty Thrifty Cheese Recipes
Brackleson's *Stoat-Breeding for Intermediates*
The Luddite's Guide to the Internet
Me & Chaos Theory, by Arthur himself
The History of Gog and Magog
Dental Evidence in Body Identification (Volume 1: *Bridge-work*)
The Vanished Rivers of London
The Mammoth Book of Druid Lore
Great Boiler Explosions of the Ukraine
The British Catalogue of Victorian Naval Signals
The Fall of Jonathan Wild, Thief-Taker
Tribal Scarification (Volume 3: *M–R*)
London's Most Notorious Highwaymen
Ordnance Survey map of London (1911 edition)
Malleus Maleficarum (*The Witches' Hammer*) (1486 edition)
The 1645 Omens of the Apocalypse
Grow Your Own Hemp
The Beano Christmas Annual, 1968
Laugh, I Thought I'd Die: Reincarnation and Comedy
Victorian Water Closets: A Social History
Sumerian Religious Beliefs and Legends
Colonic Exercises for Asthmatics
Shazam! The Adventures of Captain Marvel
Mend Your Own Pipes!
Pornography and Paganism
Courtship Rituals of Papua New Guinea

Codebreaking in Braille
A History of Welsh Vivisection
The Secret Life of London's Public Houses
Yoruba Proverbs
The Anatomy of Melancholia
Further Thrifty Cheese Recipes (Edam and Red Leicester only)
Embalming Under Lenin
Cormorant-Sexing for Beginners
Apocalypsis Revelata (Volume 2)
A Complete History of the Trouser-Press
Financial Accounts for the Swedish Mining Board, Years 1745–53
The Pictorial Guide to Chairman Mao Alarm Clocks
Letts Schoolboy Diary, 1952
Secret Codes & Urban Semiotics in Viennese Street Names
An Informal History of the Black Death
Intestinal Parasites (Volume 2)
British Boundary Lines, 1066–1700
A Guide to the Cumberland Pencil Museum
Greek Rural Postmen and Their Cancellation Numbers
The Pictorial Dictionary of Barbed Wire
Collectible Spoons of the Third Reich
Patient files for the Royal Bethlehem Hospital, Moorgate, 1723–33
The Time Out Guide to Alternative London, 1971
Mind the Ghosts: The London Underground & the Spirit World
Conjuring & Tricks With Cards (Volumes 1–6)
Mortar and Mortality: Who Died In Your House? (1923 edition)
Intestinal Funguses (Volume 3)
A User's Guide to Norwegian Sewing Machines
The Complete Compendium of Lice
Cross-Stitching in the Time of Edward the Confessor
Hungarian–British Trade Fairs of the 1950s
The International Handbook of Underwater Acoustics
Across Europe with a Kangaroo

The Complete Works of Edward Bulwer-Lytton in Braille
Churchill's Favourite Engineering Problems
Recreating Renaissance Masterpieces with Cheese
Bombproofing for Beginners
An Informal History of Cow-Staining
Stipendiary Justice in Nineteenth-Century Wales
Unusual Punishments for Sodomy (Volume 13: *Northern Portugal*)
How to Cook Bats
Take My Wife, Please: Negotiation Techniques in Abduction Cases

NB. Some of the above titles are real.

ACKNOWLEDGEMENTS

I blame Sir Arthur Conan Doyle for this book's existence. He mentioned a number of his consulting detective's missing cases in the pages of the Sherlock Holmes stories, and these were later explored in more detail by his son Adrian Conan Doyle and co-writer John Dickson Carr in *The Exploits of Sherlock Holmes*. Over the years a number of Bryant & May investigations have been mentioned in passing but not unearthed, and it seemed like the perfect time to look into them.

I can't quite remember whose idea it actually was, but between the unholy triumvirate of my editor Simon Taylor and my agents Mandy Little and James Wills (or possibly even me), the idea was born and is here in your hands. Easing it into print were Kate Samano, Lynsey Dalladay and Sophie Christopher. I'd also like to thank the book clubs, bloggers, librarians and booksellers who have supported me over the years – you know who you are. Let me know if you'd like to see more cases at www.christopherfowler.co.uk.

Discover Christopher Fowler's gloriously entertaining memoirs

PAPERBOY

'One of the funniest books I've read in a long time . . . this is the kind of memoir that puts most others to shame'
Time Out

'Anyone who remembers Mivvis, jamboree bags, streets with no cars, Sid James and vast old Odeons will love this Sixties retro-fest'
Independent on Sunday

'The book is fabulous, and I hope it sells forever'
Joanne Harris

'Paper-dry wit, natural charm, brutally funny anecdotes – Fowler's likeable memoir unearths the trail that led the schoolboy to become a writer'
Evening Standard

'Entrancing, funny, deeply moving and wonderfully written. Please read it'
Elizabeth Buchan

'An almost Morrissey-like lament . . . for a sixties childhood'
New Statesman

FILM FREAK

'Gold-plated writing: uproarious, then dark, and surprisingly moving *****'
Mail on Sunday

'An homage to pre-digital cinema, an elegy for a vanishing London . . . a tribute to friendship, gonzo-style. Two thumbs up for this triple billing'
Financial Times

'Charming, funny, perceptive . . . I found myself laughing loudly and lengthily. Above all, though, I was moved'
Daily Mail

'Brisk, chatty . . . trenchantly funny . . . he's so entertaining'
Daily Telegraph

'A master storyteller . . . a beautifully written and often hilarious book'
Sunday Express

Keep an eye out for the e-book editions of these classic Christopher Fowler novels

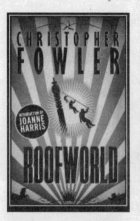

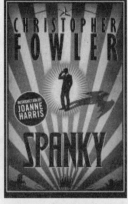

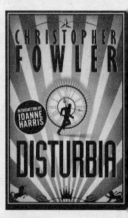

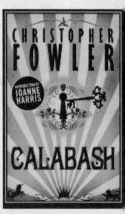